What will she bid?

Desperate for riches, penniless Michael Tremayne, Marquess of Falconridge, is willing to auction away his only possession of value—his title—to the highest bidding American father. But Kate Rose was the last woman he had in mind to marry. The willful and headstrong Kate requires from marriage the one thing Michael is unable to give—powerful, unending love.

Kate refuses to give into her husband's sensual demands until he has earned her love. Michael is not one to back down from a challenge, but neither does he believe in playing by the rules. While he is unfamiliar with love, he is extremely intimate with passion. He is determined to convince Kate that one can substitute for the other. And what better way to convince her than by patiently and skillfully seducing her? Kate never thought marriage would be so mischievous . . . or that her husband would persuade her to be so sinful.

By Lorraine Heath

JUST WICKED ENOUGH
A DUKE OF HER OWN
PROMISE ME FOREVER
A MATTER OF TEMPTATION • AS AN EARL DESIRES
AN INVITATION TO SEDUCTION
LOVE WITH A SCANDALOUS LORD
TO MARRY AN HEIRESS • THE OUTLAW AND THE LADY
NEVER MARRY A COWBOY • NEVER LOVE A COWBOY
A ROGUE IN TEXAS

*If You've Enjoyed This Book,
Be Sure to Read These Other*
AVON ROMANTIC TREASURES

BEWITCHING THE HIGHLANDER *by Lois Greiman*
CLAIMING THE COURTESAN *by Anna Campbell*
THE DUKE'S INDISCRETION *by Adele Ashworth*
HOW TO ENGAGE AN EARL *by Kathryn Caskie*
THE VISCOUNT IN HER BEDROOM *by Gayle Callen*

Coming Soon

THE SCOTTISH COMPANION *by Karen Ranney*

LORRAINE HEATH

Just Wicked Enough

An Avon Romantic Treasure

AVON

An Imprint of HarperCollinsPublishers

This is a work of fiction. Names, characters, places, and incidents are products of the author's imagination or are used fictitiously and are not to be construed as real. Any resemblance to actual events, locales, organizations, or persons, living or dead, is entirely coincidental.

AVON BOOKS
An Imprint of HarperCollinsPublishers
10 East 53rd Street
New York, New York 10022-5299

Copyright © 2007 by Jan Nowasky
ISBN: 978-0-06-112970-4
ISBN-10: 0-06-112970-4
www.avonromance.com

First Avon Books paperback printing: September 2007

Avon Trademark Reg. U.S. Pat. Off. and in Other Countries, Marca Registrada, Hecho en U.S.A.
HarperCollins® is a registered trademark of HarperCollins Publishers.

Printed in the U.S.A.

10 9 8 7 6 5 4 3 2 1

For Petra and Karen
Because you make my sons smile.

Just Wicked Enough

Chapter 1

London
1888

Michael Tremayne, the fourth Marquess of Falconridge, had always maintained, both publicly and privately, that Jane Austen had the wrong of it. The accepted universal truth to which she so blithely referred would have been more accurate had she written, "a single American heiress in possession of a good fortune must be in want of a titled husband."

Studying his reflection in the cheval glass, Michael was none too pleased with what greeted him, but only because he tended to delve below the surface. With determination, he forced himself to study nothing more than the visible trimmings. With those he could find no fault.

He'd purchased his formal clothing—silver waistcoat, white starched shirt, silver cravat, black silk trousers, and black patent-leather shoes—expressly for this important occasion. His thick black hair had been tamed, brushed back from his face, but it was only a matter of time before the rebellious wavy curls regained their freedom and became a nuisance. He knew he should probably go with the shorter style men were wearing these days, but he didn't fancy conformity. The unruly locks served notice he was his own man—even if that notice was about to be discarded in favor of greater gain.

Earlier, he'd carefully applied a straight-edged razor to his sturdy jaw, taking extra care in order to avoid any chance of a nick. It wouldn't do for any evidence to point toward unsteady hands or a hint that he was the least bit uneasy with his role in the forthcoming proceedings. Nor did he want it apparent he could no longer afford the luxury of a valet.

He'd purchased special cologne—a musky blend of lilac, lime, and citrus—and applied it liberally, almost suffocatingly so. He preferred the earthy smells associated with a man after galloping across the rolling hills, but for his plans this afternoon to succeed required all manner of civilization. He wanted to leave no doubt he was the product of sound breeding and extensive education in all matters of importance.

He slipped his black, double-breasted tailcoat—again, newly purchased—onto his wide shoulders and settled it into place, not bothering to button it as the present style was to leave it undone. It had been some time since he'd been properly attired in the latest fashion, and it had taken considerable cajoling on his part to get his preferred tailor to agree to extend him credit yet one more time when he already owed the man a substantial sum. But Michael had promised a tempting additional payment for the man's generosity and understanding.

He studied himself more critically, quite pleased with the package. Make it fancy enough to mesmerize, so no one was tempted to peel back the wrapper and peer inside. Yes, even the most unflattering of souls could be hidden in plain view, and a man who eluded confidence was a man assured of success. What better way to demonstrate confidence than with perfectly fitted clothing and exceptional grooming. He'd gone to great pains to prepare for this moment, to ensure he acquired what he so desperately needed: an American heiress in possession of a good fortune.

With any luck Michael would be debt-free before the end of the month.

No, not luck. Cunning, cleverness, and the willingness to do whatever was necessary . . . no matter how difficult, no matter how tightly his gut clenched with the implications of what the future would hold.

A sharp rap sounded on the door.

"The last of the gentlemen has arrived, my lord," his butler announced. Michael had managed to retain his butler, his housekeeper, his cook, and one footman. His outside staff consisted of the gardener, coachman, and groom. They were all necessary to keep up appearances, but the number was a far cry from the twenty-four servants who had once seen to the needs of this household and its family.

"Very good, Bexhall. Inform Farnsworth I'll be down shortly." Farnsworth, his portly solicitor, would oversee the proceedings.

"Yes, my lord."

As the footsteps faded, Michael bowed his head and released a deep breath, gathering the fortitude he would need in order to face what he had put into motion. He'd have much preferred taking the way of a coward and staying in his bedchamber until the proceedings were concluded, but he thought it important to be present when the gentlemen heard the terms of the exclusive auction to which they'd been invited.

It was Michael's resounding conviction regarding what American heiresses wanted that had caused him to face the reality of his present circumstance and dispense with the flirtations and falsehoods required to snare one. He'd accepted the truth of the matter and stopped dancing around it: he was selling, they were buying. Money talked. It was ridiculous to pretend otherwise.

Besides, courtship required a great deal of effort and was fraught with the possibility of failure. Even if he met success with his wooing, he would eventually have to meet with the heiress's father, obtain his permission to marry his daughter, and then spend days, possibly weeks, hammering out the tedious details of the settlement, its final outcome questionable from the outset.

He had no assurances when he began his court-ship endeavor—again, a long and tedious under-taking—that his efforts would be well worth his while. Quite simply put, he found the entire prac-tice of winning a lady over to be a great deal of bother, with no guaranteed satisfactory outcome. It was a gamble. Any venture involving the fairer sex was *always* a gamble.

Case in point: his trusted friend, the Duke of Hawkhurst, had expended a great deal of effort into winning the affections of the wealthy Ameri-can heiress Jenny Rose only to find himself mar-ried to her chaperone, after creating a scandal that had nearly ruined them both. And the Earl of Ravensley had been reduced to betraying his long-time friend and his sister in order to protect his interests in Jenny Rose—his betrayal adding fuel to the scandal. Michael had no idea where the man was now.

Nor did he care. At present, he was much more concerned with his own plight.

Lifting his head, he met his gaze, as green and hard as emeralds, in the mirror and squared his shoulders. "You've no other choice, old man. Let's get to it, shall we?"

With a shuddering breath, he gave himself one more nod before striding from the room and heading down the stairs to the library.

Michael's two friends had shown rather poor planning and judgment. Michael, however, had no intention of following their lead. Not when success could easily be pre-determined with a bit

of forethought, preparation, and the careful ar-
ranging of key players.

Hence the exclusive auction to be held within
his library that afternoon. Americans were known
for wanting to outdo each other. He hoped to
provide them with ample opportunity to do just
that. Place an item before them and let them fight
over it. If all went as expected, Michael would be
the victor, with enough funds to do whatever he
damned well pleased.

The footman opened the door to the library
just as Michael arrived. He strode into the room,
a man refusing to reveal what the next few moments would truly cost him. Five gentlemen
rose—as one—from the chairs circling the mas-
sive mahogany desk.

His solicitor stepped away from the tea service
set off to the side. "My lord," Farnsworth said,
with a slight nod. "I was about to pour tea for our
guests. Allow me the honor of introducing them
first."

The only thing Michael truly noted about the
gentlemen was that each wore success as though
it had been tailor-made, each stitch hand-sewn
with the wearer in mind. Resentment welled
within him, but he knew it didn't rise to the surface, wasn't visible in his face or his eyes. He'd
had years to perfect the art of not revealing his
thoughts or feelings. He was a selfish bastard
where they were concerned. He shared them with
no one.

"My lord, allow me the honor of introducing

Mr. Jeffers of New York. His interests lie in railroads," Farnsworth said.

Michael paid little attention to the rest of his solicitor's glowing praise for the man standing before him, because Michael had already researched and read the reports provided by both Farnsworth and a private investigator Michael had hired—with the promise of an enticing payment once all business was concluded. He knew *exactly* who he'd invited to this affair, their worth, and their daughters.

"I had the honor of dancing with your daughter, Leonora, earlier in the Season. Lovely lady." *Face like a horse, but in a darkened bedchamber all women look the same.*

Jeffers had two other daughters: Melanie who had recently married and Emily who would be joining the ranks of eligible heiress next Season, if rumors were to be believed.

"Thank you, my lord. She takes after her mother," Jeffers said.

Which said a good deal about Jeffers's taste in women. They ran along the same lines as Michael's—wealth over beauty—because he knew the man's wife had brought the money into the family which helped to give Jeffers the initial funds to invest in railroads. If love had entered into Jeffers's decision at all, Michael would gladly eat his recently purchased jacket.

"My lord, Mr. Blair of Boston. His passion is hotels and horses."

And his daughter, Elizabeth, from all accounts.

With only one daughter, he had but one chance to move into aristocratic circles. He wasn't quite as refined as the other gentlemen, and Michael knew his wife was the one with social ambitions. Blair simply paid the bills his wife presented. Not that Michael faulted the man for avoiding the social scene. Until recently, he'd been of a like mind. He preferred his evenings spent with a few intimates, rather than a host of jolly sorts who quickly annoyed him with all their boring trivial conversations.

"Mr. Rose, my lord, of New York. A banker with interests in Wall Street."

James Rose was the wealthiest of the lot, disgustingly so. It was rumored that in his New York residence the floors were paved with gold, the chandeliers carved from diamonds, and the furnishing imported from around the world.

He was also the man whose daughter, Jenny, had caused the downfall of Michael's two best friends. She demanded passion and both men had been determined to deliver it. Michael thought a man could do worse than a wife who fancied passion. He was also quite confident he could exceed her expectations in that regard.

Rose had another daughter, Kate. Michael had danced with her at the beginning of the Season. Her hazel eyes had sparkled that evening. On another occasion, he'd had the opportunity to play a game of lawn tennis with her. She'd smiled and flirted, albeit only a little, but he'd been left with the impression she'd make some gentleman a fine wife, as long as that gentleman could shower her with the one thing *she* demanded: love.

Michael's one experience with the emotion had taught him that it brought excruciating agony. Why any woman would desire it was beyond his reasoning. And he certainly wasn't a man capable of delivering it.

"Mr. Keane . . . Wall Street . . ."

Michael was barely listening as he moved farther down the line of expectant fathers. He knew Keane had invested heavily and invested well. The man did nothing by half measures. Even procreation. He had four daughters: Emma, Mary, Helen, and Florence. Michael had no preferences where they were concerned as there was very little to distinguish one lady from the others. As he recalled, they were all blondes with blue eyes, nothing spectacular, nothing horrific.

". . . Mr. Haddock . . ."

Who'd built an empire as a wholesale grocer, not a particularly impressive origin, but the results couldn't be argued. Haddock had three daughters: Lily, Alice, and Ada. Although Michael had yet to meet them, any one would do nicely. They met his one requirement: they'd chosen their father well.

"Gentlemen," Michael said. "I'm pleased you were able to join us this afternoon. I know your time is valuable, and I won't take any more of it than necessary. Although, Mr. Farnsworth, I do believe the occasion calls for brandy rather than tea. See to it before we begin."

As unpatriotic as it might seem, Michael didn't

understand the English fascination with tea. Unlike his opinion of Austen, however, he'd never publicly revealed his distaste of the flavored brewed concoction. There were some opinions, after all, for which an Englishman might not be forgiven for possessing.

Michael glanced over his shoulder. "Nothing for me, Mr. Farnsworth." He wasn't certain his knotted stomach could handle anything at the moment. With one more nod toward his guests, he walked to the window that looked out over the well-manicured garden. His title had bought him extended credit that had allowed him to keep his London residence from displaying his decline into poverty, but he knew he'd reached the end of all men's generosity.

With a sigh, he clasped his hands tightly behind his back. His part of the performance was over for the moment.

He heard the chair behind the desk scrape across the wooden parquet flooring as Farnsworth took his seat. Michael was aware of the sounds of other creaking chairs as the fathers sat. The moment he'd been meticulously preparing for was beginning. He was about to auction off that which he valued most.

He listened with vague disinterest as Farnsworth carefully explained the value of the item. Michael had no reason to pay attention to the details because he was intimately familiar with it and knew precisely its worth.

Facing away from the gentlemen sitting in thick

leather chairs before the desk allowed Michael not to reveal that he knew Farnsworth was embellishing the truth surrounding the item's value. It also allowed him not to disclose what he thought of the embellishments.

It would not do to give away too much too soon.

In some respects, the item being auctioned was worth very little, and yet at the same time, it was worth everything.

The odd thing was that Michael was the only one who knew what was truly being auctioned. Even Farnsworth, with his flowery prose—incomparable lineage, highly coveted, incredible legacy—had absolutely no clue.

"Have you any questions, gentlemen?" Farnsworth now asked.

Naturally there were none as the man had done an exceptional job at not only describing what was being auctioned, but explaining how this unusual auction would be handled.

Behind closed doors, with as much dignity as possible, in complete secrecy.

But for Michael, the dignity was an illusion, a pretense, something that after this meeting he would never again possess in truth, but would only possess by appearances. Yes, he could appear dignified on the outside, even if he had not a shred of dignity within him.

"Very good," Farnsworth said. "To simplify matters, the marquess has approved all amounts to be bid as American dollars, since that is the currency with which you gentlemen, as Americans, are most familiar."

Hearing the gavel banging on the wooden block resting on the desk—Farnsworth did have a penchant for theatrics—Michael took a deep breath, closed his eyes, felt his fingers biting unmercifully into his hands, and waited. He wanted to cancel the auction, wanted to explain that its arrangement had been a farce. He didn't want to part with—

"The bidding may begin, gentlemen," Farnsworth prompted, daring to reveal a bit of his irritation that amounts hadn't been immediately forthcoming.

A moment of hushed quiet ensued, as though all breaths were held—

"One thousand."

"Two."

"Five."

"Ten."

"Gentlemen, please," Farnsworth said, interrupting the bidding. "The marquess will settle for no less than a hundred thousand for so highly a prized commodity."

As the silence resumed and stretched, Michael considered facing them, daring them not to hold their purse strings quite so tightly, but in the end he stayed as he was, fearing they would see in his eyes the desperation that had brought him to this moment of auctioning off the only thing of value that remained to him. If they knew the truth, he'd lose his advantage.

"A hundred thousand," a voice finally uttered.

"Two hundred—"

"Five—"

"Damnation," a voice he recognized as belonging to James Rose growled, for the first time since the bidding began. "We could be here all day at this rate. One million."

Michael felt as though he'd taken a blow to the chest. Good God. He'd hoped for half that.

"Two million," someone else ground out.

Michael's knees actually weakened.

"Three—"

"One million," Rose stated emphatically.

"I'm afraid, Mr. Rose, we've surpassed that amount," Farnsworth said, and Michael could hear the almost giddiness in his solicitor's voice since they had agreed five percent of the final accepted amount would find its way into his pockets.

"One million," Rose repeated, "per annum as long as my daughter remains his wife, and as she has only just reached her twentieth year, I believe the marquess is looking at a rather substantial amount in the long-term."

Into the silence following that generous and unprecedented offer, Farnsworth finally spoke after clearing his throat twice, although his voice still warbled with excitement. "One million per annum is the current bid. Does anyone wish to better it?"

"And if she dies in six months, one million is all he gets, while I'm willing to pay three million, up front, now."

"Dammit, Jeffers," Rose began.

"He does have a valid point," Farnsworth interrupted. "A bird in hand and all that."

"All right, then. Five million up front with one million per annum to begin in five years."

It was all Michael could do to remain standing.

Farnsworth cleared his throat. "Do I hear a better offer?"

Michael heard quiet murmuring, an oath, a groan, and finally silence.

"Very good," Farnsworth said. "Mr. Rose, you have purchased your daughter a very nicely titled English lord."

And with that, Farnsworth pounded the gavel one last time, and to Michael it rang like a death knell.

"Congratulations, sir," Farnsworth boomed. "Gentlemen, it has been a pleasure to conduct business with you. I shall escort the rest of you out of the library as I'm certain Mr. Rose would like a few moments alone with the marquess."

Listening as the small gathering took their leave, Farnsworth at the helm, Michael stayed as he was, schooling his features not to reveal any of the emotions he was presently experiencing—relief, loss, mortification that his desperation had led him to this resolution. He waited until he heard the door click shut before finally turning around.

Rose had moved from the chair to the edge of the desk, sitting on its corner, his eagle-eyed glare focused on Michael. His graying hair, which perfectly matched his mustache, was swept back from his forehead, and Michael doubted that it would dare become unruly and fall forward. It was strange to find himself facing a man who actually had the misfortune of appearing kind—but it was well known he had the ruthlessness of a lion.

"Quite clever on your part to give the fathers of several heiresses the opportunity to bring a swift end to the husband hunting their daughters are doing this Season," Rose said.

"I merely faced reality, Mr. Rose. We can dress the whole affair up with fancy balls and dinners, but we, gentlemen, all understand we are engaged in a business venture. I merely recognized what is being sold and was quite confident exceptional fathers were wise enough to acknowledge the truth of what they were buying. You Americans are purchasing titles. We Brits are selling them."

"Money means nothing to me, Falconridge."

Easy enough for a man to claim when he had an abundance at his disposal.

"My family means everything," Rose continued. "I promised my wife our daughters would marry nobility." He shook his head like one of the bison Michael had seen at the zoological gardens. "Don't know why she got the bee in her bonnet that that's what she wanted, but there you are. It's the reason I paid an unreasonable amount to secure you as a husband for my Kate. Nothing is more important to me than seeing to my wife's happiness."

Michael's stomach, if at all possible, tightened

more than it had before the auction began. He was surprised he didn't double over.

"If I may be so bold, sir, I believe Jenny and I would be better suited." Passion he could deliver; love he could not.

Rose seemed to consider that possibility, then shook his head again in a sorrowful gesture. "My wife has her heart set on Jenny, as the older, marrying a duke. There's one who's shown some interest. It's Kate for you or nothing."

Michael bowed his head in acquiescence. "Kate will do very nicely."

"Don't be too quick there, young fellow. This arrangement comes with the stipulation that my Kate is happy. If she's not, then I don't make payment."

"You are the highest bidder, sir. Dictate the terms and I shall abide by them." Michael had given too much already to stand firm now. He was willing to do anything necessary to bring this situation to as quick a resolution as possible.

Rose slid off the edge of the desk and stood, a man confident in his position and his place in the world and among other men. "I'll be over with my lawyer in the morning to work out the finer details."

"Mr. Farnsworth and I shall make ourselves available."

He watched Rose stride from the room. Then he turned back to the garden, bowed his head, closed his eyes, and fought the need to call Rose back, to cancel the bargain struck.

But instead he stayed as he was, his hands balled into fists, his chest tightening with the acceptance of what all of this was going to cost *him*.

He'd not auctioned away his title. He'd auctioned away his pride . . .

For a woman who had never loved him . . . and another woman who never would.

Chapter 2

Standing in front of the mirror while her maid fluttered around her like a nervous butterfly, Kate Rose had little doubt that her mother, if she set her mind to it, could convince the Queen of England that the devil himself would make a suitable addition to the royal family. After all, her mother had succeeded in convincing all of London that the Marquess of Falconridge was so besotted with her younger daughter that nothing would do except for their marriage to take place as hastily as possible.

And her mother, who had never doubted both her daughters would marry an aristocrat in very short order after arriving on English shores, was fully prepared to arrange a most spectacular wedding in less than two weeks.

No reading of banns, but with the securing of a special license. Expense was no object, and as Kate was well aware, a bottomless well of gold can ensure the acquisition of *anything*.

Kate's wedding gown, a Worth masterpiece, had been designed by the master himself in the spring when he'd worked so diligently to complete Kate's twenty-thousand-dollar yearly wardrobe. Lavish invitations for the fashionable afternoon wedding, with a dinner to immediately follow at the home of the bride's parents, had been sent. A church and archbishop had been secured. American Beauty roses filled the sanctuary. Small white baskets of dark red petals awaited the guests, so they could shower the bride and groom when they took their final leave.

The entire affair had come together so quickly and so smoothly, because Kate's mother had known, just known, that her daughter would catch some lord's fancy, and here, the Marquess had been appropriately swept off his feet.

All so romantic and incredibly thrilling. Kate and her soon-to-be husband were the talk of London, their romance having blossomed right beneath everyone's nose with no one noticing.

Oh, what a secretive fellow the Marquess of Falconridge was!

So secretive in fact Kate hadn't encountered him since quite early in the Season. The last time their paths had crossed was during an afternoon tea with sporting activities that her sister, Jenny, had arranged. Kate had soundly beaten Falconridge at a game of lawn tennis. She'd not seen hide nor hair of him since. Not very sporting of him really.

Perhaps he thought she was too busy preparing for her extravagant wedding to give him any time. Or perhaps, as she suspected, he was much more interested in the settlement agreement than the bride. Clever fellow had no doubt realized what other lords had yet to learn: he need only approach the mother in order to acquire the daughter.

The Rose girls had understood at an early age that when it came to their marriages their mother would have her social ambitions realized. It might seem a strange thing to some that Kate had not even been asked her opinion on the matter of the selection of her husband, but the reality was that her overbearing mother was determined to have her way—and she was not the only American to insist her daughter settle for nothing less than a titled husband. And what Mother wanted, Mother acquired.

What choice did Kate have really except to honor her mother's wishes? She had no proven skills and without her mother's benevolence, no funds. Rebelliousness would result in her being cut off without a penny to her name. Quite honestly, life on the street held no appeal. She was spoiled, she knew it. Now she was paying the price for that spoiling.

As her maid set the veil in place with a circlet of tiny white roses, Kate couldn't help but be impressed by her mother's grand production. Kate had been informed of every detail, including the fact the marquess wanted to marry her. The man couldn't even be bothered to ask her. Not in person, not even in writing, almost as though he considered her inconsequential to the entire arrangement.

Her parents arranged the damned marriage. They spoke with the blasted marquess, he spoke with them, and now here she was, staring at her reflection in the mirror, her complexion almost as white as her bridal gown.

"You don't have to do this, Kate," her sister said quietly from behind her.

Jenny, who still fiercely held on to her independent streak, would think that. Kate almost pitied her, because she knew a day would come when her unconventional nature would be squashed beneath her mother's aspirations. As for Kate, the squashing had happened quite painfully three years earlier.

"It doesn't matter, Jenny."

"But you wanted love."

"Love is forever lost to me."

"Dear Lord, Kate. Don't be so melodramatic. You don't know that."

"Yes, I do. Wesley got married."

Kate had never before voiced those words aloud, and the unexpected pain at hearing them, of giving them credence, bringing them into the world of reality, nearly brought her to her knees. Tears stung her eyes, and she wound her arms around her waist to try to hold herself together. She didn't see Jenny move, but suddenly she was standing before her, hugging her tightly, dismissing her maid with a few quietly spoken words.

"Oh, Kate," Jenny said softly, once they were alone. "Is this the reason you've been so melancholy of late?"

"Melancholy? Is that what you call it when all the joy has been stripped from your life? Oh, Jenny, I've been nothing short of devastated. His marrying was the final betrayal, the last nail pounded into the coffin of my happiness."

"Oh, Kate, it's not as bad as all that."

"It's a thousand times worse."

"Why didn't you say something?"

Shaking her head, her chest tightening with grief, she allowed Jenny to lead her to a nearby chair, where she promptly collapsed. Jenny knelt in front of her, took her hands, and looked up at her with tears of sympathy swimming in her green eyes. "Oh, darling sister, I'm so frightfully sorry."

"From the moment Mother tore Wesley from my life, I thought if I showed absolutely no interest in anyone, if she saw how miserable I was, she'd relent, she'd consent to my being with him." The tears warming her cheeks cooled as they rolled to her chin. "Jenny, he didn't wait. I've been tormented, wondering if Mother was right. What if he didn't love me? What if he never loved me?"

"Of course, he loved you, silly girl," Jenny said sternly. "You mustn't think otherwise, but you can hardly blame him for moving on with his life when absolutely no hope was given to him. Mother would never approve you marrying the third son of a viscount."

Kate laughed bitterly. "She'd never even approve me marrying a viscount." Her mother was impressed only with dukes and marquesses, much closer to royalty than any of the others, as far as she was concerned.

"When did his marriage happen?"

"A few weeks ago. I saw the announcement in the *Times*."

"That's when you stopped attending balls."

Kate nodded. "How could I be jovial, flirtatious, when all I wanted was to curl into a ball and weep every minute of every hour?"

"I wish you'd confided in me."

"What could you have done? Nothing would change the fact he is permanently denied to me." She squeezed her sister's hand. "It hurt so badly, Jenny. And it still does. I can't believe how very much it hurts. It's as though someone is slicing into my heart, repeatedly, without mercy. I loved him with every fiber of my being. I still do, and it only makes everything worse. I can't sleep. When I try to read, I can't concentrate on the story. I feel as though I'm drifting through a fog, with no purpose."

"I'll confess I always envied your conviction that love was so grand."

"It was while it lasted, but when it dies, it's the most painful experience on earth."

"I hate seeing you go through this with your beliefs shattered. Whom did the wretch marry?"

"Melanie Jeffers."

"She has the face of a horse and the personality of a wilted rose!"

Kate released a tiny giggle, wiping her tears. All the Jeffers sisters had the misfortune of inheriting their mother's rather identifiable mouth. "I know. Isn't that awful? That he would throw me over for someone like *her*?"

"You do realize he married her expressly for her money."

"Mother believed he wanted *me* for only my money. That he was a fortune hunter. It's the reason she insisted she would deny him any funds." She laughed bitterly. "Ironic that she has ensured I marry a man who does want me for *only* my money. But he comes with a title so his reasons are acceptable."

"He *chose* you, Kate. There's something to be said for that. He could have asked for the hand of any American heiress and he asked for yours."

"Has he even spent a total of twenty minutes in my company? He didn't bother to court me or attempt to win me over."

"You weren't around to be courted or wooed. You've stayed in your room, reading your books. I've been most worried about you, but you've barely given *me* the time of day. I can hardly fault Lord Falconridge for losing patience with your absence and going directly to Mother and Father. You've been a recluse, and now you're finally leaving your room . . . only to be married."

"More irony. It seems to be the way of my life of late."

"As I suggested earlier, you could always refuse to marry him."

"I'm weary of fighting Mother, Jenny. This marriage today will make her deliriously happy. At least one person in this family should be happy. And what does it matter, really? I can never have the man whom I love now. If I must marry, I might as well marry Falconridge. At least I'll have a reason to get up in the morning: to see after his household. I won't have to attend balls anymore. I won't have to go out at all. I won't have Mother pestering me. I can simply sit in my room and do as I please. And if I please to do nothing at all, that is my choice. Mother won't be about to scold me."

"Oh, Kate, I hate that all this has happened to you, but you shouldn't marry Falconridge unless it's what you want."

"I don't know what I want anymore, but I must admit I'll take some satisfaction in imagining what Wesley will feel when he sees the announcement of my marriage in the *New York Times*, and I know Mother will ensure it appears there."

"You don't think he saw the announcement of your betrothal in the *Times* here?"

"Wesley and Melanie are in America. On their honeymoon."

Dear God, she thought she would die from the pain of imagining Wesley kissing Melanie, of taking her in his arms, of taking her to his bed.

"You're marrying for all the wrong reasons," Jenny said quietly.

"How many women of our class marry for the right ones? We came here, Jenny, to find and marry an English lord. Why should I now fault Mother for accomplishing her goal?"

"But you wanted love," Jenny repeated.

"Perhaps you had the right of it. Perhaps I should settle for passion."

"How do you know Falconridge can deliver passion?"

"I shall insist upon it. As explained to me, Father made a very generous settlement which includes provisions for me to oversee our finances. I shall have more independence as a wife, and if Falconridge wishes for me to loosen the purse strings, he shall have to keep me very, very happy."

"I can't believe you actually managed to pull this off."

Standing at the front of the church, Michael glanced at his best man, the Duke of Hawkhurst. He knew it was poor etiquette—frowned upon by those who determined such things—to have a married man serve as best man but etiquette be damned. His only unmarried friend had disappeared, and during the worst possible moment of a man's life—the day he took a wife—even the most courageous of men needed someone at his side whom he trusted, someone with whom he had some history. "I *can't* believe how quickly this all came about."

"Did you really think Mrs. Rose was going to wait until the ink dried on the settlement papers to get her daughter to the altar?"

Michael wasn't certain what he'd expected: Mrs. Rose not to be quite so formidable or in such a rush. It all worked to his advantage, of course. And he wasn't complaining. Following the ceremony, they'd go to the vestry where they'd sign the marriage documents, and in short order, an incredibly large sum of money would be transferred to Michael's bank, into his account. For the first time in his life, he'd not have debt pressing down on him and he could spend without worrying about consequences.

Why in God's name wasn't he anticipating the future with more enthusiasm?

"I just . . ." Good God, if he didn't know better he'd think he was terrified. "I just . . . I haven't even spoken with her."

"Mrs. Rose?"

"Kate."

Hawk wasn't a man easily flummoxed, not even when he'd been caught making love to the Rose chaperone in another duke's library a little over a month ago. But he certainly appeared flummoxed now. He quickly schooled his features so his thoughts were again unreadable. "I'm not quite certain I understand what you're saying. You're marrying the girl in a few moments, and you've not spoken to her . . . what? Today? In the past week?"

"Since near the beginning of the Season."

"So you're not certain she favors marrying you?"

"I assume we'd not be here if she didn't."

"Good God, man, you don't know her mother if you believe that. The stories Louisa has told me . . . I admire her immensely for being willing to help the family secure a duke for Jenny."

"You'd admire her in any case. You love her."

"Yes," he said quietly, "I do."

Michael watched as Hawkhurst's gaze shifted to the third pew where his wife sat, her gaze never wavering from her husband. All these years, Michael had paid little attention to the Earl of Ravensley's sister, had assumed Hawk had done the same. What an amazing turn of events.

Michael couldn't deny she was lovely, with blond hair and blue eyes that shone with so much love that it was rather disconcerting to witness— as though he were a voyeur who would only ever be able to watch from afar but never experience that depth of sentiment. He found himself wondering if his wife would ever look at him with half that much affection. He cursed himself for even entertaining such ludicrous thoughts.

Their marriage was business, and a successful business was usually managed without emotion, the arrangement based on an even exchange of desired acquisitions: in their case money and a title. Nothing more.

If Miss Kate Rose had any expectation of something more, then surely she'd have insisted on speaking with him prior to this hour. Instead it had been her mother who'd paid Michael a visit and set out expectations regarding the wedding: the speed with which it was to take place and the rumors she'd instigate concerning the necessity for haste: his besotted state.

He'd never been besotted in his life, but considering that her husband was making funds available to Michael, Mrs. Rose was free to start any damned rumors she pleased.

Yet, he knew in spite of the circulating gossip Mrs. Rose had successfully instigated, other rumors had begun to surface: that, in the same manner as his trusted friend, Hawkhurst, he'd compromised the girl in order to secure her hand in marriage. Wagers were being made on how shortly after the vows were exchanged the first child would make his appearance. Most were betting in fewer than eight months.

Michael had made his own wager, selecting eleven months from today. He knew all the gentlemen believed he'd made the wager for his lady's honor, but the truth was he had a weakness where wagering was concerned, and in this matter, he had an advantage. He knew the heir wouldn't arrive any earlier than he should.

Nor could he deny that perhaps he *had* wanted to make a stand for his lady. Guilt was a strong motivator, and he was feeling a tad guilty for not approaching her before now.

Rather poor planning on his part, especially since he prided himself on his ability to plan.

The organ suddenly rent the stillness of the sanctuary, and Michael felt as though the chords were vibrating through his chest. The moment was upon him, the final step. Signing the settlement papers had committed him to this course, but still the arrival at his destination was almost unexpected. He'd kept thinking something would happen, that Rose would make further inquiries, would discover the truth, would renege on the arrangement . . .

But there they were, with the music reaching the rafters, a small girl walking down the aisle tossing out red rose petals, the beautiful Jenny Rose following behind her.

And behind Jenny . . . the doorway . . . empty.

At what point was his bride supposed to show herself? Was she sitting somewhere, waiting for him to propose? Everyone had consented except her. Had he really thought she'd show with no encouragement from him?

A woman who wanted love, marrying a man unable to give it?

Jenny gave him an appraising glance, before taking her place, and he was struck once more by her beauty and reminded of her quest for passion. He should have insisted she be his wife. With his pride in tatters, he'd forgotten himself, forgotten his position in Society.

And now it was too late. Too late for them all.

Chapter 3

He was older than she remembered.

When Kate finally came to stand before him, she was surprised by his appearance. Not his clothing necessarily. The wine-colored morning coat enhanced his dark features, and she couldn't deny he was also more handsome than she'd remembered. But something about him was decidedly different. Perhaps it was that the occasion was more like a funeral procession than a wedding ceremony. In the vestry her father had seemed almost as hesitant as she to step into the sanctuary. Then he'd looked at her and displayed a soft, gentle, almost shy, smile that seemed so out of place on a man with his determination and drive.

"He's a good man, Kate."

"Is he, Papa?"

He gave her a brusque nod. "And you'll hold all the financial power."

He'd explained the terms of the settlement to her last night. She'd barely listened. Last night she hadn't cared. Suddenly, she was beginning to care a great deal.

Her father had leaned over, kissed her cheek, and brought her veil down over her face. "It's going to be all right, sweetheart. Now, let's go make your mother happy."

And so she'd squared her shoulders and allowed the first man she'd ever loved to walk her down the aisle toward a man she doubted she'd ever love.

She was vaguely aware of the archbishop speaking in a low voice that still seemed to boom around her, her father responding with his usual confidence as he gently lifted her hand from his arm and placed it on Falconridge's. The bridegroom neither smiled nor seemed pleased. Rather he appeared to wish he was somewhere else.

Had he suddenly realized he'd asked for the hand of the wrong Rose sister? Had he forgotten she was not the beauty? Not the one who drew the attention of princes? Not the one who would one day, without question, become a duchess?

Falconridge gave her only the barest of nods, before facing the archbishop. Kate found herself wondering what sort of punishment her mother might mete out if she suddenly spun on her heel and marched back down the aisle. No doubt, she'd be entirely cut off. It had happened once before. Mercifully, through the efforts of her father and brother, she'd been brought back into the fold. She doubted she'd be forgiven again for such an embarrassing transgression or another scandal. The first had been private and easily hidden. This one would be quite public and not so easily swept under the rug.

Briefly she wondered if her parents had revealed her sordid history to the marquess. Did he know everything about her? Or when he had asked for her hand, had her parents breathed an enormous sigh of relief, held their tongues regarding her past, and set about making the arrangements to bring this union to fruition as quickly as possible—before the aristocrat learned the truth of her disreputable behavior.

While an abundance of money could undo a great many things, it was powerless to change one thing: it couldn't return to a woman her innocence.

Was Falconridge expecting to find a virgin in his bed tonight? And would he be furious when he didn't? Had they considered that aspect to this whole arrangement? Had they been forthcoming or had they hoped it wouldn't matter?

She knew men prided themselves on being a woman's first, and she knew when he realized he wasn't that he might forever doubt being the father of their first child if he—or she—arrived too soon. And so much emphasis was placed on the birthright of the heir. He would inherit everything. She couldn't risk her husband doubting the child's legitimacy.

Why hadn't all these realizations and ramifications occurred to her sooner? What in God's name was she doing standing there, exchanging vows with a man who knew nothing at all about her, who couldn't be bothered to do anything more than acquire a cursory introduction. One dance, one blasted dance, and a game of lawn tennis, and he'd deduced they were well suited?

He'd never even taken the time to call on her. And how would he react when he discovered she'd been *well suited* with someone else before him? Would he respond with heated anger or cold fury? He looked to be a man capable of delivering both in equal measures.

Standing in front of God and London was an odd place and time to suddenly awaken from an incessantly deep lethargy and begin questioning everything that had occurred to bring her to this moment. She trusted her father's judgment, she always had, but she knew he could be influenced by her mother, and she had no doubts that it was her mother's desire to see her daughters marry into the elevated ranks of the aristocracy that was responsible for the path she found herself traveling.

She was vaguely aware of responding to the archbishop's questions, of Falconridge gently removing her glove, and placing a gold band on her finger.

". . . pronounce you man and wife. You may kiss the bride."

Falconridge turned to face her more squarely, and she suddenly found herself gazing into his green eyes. What did she see there? Regret, sorrow, remorse? He'd asked for her hand in marriage, was obtaining what he wanted. Why wasn't he more joyous?

"I thank you," he said quietly, before brushing his lips lightly across hers, with as little substance as moonlight passing over the lawn.

His thanking her was her undoing. She didn't know what had prompted his words. If he'd read the amassing doubts in her eyes. If he knew she was questioning whether or not she could actually sign the marriage register.

Whatever the reason, the words spoken gave another meaning to the expression reflected in his eyes. He didn't want to be here anymore than she did. And just like her, he had no choice.

And with a startling clarity she realized they'd condemned each other to misery.

"Why did you thank me?"

As the open carriage rumbled along the London streets toward the Rose residence, Michael gazed over at his . . . wife. He could hardly fathom he was actually married. She'd hesitated but a single breath before signing the registry, a moment during which she'd glanced up at her mother's formidable expression before promptly applying ink to paper.

During the ceremony, he'd noticed a good deal about her that had escaped his attention before. Or if he had noticed on the previous occasions when their paths had crossed, he'd forgotten. The top of her head did not quite reach his shoulder. She had a light smattering of freckles across her nose and just along the inside of her cheeks. He shouldn't have been surprised. Her hair was a brilliant red that no doubt attracted the sun, as well as other men. She was sturdy, and he thought her breasts would make for a nice pillow upon which to rest one's head after a weary day. However, based upon the manner in which she fairly managed to distance herself in the carriage, he assumed she'd not welcome him there.

He cleared his throat. "I assumed any besotted fool would say something unprompted to the woman he was marrying. And as I am supposedly besotted, with any luck, my words were not heard and yet they may have been interpreted to be another sentiment entirely." At the altar, leaning in for a kiss, he'd felt a strong need to say something. *I thank you* was his true sentiment, but his hope was that those in attendance would think he'd said *I love you.* Words he'd never spoken aloud and never would.

He didn't know why he suddenly wanted everyone to think he was besotted.

"But you're not besotted, are you? It was only a rumor my mother started. Part of her fantasy regarding this marriage."

He saw no reason to fill her with false hope that their relationship would be anything other than what it would be. So he'd made no previous attempt to encourage her affection with flowers, sweets, or poetry. And he saw no reason now not to remain true to his pragmatic attitude. He needed to be clear without being cold, to the point without being abrupt, while giving the impression he fancied being married to her without appearing to fancy *her* overmuch.

"No, I'm afraid not, but please don't take it personally. My failing lies with me, not you. I'm acutely aware of how fortunate I am to have you as my wife."

She studied him for a moment the way his man of business often scrutinized his ledgers. It was at once thorough and disconcerting.

"When my mother said you asked for my hand in marriage—"

"She said I asked?"

"Yes. Did you not?" Horror swept over her lovely face. "Oh, dear Lord, don't tell me she approached you."

Damn it all! They hadn't told her about the auction. They hadn't told her the truth of the arrangement. Was it because they knew she'd balk at the prospect of having a husband who'd been so flagrantly purchased?

A pity they'd not alerted him regarding exactly what they would and wouldn't reveal to their daughter. What other surprises lay in wait?

"No, I assure you that your mother did not approach me. I approached your father." That, at least, was true. He'd approached her father *and* invited him to the auction.

"Why not approach me?"

"Courtship requires a great deal of effort and is fraught with the possibility of failure. Even if it were successful, we would have to delve into the realm of working out the details of the financial settlement, at which point much of the affection would no doubt be diminished. Quite simply, I find it to be a great deal of bother, especially when the final decision and the bargaining are handled by the father. I sought to expedite matters, by approaching your father and obtaining his approval."

Her eyes held censure, her lips were a straight line that he thought even a kiss might not reshape. "You're not terribly romantic, are you?"

"Romance is for novels and poetry."

"And affection?"

Was a stranger to him.

"I believe you'll find I'll make a most agreeable husband."

"A pity agreeable is not what I desire."

What the devil did she mean by that comment?

Unfortunately, the driver brought the carriage to a halt. A liveried footman stepped forward, opened the carriage door, and assisted the new marchioness as she descended to the drive. Michael followed her out and offered her his arm.

"This is a conversation we need to finish later," he told her.

"We have the rest of our lives, my lord."

He wasn't certain that boded at all well.

"Oh, my dear, you're here!"

Surrounded by her father, her brother, and her sister, Kate endured her mother's enthusiastic greeting and hug, because she knew it would embarrass her mother if she didn't, and although the woman irritated her more often than not, Kate still loved her beyond measure. She knew her mother's heart was in the right place, even if her actions weren't.

"Or I suppose I should say, *my lady*." Her mother hugged her again and whispered near her ear, "You have no idea how very happy I am for you."

"I'm happy for us both," Kate murmured. She wasn't going to ruin this day for her mother. If she did then what was the point in having suffered through any of it at all?

Her mother released her hold, dabbed at her eyes with a silk handkerchief, and tapped Jeremy on the arm. "Hug your sister."

"I think a bow is more in order. You're nobility now, aren't you?" His hazel eyes offered a teasing glint as he bent at the waist, took her gloved hand, and pressed a kiss to the back of it. He'd taken after their father with his dark hair and handsome features. Kate didn't like to admit it, but she'd always envied him his freedom as the son and the opportunities afforded him. He would no doubt manage the family businesses in time. As though deciphering her thoughts, he winked at her and said, "It's damn close, Kate, damn close to ruling an empire."

"You're ruining the moment," Jenny said, shoving playfully on his shoulder, before taking Kate into her arms. "I think you're the loveliest bride this Season."

"Only until the honor falls to you," Kate said.

"Not this Season." Jenny turned to Falconridge. "My lord, welcome to the family."

Falconridge bowed slightly. "It is my honor and privilege."

"An honor all the way around," her mother said, before facing the crowd in the parlor. "Everyone! Lord and Lady Falconridge have arrived!"

Enthusiastic clapping resounded throughout the room. Kate was suddenly very much aware of her husband standing beside her. Her husband. Why was it that the phrase was suddenly so shocking?

"Smile, sweetheart," her father said in a low voice. "Remember my words in the vestry."

In the vestry, right before they'd entered the sanctuary, when she'd begun to shake, he'd told her that he loved her and then dared to promise her she'd be happy. Her father had never in his life gone back on his word, although she thought he might be overstepping his bounds with this latest vow. How could he promise what he wasn't the one delivering?

Kate forced herself to smile. "I think I'm simply feeling quite overwhelmed."

"Jeremy, fetch your sister some tea," her mother said. "It wouldn't do to have her swoon in front of our guests. A rather deplorable habit the English women have of swooning."

"Certainly, Mother."

Kate wasn't sure if her brother was answering her mother's summons or agreeing with the assessment of swooning English women. She watched as Jeremy rushed off, cutting a fine figure as he made his way through the crowd, obviously catching the attention of several ladies.

"Maybe it's Jeremy who'll be getting married next," Jenny whispered near Kate's ear.

"And give up his wanderlust ways? I doubt it."

"My lord, I was surprised your mother wasn't in attendance," Kate's mother suddenly said, effectively jerking Kate's attention away from her brother and speculation regarding his love life. "She wasn't was she? Did I overlook her?"

"No, madam, she's not in London."

"Why ever not?"

"Mama," Jenny scolded. "The English don't appreciate such personal questions. Besides, it's not at all unusual for aristocratic parents not to attend their children's weddings."

"But her son has married into one of the wealthiest families in America. Surely she could be bothered to make an appearance."

"She's ill, madam," Falconridge said, and Kate thought she actually heard his teeth grinding.

"I'm so sorry," her mother said. "Is it the cancer?"

"I'd rather not discuss it, madam."

Kate saw true sympathy wash across her mother's face. "I'm dreadfully sorry. Truly I am. It's such a horrid disease," she said, as though his answer confirmed her worst fears. "If there is ever anything—"

"Thank you, madam. I'll convey your concerns.

But this afternoon is all about the bride's happiness, so shall we move on to accomplishing that goal?"

"Of course, my lord. How very noble and considerate of you to place my daughter above all else, when you have your own worries."

Kate cast a glance at Jenny who simply mouthed, "Be happy."

If only it were that simple.

Jeremy reappeared with a footman carrying a tray of champagne-filled flutes and winked at Kate. "I thought we might as well get into the spirit of celebrating."

He passed around the glasses, then held his aloft. "To the health of my dear sister and her new husband. To the health of the Marquess and Marchioness of Falconridge."

As far as Kate could tell, everyone in the room lifted their glasses and repeated the toast. Her husband clinked his glass against hers, held her gaze, and toasted, "To a long life."

She drank the champagne. Not a sip. But a gulp. A long gulp. She handed the emptied glass to her brother. "Fetch me another."

The reality of what she'd done was suddenly hitting her and hitting her hard. She felt as though she were awakening from a long sleep.

"You have guests to greet, Kate," her mother said.

"I'm the bride, Mother. I think we'll dispense with that particular practice. People should simply enjoy themselves. We know they wish us well.

Otherwise they wouldn't be here. I see no reason to be so formal."

"Kate—"

"My wife has spoken," the marquess said. "It shall be as she wishes."

Kate looked at him. He lifted her gloved hand and pressed a kiss to her knuckles, holding her gaze as though her eyes were the most mesmerizing in the room, when she knew they were far from it. His, a deep emerald green, were far more intriguing while hers appeared as though unable to decide if they wanted to be brown, green, or blue, so they'd ended up being no distinct color. Rather they were a boring dullness.

She was quite quickly struck with the notion that this incredibly handsome man could have any woman in the world and he'd chosen her. Why? What did he know of her? What did she know of him?

"Something we tend to overlook when considering marriage is that not only do we marry the daughter, but we marry the family," Hawkhurst said drolly.

Michael fought not to visibly shudder at that poignant prophecy that came much too late to be helpful. He noticed that the Set was well represented by the guest list. It was the English fascination with Americans. Whether they despised, tolerated, or adored them, his fellow countrymen were always intrigued by them.

"Taking them to the country estate with you?" Hawkhurst asked.

"Good God, no. I'm not certain I've ever known a more forceful woman than Mrs. Rose. She's hardly circumspect in her behavior."

"At least you didn't have the misfortune of throwing over her daughter for the chaperone. Truly, if you hadn't honored me by asking me to stand with you, I doubt we'd have been invited."

"She'd have invited you. Having a number of dukes in attendance is a feather in her cap, and she seems determined to collect all the feathers she can."

"What of your wife? They say a man can see the future of his wife by studying her mother."

Michael couldn't repress the shudder that rocked him with that statement. "I'm certain Kate won't be as bad as all that. Besides, look to your own wife. Her mother was an acknowledged spendthrift. But Louisa seems to be far more conservative in her spending habits."

"Indeed, she's frugal, wise, and not above working if need be to make ends meet. It's her brother who is addicted to spending what he does not have."

"Have you heard from Ravensley?"

"No. Nor has Louisa. She pretends it doesn't matter, but how can it not? To be forgotten by your own brother?"

"She's not forgotten," Michael ground out. He knew too well the pain of being forgotten, overlooked, abandoned. His wife had already chosen to leave his side. Her excuse was that she needed a moment alone. But she wasn't going to find solitude within the confines of this crowded room, and he'd done little more than watch her wander from guest to guest. "Ravensley is no doubt steering clear because of embarrassment over his own abhorrent behavior. He spread the rumors that resulted in you're having to marry the girl."

"Honestly, I'm quite glad he did."

"Because marrying Jenny would have been a dreadful mistake?"

"No, because not marrying Louisa would have been. If you come to love Kate half as much as I—"

"You've become quite disgusting with all your romantic notions of late."

Hawkhurst chuckled low. "I suppose I have. But I'm happy. Even if I'm still impoverished."

"If you have any money at all, make a wager on when our first child will arrive. I assure you it will be no sooner than nine months from tonight."

"Quite confident of your prowess?"

"I simply know the haste with which our marriage was arranged had nothing at all to do with her being with child. So it's a safe bet."

"I'll consider it."

Even as he was talking with Hawkhurst, he couldn't seem to take his eyes off Kate. She was undoubtedly one of the most graceful creatures he'd ever seen, and he wondered why he'd paid so little attention to her earlier in the Season. "Her parents told her I'd asked for her hand in marriage."

"Did you tell her the truth of it?"

Michael shook his head. "Her not knowing works to my advantage. She is likely to be more generous with her affections."

"And when she learns the truth?"

"She shan't. If her parents didn't already tell her, they have no reason to tell her now. Besides, the auction was handled with a good deal of discretion. I doubt any of the participants would care to admit he'd been outbid. It's a secret that will go the grave."

Hawkhurst raised his glass. "A toast, my friend. May you have better success keeping your secrets than I did keeping mine."

Kate thought she might cause bodily harm to the next person who told her how fortunate she was to have snagged the Marquess of Falconridge. The ladies, of course, wanted details. Kate did little more than smile mischievously.

He had, of course, remained by her side during the first part of this dreadful affair, while they'd accepted congratulations together. But once it was clear that all their guests had arrived, they'd parted ways, he to speak with Hawkhurst and she . . . to just slip away. But ladies kept delaying her progress.

She'd almost made it to the door leading into the garden when she heard a familiar voice.

"Kate?"

She turned and smiled at the Duchess of Hawkhurst. "Your Grace."

"Oh, please. We've been through far too much

to be so formal." She reached out and took Kate's hands, squeezed gently. "I must say I was rather surprised by this sudden event. I thought you were going to let *me* find you the perfect lord."

"Are you saying my husband isn't perfect?"

Louisa blushed. "Of course not. I simply didn't realize that Falconridge had caught your fancy."

"Quite honestly, he hadn't. Nor had I realized I'd caught his. I've had other matters on my mind, and until today I don't think I was truly aware of the momentous path I was traveling. I have to admit to suddenly feeling quite overwhelmed."

"Well, at least you had no scandal associated with the gossip surrounding you."

"You seem to have weathered your own scandal admirably."

"We do what we must."

While Louisa was sister to the Earl of Ravensley—possibly the most impoverished lord in all of London—she'd not been above seeking employment as a lady's chaperone. It was a reputable undertaking for ladies of quality, and Kate's parents had hired then-Lady Louisa to serve as their daughters' social chaperone, because she was well acquainted with the lords, knew who was suitable and who was not.

"At the beginning of the Season, when we were making rounds among the Set, you didn't recommend Falconridge. Why not?"

Louisa glanced around, as though wanting to ensure that no prying ears would hear what she had to say. When she seemed content with their

seclusion, she said, "As you know, he and my
brother are very good friends. And my brother
and his friends tended to stay out until all hours,
engaging in . . . debauchery. Or so I assumed.
Hawkhurst, too, was part of their inner circle. I
judged him as harshly. And I've come to realize
that I judged him unfairly. It's quite possible I did
the same with Falconridge."

"Do you know anything at all about him?"

"Alex and his friends wanted me to put in a
good word for them with you and Jenny. I told
them I would only do it if they proved themselves
suitable. Falconridge thought I asked too much.
But I'm not certain I can find fault with his attitude any longer. I've come to discover men are
such prideful creatures."

"And we're not?"

"Of course we are. But we're more capable of
bending. Men tend to break."

"Do you believe the rumors that he's besotted
with me?"

The duchess glanced down.

"Louisa?"

She lifted her gaze, and Kate could see the answer in her eyes. "Let me ask you this, then. Do
you think there is any chance he could become
besotted with me?"

"If anyone at all has the power to steal his heart,
it is you."

Kate couldn't help herself. She smiled. "That
was very diplomatic."

"If I may be so bold, Kate, I worried about you

while I was your chaperone. You don't enjoy the parties or the attentions nearly as much as Jenny. Perhaps marriage to Falconridge will give you whatever it is you're looking for."

Kate glanced across the room to where her husband stood watching her. He lifted his glass, a silent salute.

"I also think you could very well be what he's looking for," Louisa said.

"I doubt it," Kate said, before turning back to Louisa. "And unfortunately for him, he may have to learn that fact the hard way."

Chapter 4

Michael had recently decided there were three times in his life when he needed to take extra care in preparing himself: when he was to be auctioned, when he was to be wed, and when he was to bed his wife for the first time. As he stood in his bedchamber, he couldn't help but think a little extra care might be needed for the last situation.

From the moment they'd left the Rose household—following a rather unimaginative and tedious dinner with far too many celebratory toasts—a tenseness as brittle as ice had surrounded them. Neither had spoken a word as the carriage had conveyed them to his London residence. He couldn't help but believe she was as pre-occupied with thoughts of the coming night as he. Every event throughout the day had been only a prelude to the upcoming consummation.

All her things, including her lady's maid, had been delivered by the time they'd arrived at the residence. He'd taken Kate on an incredibly dull tour of the place, naming rooms as though she didn't have the good sense to properly identify them herself, introducing her to the small staff, certain her first order of business would be to increase its numbers.

She'd taken inordinate interest in the library, making her first comment to him since their arrival. "I'd like to fill all these shelves with books."

"If it pleases you," he'd responded.

They'd remained in the library for a bit of reading before bed. Well, she'd read; he'd merely stared at the page in his book, wondering how best to approach her. He knew exactly how to approach a mistress . . . but a wife?

How did one lure a wife into his bed?

His mistress had required nothing more than a tilting of his head toward whichever piece of furniture he desired to take her on. His mistress had been an expert at bringing him unparalleled pleasure.

But his wife . . . by God, he was saddled with the burden of introducing her to the ways of the flesh, and the embarrassing truth was he hadn't a clue where to begin. Not that he wasn't well acquainted with passion, but he was accustomed to women who needed no instruction. How delicate were a virgin's sensibilities? What were his wife's expectations? Did she even have expectations? Was she aware of what passed between a man and a woman? Had her mother spoken to her? Most likely not. Certainly Michael had never received any instruction. He'd gone at it with the instincts of a young stallion. But women of quality didn't have the luxury of experience. No, their first time was reserved for their husbands—and rightly so.

Particularly among the aristocracy where there could be no question as to the father of the heir.

He wanted to put his wife at ease. He didn't want to frighten her, although the potential to do so was certainly there. He had to keep his ardor in check until he had properly prepared her for what was to come. He wanted her to have no regrets that he was in her bed. He wanted her to welcome him there in the future.

Releasing a groan of frustration, he realized that for the first time in his life, he might have an inkling of what his mistress had experienced: the doubts, the worry over pleasing him. In a way his position was no different than hers had been. He'd been bought to serve as a husband for a wealthy American heiress.

He tightened the sash of his emerald green silk dressing gown as he approached her door. He supposed a nightshirt was in order, so as not to frighten his virgin bride, but the truth was he didn't own any. He couldn't stand feeling confined or crowded. It was the reason he'd never actually slept with his mistress . . . or she'd never slept with him. She knew to leave his bed once passions cooled.

How fitting that with his wife, he would be the one approaching her and the one leaving when all was done. He shook off the resentment that threatened to overcome him. Going into this venture with both eyes wide open, he had no cause to regret where he now stood. Life would be better all the way around—and he'd thank her for it. Repeatedly. While not her specifically, marriage to her and the funds it would provide would lift him from the depths of despair and poverty into which he'd plunged.

It was time to pay the devil his due.

Or *her* due as the case may be. Not that he considered Kate Rose Tremayne a devil, but he certainly felt as though he'd made a bargain with that very creature in the form of her father.

He rapped his knuckles once on the door separating their bedchambers, before opening it. The gaslights were lit. She was lounging on a chaise longue near the window, a book in her lap, a box of chocolates beside her. She was dressed for the night in a white gossamer nightgown, a shawl draped over her legs. Desire slammed into him, almost destroying his resolve to go slowly. He'd been physically attracted to Kate Rose from the first moment he'd met her. He assumed she couldn't make the same claim. She didn't seem the least bit interested in his arrival. She barely lifted her gaze from the book as he strode farther into the room.

"I've come to say good night."

"Good night." She plucked out a chocolate and popped it into her mouth.

He studied her, trying to decipher the meaning of that concise reaction. She was either more naïve than he'd realized or it was a damned intriguing story that she was hesitant to set aside. He cleared his throat. "I think you'll find it'll go more pleasantly if we say good night in bed."

She gave him her complete attention then, the tiniest of creases etched between her brows. "Do you wish to *say* good night or to *show* me good night?"

Maybe not as naïve as he'd assumed.

"Show you, I suppose."

"And by showing me, I take it to mean you'll lift the hem on my nightgown and wedge yourself between my thighs and take to rutting like a wild boar until your husbandly rights are satisfied."

No, not naïve at all. American ladies were vastly different from English ones. He couldn't imagine any other lady of his acquaintance speaking with such forthrightness. It took everything within him not to shift with discomfort at her brazen description, nor take exception to her opinion of his prowess. He couldn't deny there were times when his enthusiasm bordered on the feral, but he certainly never grunted, snorted, or rutted. "I'd planned to use a bit more finesse."

He'd not intended to growl the words but they sounded rough even to his own ears, which unfortunately gave them an uncivilized cadence.

"Do you love me?" she asked.

She couldn't seriously be posing that ludicrous question, and yet her expression contained no hint of teasing. Rather she appeared to be incredibly sincere. Why was she making this moment so blasted difficult by referring to matters of the heart with which he had no experience? Why did she look so damned hopeful as though the answer could be anything other than what it was?

He averted his gaze, studying the pattern on the faded wallpaper. He should have it replaced. He *would* have it replaced. *If* she approved the funds. That was the bargain he'd struck with the devil.

"As I thought," she said rather smugly. "Your answer and mine, my lord, is no."

He turned his attention back to her. She popped another chocolate into her mouth and returned to reading her book, apparently dismissing him as though he were of little or no consequence.

"I beg your pardon?" he asked.

She looked at him as she might some dim-witted fool. "No. I will not spread my legs for any man who has not earned my love."

"This was not the arrangement I made with your father."

"More's the pity. You should have discussed the arrangements with me."

"You are my wife. You have a duty to give me an heir. I have rights as your husband—"

"I believe you will find, my lord, if you closely read the settlement papers that I hold the reins on our finances."

"As I did read the damned settlement papers closely, I *am* well aware of the arrangement."

An arrangement Farnsworth had argued vehemently against. He favored English law, which, upon marriage, allowed that all belonged to the husband.

Rose had merely studied the smoking end of

his cheroot. "I favor Rose law. The marquess has already proven he has no prowess where money is concerned. Kate was raised on my lap and her banking acumen is unparalleled for a woman. I'm handing over an unprecedented amount of my hard-earned money, gentlemen, and I don't do so lightly. It is done on my terms or not done at all, English law be damned."

Michael had considered walking out, hosting another auction, but he had no desire to suffer through the indignity again. And so he'd consented to giving his wife power over him. It was the shortest, least troublesome route. She'd seemed an agreeable sort when he'd danced with her, but now he had to wonder if he might have misjudged her. He had little doubt her father had acquired his wealth through ruthlessness. Had he passed that particular trait on to his daughter as she'd sat upon his lap?

"I will only loosen the reins on our money if I am happy," she said, breaking into his thoughts. "I assure you that I will not be happy if you crawl beneath the sheets with me before you have earned my love."

"And how in God's name do you expect me to do that?"

"Speak with Lord Bertram. I have great affection for Lord Bertram."

"The man is a toad!"

"He is most kind and generous."

"Generous? How generous can I be when I have to ask, 'My dear, may I have a few shillings so I can purchase you some trinkets?' You will dictate my generosity."

"Generosity is not measured by the number of *things* one is given. Generosity of spirit, of heart—"

"I don't bloody well believe this!"

"Believe what you will, but know this. Love-making is an extremely intimate act that should transcend beyond the physical to include the emotional. We have spoken hardly at all. You cannot possibly believe I would bare my body to a man who has yet to discern my favorite color."

"Good God, woman, what has colors to do with bedding?"

"They both speak of intimacy, of knowledge regarding another's preferences."

"Then what is your favorite color?"

"That's for you to deduce."

Was she saying that announcing her favorite color was the key to unlocking her body?

"Red."

She gave him an indulgent smile. "You have to know, not guess."

Damnation! "I've given you a blasted title!"

"My mother wanted the title, not me, and I believe you were well aware of that fact as I mentioned it the night we met."

"If you didn't want"—in frustration he waved his hand toward the bed—"*that* with me, then why didn't you tell your parents you wouldn't marry me?"

She laughed lightly. "I could have sworn you were acquainted with my parents. They think they know what is best, and they are not easily swayed otherwise. You can't possibly believe my opinion on this marriage was of any consequence."

"But you've been most pleasant throughout the afternoon and into the evening—"

"And I'll continue to be pleasant during the day and into the evening. As a matter of fact, I don't think you can deny that I'm still being most pleasant. I simply won't be bedded just because it is *your* husbandly right."

He began pacing in front of the bed, panic settling around his heart. How could matters have come to this? He came to a thunderous stop with his back to her, gripped the bedpost, bowed his head, and ground out, "What about the money?"

"What about it?"

He glanced over his shoulder at her, sitting there all smug and knowing, as though she sat upon a throne and held the fate of her subjects in her hand. "Do I have to earn your affection before you release any to me?"

The only sound in the room was the hissing of the gaslights. He thought for an indescribable moment that he might have seen consternation in her eyes, but it was no doubt only a flickering of the shadows in the room. He felt as though he'd walked into a torturous realm where a man's pride was flayed over and over for eternity. He'd already paid his price and she was demanding more.

Slowly she shook her head. "No, we'll see to your debts in the morning."

"And beyond the debts, I have affairs which require funds."

"I'm not paying for your mistresses."

She fairly bristled, the first bit of real emotion he'd ever seen in her. As angry as he was at her, he was also pleased to see she could elicit fire as well as ice. And damn it all, if the fire didn't make him more determined to get her into bed.

"I'm not referring to those types of affairs. I was referring to personal matters."

"We can discuss them in the morning."

He spun around and glared at her. "I could spend a thousand pounds for a thousand days and still have money to burn."

"It is that attitude, my lord, which resulted in your having to *marry* for money. We will not spend frivolously simply because we have an abundance of coins at our disposal."

He slapped his palm against the bedpost, relishing the stinging pain that served to anchor his fury so he didn't strike out at her. "This is not what I bargained for."

"Quite honestly, my lord, I don't give a damn. You couldn't be bothered to call on me before today. You've never even addressed me by name. You will find that I'll be quite generous when it comes to dispensing our funds, but as for everything else you acquired by marriage, it is not easily given. I will not be merely money and a means by which you can effortlessly dispense your lust."

"Lust requires desire."

He regretted the harsh words the moment they

flew from his mouth without thought, a second before she looked as though he'd struck her a physical blow.

"My apologies, my lady. Those words were uncalled for and their implication untrue." With a sigh, he banged his head against the bedpost. "We've gotten off to a most unfortunate start."

"Because nothing lies between us except my father's money. If you're discontent, my lord, we may seek an annulment. My father is quite handy at obtaining them."

No, her solution wasn't an option.

"I'm not in the mood to seek an annulment."

"Then you accept the revised terms of the agreement?"

What other choice did he have? He wasn't in the habit of forcing women to welcome his attentions, and he couldn't risk causing her unhappiness. Rose, damn him, had been very explicit in the terms he'd laid out regarding the settlement. His daughter, first and foremost, must always be happy.

Michael nodded brusquely. "I do."

"Good night, then. I'll see you in the morning."

She popped another chocolate into her mouth, and he almost hoped she'd choke on it.

Kate almost choked on the chocolate. Her throat was knotted so tightly with tension she couldn't swallow. As soon as he'd stormed from the room and slammed the door in his wake, she spit out the confection and took several deep calming breaths until she began to relax.

She'd almost ruined everything by laughing out loud at the incredulity expressed in his voice regarding her opinion of Lord Bertram. He did very much resemble a toad with protruding eyes and lips that looked as though they'd been stung by a swarm of bees. But for all his unattractive appearances, he was indeed kind. Not that Kate had ever entertained taking him as a husband. Still he was an example her own husband could follow, although she suspected he wouldn't welcome any further suggestions from her.

He'd been livid before departing her company.

Although she'd achieved her end result, keeping him from her bed, it hadn't gone at all as she'd planned. Perhaps she should have let him bed her, let him discover her secret, but she had no idea how it would affect him. And the truth was, while she'd blithely suggested annulment, she wasn't quite certain she wanted one.

She would be more independent here under his roof than she'd be under her parents'. She and Falconridge could work out an agreeable arrangement. In time, as their affection for each other grew, then she could allow him into her bed knowing he would forgive her sins. And she would give him an heir eventually. They had plenty of time. She was only twenty after all.

On the other hand, his reaction had confirmed that his *only* interest in her was the money. He'd offered no words of undying love, no words of deepest desire. He'd shown no disappointment that she wasn't willing to be bedded. He'd not tried to convince her that within his arms she'd find bliss. She was the means to two ends: the obliteration of his debt quickly followed by further spending and the obtainment of an heir.

She'd known that of course, but still the reality of it was painful to admit. He cared only for his own needs, not hers. Not once did he ask her what she wanted, not once did he inquire as to the key to her happiness. She required time for her heart to heal. She needed to be more than coins jingling in his pockets. While she'd spoken of love, she didn't truly expect to ever again acquire it, but she thought they could develop affection for each other, could at least come to care for each other's happiness. They simply needed a little bit of time to come to know each other.

The slamming of another door rang out. The door to his bedchamber?

She heard the harsh beat of feet guided by fury making their way down the stairs. She rose, not certain what she planned to do, but her curiosity—

Another thundering bang from below.

She hurried to the window, drew back the drapery, and glanced down in time to see her husband sweeping down the path toward the street, his cloak billowing out behind him in a rather ominous way, as he disappeared into the fog-shrouded night. Her imagination fueled by far too many novels conjured up unflattering scenarios regarding his plans.

Was he off to find a woman to sate his lust?

Was he off to drink himself into oblivion?

Was he off to vent his anger on some unsuspecting soul?

Lord, she knew nothing at all about his temperament, about what harm he might be capable of inflicting.

She'd watched his knuckles turning white as he'd gripped the bedpost, and she couldn't help but believe he'd been imagining that thick wood was actually her slender neck.

Her father had never been prone to violence, and she'd been incredibly sheltered. Wisely, her father had put safeguards in place to ensure the marquess never brutalized her, but a man could exact his revenge in any number of ways that didn't involve physical violence.

Leaving her alone and lonely was one of them.

But then she'd been lonely ever since her mother had torn Wesley from her life. And now he was married, forever lost to her. And so she'd married expediently, partly for some sort of twisted revenge. What a misguided sense of retribution that decision was turning out to be.

The marquess had so few books on his shelves. Was the man even literate? They'd sat in the library for an hour reading, and not once did he turn a page. She could think of little worse than living with a man who did not value books.

All right. Something was far worse. Living with a man who held no affection for her whatsoever.

Wesley had been the first and only man who had truly wanted *her*. It was Jenny the men fawned over, Jenny the men wanted. Kate had always protected her heart by burying her nose in her books and pretending it didn't matter that she wasn't the Rose daughter unattached men favored.

And then Wesley had come into her life, and she'd known the splendor of love. He'd written her poems, brought her flowers. Almost from the start, he'd coerced her affection to life by never shying away from sharing his own feelings. They'd arranged secret trysts. He'd whispered sweet words of longing in her ear. He'd won her heart over in such a short time.

But her mother had declared him a fortune hunter and his love false. But she was wrong. With all her heart, Kate knew her mother was wrong.

Now she was free of her mother, but shackled to Falconridge. A man who truly did want her only for her money. But Falconridge came with a title, while Wesley had not. Amazing how the direction of her life was influenced by an accident of birth.

Not once had Falconridge spoken sweet words. Not once had he even bothered to lead her to believe she—and not money—had been his reason for asking for her hand.

Kate longed for a man who cared about the yearnings of her heart.

* * *

"She is insisting I earn her love."

Standing within Hawkhurst's library, Michael downed the whiskey from the glass like a civilized man when all he truly wanted was to drain every drop from the bottle. He looked at his rumpled host and didn't want to contemplate that he might have taken his friend from something other than sleep.

"I must confess from the outset, when you told me you had devised a plan to acquire an heiress with little or no effort, that I had doubts you would meet with success," Hawkhurst said.

"So you're saying her insistence is a just punishment?"

"I'm saying I'm not surprised the arrangement isn't turning out to be as effortless as you anticipated."

Michael dropped into a nearby chair and sat facing his friend. "How do I do it? How do I make her look at me the way your duchess looks at you?"

Hawkhurst seemed surprised. "How does Louisa look at me?"

"As though you are her entire world." He averted his eyes from the duke's self-satisfied smile, ignoring the way his friend's gaze had shot to the doors that would lead to the stairs that would lead him back to his wife. Michael could well imagine the duchess was going to find herself aroused from slumber if she wasn't already awake, awaiting her husband's return. Michael, on the other hand, had never held a woman's heart, not even his mother's. Certainly no woman had ever anticipated his arrival, his return to her side. He wasn't particularly proud of the fact he found himself envying Hawkhurst.

"Honestly, Falconridge, I believe you underestimate your ability to earn her affection. After all, I like you well enough."

With disgust, Michael shifted his gaze back to Hawkhurst. "Hmm, so I should take her drinking, gambling, and whoring?"

Hawkhurst grinned. "It's not merely the things we do together. We have a bond, a history. I trust you."

"What's my favorite color?"

Hawkhurst blinked several times. "Pardon?"

"She says I should know her favorite color. If I cared for her at all, I would know it. I've known you for thirty years, and haven't a clue regarding your favorite color. Devil take her! I've never heard of anything so ludicrous in all my life. I may very well have married a mad woman."

And wasn't that jolly well marvelous to contemplate: that he might find himself dealing with another lunatic.

"Women do have a tendency to look at the world slightly differently than we do," Hawkhurst confirmed.

"So what am I to do?"

"What you should have done from the beginning: court her."

"I'd hoped to avoid that tedious process."

"At least you go into it knowing you've gained the prize."

"As much as I hate to admit it, I've never had much success with gaining a woman's favor. I bought my mistress all sorts of baubles and yet she left. What do women want?"

"Perhaps we should bring Louisa into the conversation."

"No, God, no. It's humbling enough discussing it with you."

"But she served as Kate's chaperone for a while. Lived with her, observed her. Surely, she'd know the girl's favorite color."

Kate Rose Tremayne's favorite color?

Louisa Selwyn, the new Duchess of Hawkhurst, stared at their guest, while trying to decipher the purpose of his question. Her husband had returned to their bedchamber to announce Falconridge was in need of some assistance, and she needed to dress posthaste—although she hadn't. She'd taken her sweet time, tormenting him with the reminder of what he'd abandoned, as she slipped back into her nightgown and wrapper. She'd taken some satisfaction in the low curses he'd thrown at his friend, the way he'd gripped the door handle to prevent himself from crossing the room to her—which surely would have resulted in their delay in returning to their guest—and the ardent kiss he'd delivered, filled with the promise of passion to be shared once they dispatched with their midnight caller.

Now her husband stood leaning against the

mantel, seemingly amused by Falconridge's discomfiture, while Louisa sat across from his friend.

"Her favorite color?" she repeated.

"Yes." Falconridge leaned forward expectantly, as though she held the solution to ending the world's troubles.

"I'm sorry, my lord, but I haven't a clue."

He flung himself back in the chair with such force that it scraped across the floor. "You were my last hope," he grumbled.

"May I inquire as to why it's such an important thing to know?"

"It's important to her that I know. It's a riddle she has set before me, and until I solve it"—he cleared his throat—"it is simply important I solve it. Your husband thought you might have the answer since you lived with her for a spell. Since you don't, allow me to ask you this: how might I earn her favor?"

Ah, now she was beginning to understand Hawk's amused expression. She did know Kate well enough to know she'd not settle for less than love; and if Louisa were a wagering woman, she'd wager Falconridge was just now learning the truth of his wife's obstinacy and facing the consequences.

"Well, she loves to read. Perhaps a book—"

"I am presently without funds."

"Oh, I see. Well, you could pick some flowers from the garden."

"I don't see that action as being of any consequence. She can go into the garden and enjoy all the flowers she wishes."

"Your selecting the ones you think she would enjoy would be the gift."

He shook his head, obviously failing to grasp her point.

"You could take her rowing on the Thames."

He grimaced.

"You could read her poetry."

He looked as though he might be ill.

"Take her on a walk, talk with her. Be kind."

He released a deep breath and came to his feet. "This is accomplishing nothing. I'm sorry to have disturbed your sleep."

"You told me once that you'd been accused of having too much pride. Perhaps, for her, you simply need to swallow it."

"Your Grace, please don't take offense at my impatience, but it is unconscionably late, my wedding night, and I am here seeking counsel. How much pride do you think remains to me? Again, my apologies for interrupting your evening. I shall see myself out."

He strode from the room as though the hounds of hell nipped at his heels. When he closed the door behind him, Louisa rose and went to her husband, relishing the swiftness with which he drew her near. "He's quite miserable, isn't he?" she asked.

"Afraid so."

"And you find his suffering humorous?"

"Not at all, but I must confess to being entertained by his attempts at finding quick solutions to complicated problems."

"Why do I have the feeling your words contain hidden meaning, perhaps insult?"

He lifted her into his arms. "Women, my love, are not easily understood and he wishes to understand them easily."

"We are not that difficult to comprehend."

He began carrying her toward their bedchamber. "Louisa, my darling, you have no clue how hard it is for a man to understand a woman's mind."

Chapter 5

"Lavender."

Kate looked up from her buttered eggs with tomatoes to stare at her husband who sat at the far end of the ridiculously lengthy table. Eight chairs lined either side of it, as though he frequently hosted breakfast parties. He'd already been eating when she'd waltzed into the breakfast room in her *lavender* day dress. He had, of course, come to his feet and waited while she took her time selecting the items for her plate. He'd not spoken a word until the butler had pulled out her chair and she'd taken her place.

"You're guessing again," she said tersely.

"Did I guess correctly?"

"No."

He gave her a disgruntled look, rattled his newspaper, and returned to reading whatever article had snagged his attention.

"What news are you reading about?"

"A couple of footpads have taken to robbing people at gunpoint. They shot a fellow recently."

"Why does anyone do that?"

He gave her a sharp look as though he didn't understand the concept of conversation before turning his attention fully back to his paper. Kate looked over at the butler who stood smartly nearby, as though there was more than the single footman to oversee. She would need to see about increasing staff immediately. "Beginning tomorrow morning, I'd like a newspaper set out for me as well."

Out of the corner of her eye, she was aware of Falconridge lowering his paper. The butler's eyes shifted to his master, and she thought she saw Falconridge nod before the butler shifted his attention back to her. "My pleasure, my lady."

"In the future, you need not look to my husband for approval of my requests." She smiled sweetly at Falconridge. "Isn't that so?"

"Bexhall meant no disrespect. It's simply that we've never had a marchioness who read the newspaper over breakfast."

"How else can I keep up with the affairs of the world?"

"The gossip?"

"The business."

He seemed surprised she'd care about world affairs. She could see him debating internally whether or not to give up the enjoyment of his morning paper, so she might have an opportunity to read it before he was finished with it. It irritated her that he had to consider it at all.

"You left the house last night," she said.

Lowering the newspaper completely, he gave

her a cool look of disdain. "I don't believe the settlement agreement included the necessity for me to keep you apprised of all my comings and goings."

"I would think, considering the fact we will be meeting with your man of business this morning to discuss monies owed, that you would do all within your power to avoid earning my displeasure."

Even from this distance, she could see his jaw tightening, his eyes hardening even further. She thought he could cut diamonds with that stare, but strangely, she wasn't intimidated. Her father had, with a mere signature, given her power she'd never before possessed. She wouldn't have said anything at all about her husband's late-night adventure if she hadn't worried herself silly that he'd sought another's bed. She would have a faithful husband, by God, if nothing else.

He nodded toward the butler, then the footman. "You're both dismissed to see to your other duties."

Both men bowed and left without saying a word.

"I thought it was acceptable to speak in front of servants," Kate said.

"I'm not accustomed to doing so when the matters are of a personal nature."

"So last night—"

"I paid a visit to the Duke and Duchess of Hawkhurst."

"It was hardly an appropriate hour for calling."

"Hawkhurst's friendship is not governed by the hour hand on a clock. I sought his counsel in an attempt to understand your demands. Ask your former chaperone if you doubt I spoke with him."

"I don't doubt you." She looked back at her eggs, having lost all appetite. It wasn't like her to be small and petty. Jenny was right. She shouldn't have agreed to this marriage. It was bringing out the worst in her. She shifted her gaze to the single red rose resting beside her plate. It had been there when she'd arrived. "Is the rose from you?"

"The duchess suggested I give you a flower as a way to earn your affection, which I suppose makes the gesture meaningless."

"Not entirely, no." She couldn't fault him with trying and she respected that he was a man who wouldn't take credit that belonged to another. Yet based upon his reputation, his exceptional good looks, and the prestige of his title, she was somewhat surprised that he didn't have the art of wooing women down to an art. Why did he find her demands so baffling that he'd need to seek counsel?

She glanced up, surprised by the tautness of his features. Did he ever laugh or smile? Strangely she had no memory of him ever doing either in her presence. Surely she'd not married a glum and broody sort. "If I may be so bold, I'm not certain it's a wise course to seek advice from a man who sought to gain my sister's hand in marriage by ruining her reputation."

"Rather you think I should follow Lord Bertram's preference for boring conversation."

"He enjoys discussing the arts—literature, painting—"

"Conversation about the arts is equal to discourse on lovemaking. No words can do either justice. I find both must be *experienced* to be fully appreciated."

Grateful he'd dismissed the servants, she felt the heat warm her cheeks. She should have known he'd work what he'd been denied last night into the conversation, although she couldn't admit to being too scandalized. As a matter of fact, she was rather intrigued by his comment. "Perhaps our experiencing the arts together will lead to us experiencing other things in time."

"In time . . ." he fairly growled.

"I don't mean to be difficult, but I always longed for something more in a marriage than convenience. You're quite right that I should have voiced my objections to my parents, but as much as you desired money, I desired freedom. For as long as I can remember, every aspect of my life has been my mother's dictate. What I was to wear, where I was to go, how I was to behave. And almost always I was the good daughter, because not being the good daughter brought even harsher, and more painful, punishments. I cannot give myself to a stranger. I simply can't. It would be torturous to be intimate with someone for whom I have no affection." She lifted the rose and sniffed the delicate fragrance. "I think you'll find I'm not too terribly difficult to please, but I do want to be pleased. Surely when you approached my father and asked for my hand in marriage, your request was spurred by more than simply receiving money. You must have seen the potential for a pleasing relationship between us."

"I expected you to be more biddable."

She lifted her gaze to him and smiled. "You vastly underestimated American women if you expected that. I'm asking only for a bit of time and patience, an opportunity to come to know each other."

"If that would please you, then I shall abide by your wishes."

She broadened her smile. "There, you see? I believe we're making great progress. That wasn't too difficult was it?"

"Quite honestly?"

She nodded.

"For me, it was hell."

She felt her stomach lurch as he came to his feet. "If you'll excuse me, I need to arrange some things before my man of business, Mr. Giddens, arrives."

He strode toward her, folding the newspaper as he came, set it down with a *thwump* beside her plate, and walked from the room without another word. She didn't know whether to take the rose *and* the newspaper as a beginning or their conversation as an ending to what might have evolved into an agreeable arrangement.

* * *

Michael could scarcely signify that he'd interpreted his wife's comments during breakfast correctly. She wanted a sensitive buffoon who routinely engaged in conversations about art, emotions, and sentiments? She wanted them to sit around and . . . *talk?*

He'd made a ghastly mistake, and if he weren't standing at the window, listening intently as Kate discussed matters with Mr. Giddens, he might have taken her up on her suggestion from the night before that they get an annulment. But dear Lord, before the day was over all his London debts would be cleared. He couldn't very well turn his back on that achievement.

She was correct in her assessment. She wasn't being terribly difficult. He'd just never met a woman who seemed quite so determined to have her way. As a matter of fact, he wasn't certain he'd ever met a woman who knew what she wanted beyond fancy hats and expensive baubles. He'd certainly never known a woman who looked as comfortable sitting behind a large desk as his wife did. Sitting at a delicate writing desk while penning letters—certainly. But looking over ledgers and statements? Occasionally making marks, adding up sums?

If it weren't for the fact it was his personal affairs she was periodically raising eyebrows over, he might have never turned his attention back to the garden.

Sitting at the desk in her husband's study, with

Mr. Giddens sitting in front of her and producing from his satchel a set of statements of monies owed from one merchant after another, Kate was very much aware of her husband's brooding silence as he stood in front of the window, gazing out on the lawn. If she'd discovered anything during their morning conversation, it was that he was an incredibly private person and not prone to revealing much about himself at all. She could well imagine how difficult it was to have his personal affairs reviewed by his wife, to have her approve which merchants would be paid and which wouldn't. Not that she had any intention of not paying any of his debts. It was unfair to withhold payment from anyone who had possessed the idiocy to continue to extend credit to a man who had, in many cases, not paid a cent in over five years. She knew merchants tended to make exceptions for the aristocracy, but still, how did they pay their own bills?

As she carefully reviewed her husband's expenditures, she couldn't help but think they weren't excessive. But then excessive was relative. She was, after all, accustomed to purchasing twenty thousand dollars worth of clothing in a single year.

She was familiar with the names of the shops that catered to women's needs: exquisite gowns, fans, gloves, hats . . .

"Your mother seems to have rather expensive tastes."

Out of the corner of her eye, she caught sight of Falconridge's back stiffening. "Those items were for my mistress," he ground out.

Mr. Giddens cleared his throat.

Kate, on the other hand, wanted to clear the room. He had a mistress. Now doubts and anger assailed her. Even if he had gone to Hawkhurst's last night, he could have dropped in on his mistress afterward. She didn't want to think of him crawling between the sheets with another woman.

"I will approve payment of these items, of course, as they were made before I came into your life. However, you will need to make other arrangements where your mistress is concerned."

He looked over his shoulder and glared at her. "You have no worries there. She left me weeks ago."

"I'm sorry."

He seemed as surprised by her words as she was. They'd popped out before she'd had a chance to stop them, guilt at her considerable relief no doubt spurring her on to show some compassion for his loss. She straightened her shoulders. "I know how difficult it is to be cast aside."

"It wasn't personal, it was business. I could no longer afford the trinkets she required in order to service me."

She flinched. Did he view all bedding as being cold, meticulous . . . business? Is that the reason he was able to come so brazenly to her bedchamber, even though they barely knew each other? To be serviced?

She released whatever bit of guilt that had been nagging at her because she had sent him away. After Wesley's tender lovemaking, she had no desire—nor would she tolerate—being treated as though she were an object to be used for his carnal desires. Not when she had a few of her own.

"Are you being deliberately crude?" she asked tartly.

"You expressed your sorrow at her leaving as though you thought she meant something to me, as though you thought I might have suffered some emotional pain at her moving on. I assure you, madam, I saw her leaving as little more than an inconvenience."

She almost asked, "Why, then, did you say she left *you* rather than just saying she left?"

But she held her tongue because Mr. Giddens cleared his throat again, and she sensed her husband would deny any suffering simply because it was a matter of pride. Dear Lord, but he was almost too proud, too stoic, too distant. What was he trying to protect?

She was taken aback by the thought. Why had she deduced that he was trying to protect anything at all? More importantly, why was she suddenly so intrigued by him?

Granted he was handsome beyond measure, but he was so damned mysterious, seemingly constantly on guard for fear he might reveal something he didn't wish her to know.

With effort, she turned her attention back to the boring debts rather than scrutinizing her fascinating husband further. She could study him all she wanted, but she doubted that would be enough to reveal anything of any significance where he was concerned.

Before the meeting, she'd changed into a rather plain blue dress that buttoned all the way to her chin, because she thought it gave her a no-nonsense appearance, and she wanted Mr. Giddens to take her and her status in this household seriously. She'd also wanted to see if her husband would blurt out, "blue" upon first seeing her.

He hadn't. He'd barely turned from the window when she'd entered the room.

She didn't know why it tickled her that he was trying to guess her favorite color. Especially since she knew it wasn't the key to getting into her bed. She'd merely used it as an example to demonstrate how little they knew of each other. He seemed to have taken it as a challenge. Discover her favorite color, leap into her bed.

No, she'd learned the hard way not to be that easy.

All in all, it took her three hours to review all the information Giddens provided. It would have been simpler to have him give her a grand total and approve all payments in one magnificent gesture, but in truth she was curious regarding what sorts of purchases had led to her husband's great debt. To her surprise, she discovered an inordinate amount of costly "trinkets" which she assumed he'd given to his mistress and she wondered if he'd been attempting to purchase her affections. She wasn't really certain how the mistress business worked. Maybe she'd pay a visit to Jeremy and ask him to explain it. She didn't think her brother had ever had a mistress, but it seemed like the sort of information men knew instinctively, so perhaps he could enlighten her.

She authorized a draft from the bank and handed it to Mr. Giddens. She also authorized an additional payment for him as an acknowledgment for his excellent record-keeping and because she didn't want him absconding with the funds himself. If he continued to be honest, he would continue to be paid honestly.

"Thank you, my lady. It has been a pleasure to meet with you and see to my lord's business."

"I should like for us to meet monthly in the future."

"I hardly see a need. It is the British way to extend credit to the aristocracy until the end of the year."

"Yes, well, I'm American and I prefer to settle all debts monthly. Less chance of them getting out of hand that way."

"As you wish." He bowed to her and to Falconridge. "Good day, my lady, my lord."

When the man had quit the room, she sighed, sat back, and looked at her husband. He didn't look happy, but then she was beginning to think he never did.

"Did you enjoy that?" he asked.

"Not particularly. You've been in debt for some time."

"Unfortunately, that wasn't all of it. The servants need to be paid."

"I'll take care of it."

He nodded brusquely. "Tomorrow I would like to leave for my country estate so we—you—can set matters to rights there."

"All right."

He tilted his head slightly. "You acquiesce that easily?"

"I've never been overly fond of London. I look forward to visiting your ancestral home. I would like to visit with my family this afternoon to let them know of our plans."

"If you've no objections, I won't accompany you. I have some personal matters to attend to before we leave."

"Of course."

He lowered his gaze to the Aubusson rug beneath his feet, and she observed a muscle in his cheek tightening, imagined his jaw clenching to the point of discomfort. And she knew, *knew*, what it was he was struggling with.

"How much do you require in funds to take care of these personal matters?" she asked.

He lifted his gaze to her, and she thought she might weep at the despair she saw there, and she knew that it was this debt more than any other that had prompted him to ask for her hand.

"A thousand pounds."

It was much less than she'd already approved for his other debts. Why was he so bothered by this? She considered asking, but instead, simply said, "I'll write you a draft."

"With no questions asked?"

"You said it was personal."

He turned away, but not before she caught relief washing over his face.

"Thank you." His voice sounded hoarse, strained. He cleared his throat, and she thought he might say something else, perhaps explain the need for his funds. Instead, he simply remained silent.

As she set to writing out the draft, she wondered if a day would come when he would share with her the burdens he carried, and if his doing so would mean sharing with him the secrets she held.

Chapter 6

❦❦

"I wanted to let you know that I've married."

The silver-haired woman sitting on the bed stared at Michael as though she was unable to comprehend the meaning of his announcement or didn't quite trust him.

He cleared his throat. "She's an American. A very wealthy American. I think you'd approve of her. Her eyes are not a distinct color. They seem to change shade with her mood. I haven't quite determined the pattern yet. Mostly because she's been put out with me more than anything else. And under those circumstances they tend to appear green. Her hair, however, is quite the opposite when it comes to color. No question there. It is as bright a red as I have ever seen. I can't say I particularly fancy the shade but—"

"Who are you that I should care?"

She studied him, bafflement clearly visible in her expression. She'd once been a beauty. Now, she was merely lost. He was incredibly weary of telling her who he was, only to be told his claim was impossible.

She had no son.

The truly sad thing was that she made the claim not because she had disinherited him, but because she truly had no memory of him. What sort of lunacy was it that caused a person to forget those she loved? The cruelest kind. Or perhaps, as he often feared, he was easily forgettable, because she'd never truly loved him.

"No one of any importance," he finally murmured.

"Then why are you here?"

He shook his head sadly. "I'm not certain. It seemed the sort of news one would share with family, and as I have no . . . family . . . I thought to share it with you. Are they treating you well here?"

She shrugged, her gaze beginning to lose its focus. "Why hasn't Falconridge come for me?"

Because he's been dead for more than twenty years.

"He doesn't usually hunt with Albert this long," she continued.

Prince Albert, too, has been long gone.

"Who are you again?" she asked.

"Michael."

"Lovely name."

She began to study her wrinkled hands, and Michael wondered if they frightened her. He hated that sometimes she became so frightened and nothing he did made her feel safe.

He unfolded his body from the wooden hard-backed chair. "I must go now."

"You mustn't let my husband catch you here. He gets terribly jealous."

"Good-bye, my lady."

He never knew what was more difficult, the arriving or the departing. He walked from the room, no longer hesitating while the attendant locked the door. The doctor was waiting for him.

"Must you lock her in?" Michael asked.

"As you know, my lord, she tends to wander, with no rhyme or reason, no obvious destination in mind. Locking her in is for her own good," Dr. Kent said. "She's not bothered by it, I assure you."

"How can you know what she is bothered by?"

"There are no signs she's bothered. She doesn't get agitated. She seems quite content."

"How can she be content when she cannot remember?"

"The mind is a strange thing, my lord. We've admitted a new Duke of Wellington. Why does this man honestly believe he is Wellington? And he is content to be so."

"Until you cure him."

Kent nodded. "We cured a Napoleon last week."

"Why would any respectable Englishman have delusions of being Napoleon?"

"As I said, my lord, the mind is baffling. If I may have a word—"

"I'm here, aren't I?"

"In my office."

"I have paid all I owe." He'd been both astounded and grateful when Kate had approved the funds without requiring an explanation for their need.

"Yes, my lord, but as you know asylums exist for those who can be cured. Generally our residents stay no more than a year. If they can't be cured, other arrangements must be made."

"Yes, I'm well aware of that. I'm working on other arrangements. I need a bit more time."

"I'm sorry, my lord, but so many need help, and most of those can be cured, if we can only have them with us for a short while. Your mother's dementia shows no signs of improving. To continue to house someone who is incurable . . . it's simply not fair to those who could be cured."

Michael gritted his teeth. "I beg of you. I will pay three times what you are asking."

Dr. Kent smiled. "I suppose we could see our way clear to keep her for another year."

Michael nodded. He could probably purchase the whole damned place, but he didn't want her here. He had other plans. He only needed a bit of time to bring them to fruition. Although considering how his plans to acquire funds had gone, he could only hope these would go much more smoothly.

"So explain to me how the mistress business works."

Kate had found her brother in the library. It was the first room she'd gone to. Someone in her family, usually her father, could always be found in the library.

Jeremy, lounging in a chair near the window, closed *The Guidebook of London*, and stared at her.

Like her, he was fascinated by details and never undertook any venture without careful planning—even touring a city he was visiting.

"Pardon?" he asked, with a raised eyebrow.

Kate sat in the chair opposite him, wishing she had the option of lounging, but the bustle on her dress prohibited such casual posture. "Falconridge had a mistress, so I'm trying to understand how this mistress business works. He purchased an inordinate number of trinkets for her. Would the amount indicate the depth of his affection for her?"

"Could mean any number of things."

"Such as?"

He sighed, reached for his cigarette case on the nearby table, and proceeded to light a cigarette.

"Mother doesn't like for you to smoke in the house."

"Good thing she's not here, then, isn't it?"

"Where is she?"

He shrugged. "She wanted to go out for a ride in the carriage so Father took her. Did you really want her here to ask how your marriage was going?"

"I suppose not and don't think for a moment that you've distracted me from seeking an answer to my question."

He inhaled on his cigarette and blew the smoke out in a way that created little rings. "I suppose he could have held affection for her."

"He says he didn't. He said it was just a business arrangement."

"He discussed his mistress with you?"

"I spent more than three hours going over his expenditures this morning and seeing to his debts. I questioned the purchasing of all the trinkets."

"If it was just business, then they were probably no more than payment."

"He leased a house for three years and had additional servants"—the expenses for which had ceased "weeks ago"—"would they have been for her do you think?" The timing fit.

"I have no way of knowing. Ask him."

Only she wasn't as comfortable with Falconridge, couldn't bring herself to ask him about the intimate details of the life he'd shared with his mistress. "Do men, as a habit, provide the lodgings for their mistresses?"

"Kate—"

"Jeremy, please. It's a simple enough question."

He looked none too pleased, but he did answer. "Generally, yes. You don't want to have to go searching for her when you have a need."

"I see." She worried her lower lip. "So a mistress is a paid companion?"

"In a manner of speaking, yes."

"So he might not have had affection for her?"

"You're not jealous of a mistress, are you?"

"Should I be?"

"No."

"Do you have a mistress?"

"I can't believe you're asking me this." He took a long drag on his cigarette.

"I thought I smelled something delicious in

here," Jenny said, strolling in through the open door, interrupting what Kate thought could have turned into a very interesting conversation. Jenny snatched the cigarette from Jeremy—who knew better than to object—and sat in a nearby chair, taking a puff. "Kate, my dear sister, why aren't you spending the day with that incredibly handsome husband of yours?"

"He had some personal matters to attend to, so I wanted to come by to let everyone know we're leaving for the country tomorrow."

"Oh, the ancestral estate. I wonder what it's like."

"If it's like other ancestral estates, it won't be very modern. I've heard of some that are still lit with candles."

"You'll have enough money to change all that," Jenny said.

"I suppose. The London residence needs some upkeep as well."

"That's what you must expect when you marry an impoverished lord."

"Do you believe everyone has only one true love?" Kate asked, fearing she might never feel for Falconridge what she'd felt for Wesley. He wasn't nearly as charming or fun. But then, in all fairness, along with his title, he'd no doubt inherited an inordinate amount of responsibilities, the likes of which would never be passed on to Wesley. Younger sons had more freedom to play than their older brother. It certainly made them a good deal more entertaining.

"Of course not. Love is infinite. You love Mother, Father, Jeremy, and me, and I daresay if you had other siblings, you'd love them as well."

"Don't you think you're being a bit presumptuous to assume Kate loves you?" Jeremy asked.

Jenny handed the cigarette back to him and smiled mischievously. "Don't you have something important to do? Like take a tour of an old museum or something?"

"Quite right." He stood. "I'm intrigued by the Chamber of Horrors at Madam Tussaud's. From what I understand the exhibits display such gruesome images that it's quite horrifying. Naturally, women are too delicate to be admitted into that particular room."

"Oh, rubbish," Kate said, annoyed that he seemed quite gleeful over his perceived superiority—which was no doubt his intent. To annoy her. She suspected he'd be a challenge to his future wife, teasing her unmercifully. "I despise that women are viewed as having such weak constitutions."

"Care to accompany me and put yours to the test?"

"I have a household to see after. I can't go gallivanting around London."

"Pity. Tell Mother not to expect me until dawn."

"The museum closes long before that," Jenny said.

Jeremy winked and grinned. "I'll find other entertainments."

He strode from the room with the confidence

of a man who could do anything he damned well pleased.

"Sometimes I wish I'd been born a man," Kate said, trying not to let the familiar resentment build within her. She'd never envied Jenny her beauty, but she'd always envied Jeremy his freedoms. "I could have taken over managing Father's bank. I think I would have enjoyed that."

"I don't understand you, Kate," Jenny said. "I can think of nothing more boring than sitting in an office all day, studying numbers."

"I find it boring sitting in a room all day being measured for gowns. My God, Jenny, we spent more than twenty thousand dollars on our wardrobe for the year when we were in Paris. That's an embarrassment of excess."

"You've been married less than twenty-four hours and already you're talking like a miser. What is the point in having money if one doesn't spend it? Besides, I believe we have an obligation to spend it, to spread it around."

Perhaps it was looking over the list of all the baubles and trinkets Falconridge had purchased that had Kate questioning her own spending habits.

Jenny got up, grabbed Kate's arm, and tugged on her. "Come along. You're far too melancholy, and it's beginning to rub off on me. Let's join Jeremy on his outing."

"I'm no longer carefree, to do as I please. I need to hire some additional staff before we leave." She planned to go to the Metropolitan Association for Befriending Young Servants. It had several branch offices and had established quite a reputation for successfully placing young ladies.

Jenny got a wicked gleam in her eye. "Are you in need of any footmen?"

Rolling her eyes, Kate smiled at Jenny's mischievousness. "I plan to hire several in fact. Presently we have only one."

"Lovely. Then I think I'll spend the afternoon with you instead. I like nothing better than having an excuse to study the turn of a young man's calf."

Footmen were generally chosen based on how good they looked in livery. A well-turned calf gave them a definite advantage.

"You'd rather ogle young men than gory figurines?" Kate teased.

"Without question. I think you should go with tall, dark, and handsome for your servants. And I'll enjoy helping you select them."

"Tall footmen can demand a higher salary."

"Which you can well afford. Indulge yourself. I certainly plan to when I have my own household."

"Perhaps I will, although I was thinking gentlemen of a fairer persuasion. My husband satisfies the tall, dark, and handsome needs of our household."

"The dangerous part as well, I suspect." Jenny leaned forward. "I'd promised myself I wouldn't ask, but the curiosity is killing me. Did Falcon-ridge make you happy last night?"

Kate felt the heat burning her cheeks and feared they might actually scorch.

"That good, hey?" Jenny asked, smiling.

Kate swallowed hard. She didn't want to discuss last night with Jenny, didn't want to explain her decision to delay being bedded. "This is hardly a topic for discussion, but I will say I was very pleased with last night's outcome. However, don't ask for particulars as I won't share them."

"You're absolutely no fun at all. Still, I knew he'd be scrumptious in bed."

"Why would you say that?"

"He just has that look about him, the look of a man who knows his way very well around a bed-chamber."

Kate wasn't at all pleased with the image that statement provoked or the spark of jealousy it created. She shot to her feet. "I really need to see about getting the servants hired."

"Give me a moment to change?"

"A moment? It takes you at least an hour."

"Then join me upstairs and I'll tell you all about the costume ball I'm planning."

"When is this?" Kate asked, following her out of the library.

"In two weeks. You will come back for it, won't you?"

"I'll certainly try. It'll all depend on what I discover at my husband's ancestral estate."

* * *

Michael needed a woman. He always did after visiting with his mother. Just for a few moments to escape the agony of not being remembered, the anguish of wondering if she suffered or was frightened, and the torment of not being able to do a damned thing for her.

Traveling in his open carriage with his groom at the reins—he'd left the coach and its driver for Kate—through the streets of London, he couldn't help but feel the tension coiling tighter. For some time he'd not had the surcease of a woman's body. He didn't truly blame his mistress for leaving him. He knew he was a selfish bastard. Their relationship had centered on his needs: his need for distraction, his need for pleasure, his need to forget while forgetting was a choice.

Would his mother's affliction visit him in time? Was it passed on through the blood? Some nights he didn't sleep for fear he'd awaken unable to remember. He could hardly think of anything worse than not remembering.

And why couldn't she remember?

The physician had told him sometimes a blow to the head will cause one to forget. But she'd taken no blow to the head.

Sometimes a traumatic experience—surviving a fire, a rape, an attack—no, no, no.

She'd been sheltered, pampered, cared for.

Then one day he'd returned home to find her hysterical, crying, terrified, lost . . . within her own home. Not that it wasn't difficult to become confused. Their country manor was a labyrinth of corridors, a maze of rooms. But she'd lived there since she'd married at sixteen. How could she suddenly not recognize the hallways, the rooms? How was it that she'd seemed to have no idea where she was?

And the next day she'd been fine. No repercussions. No worries.

But slowly over time other signs of forgetfulness had begun to appear. Until five years ago, when he'd finally recognized that she needed more help than he could provide, and he'd had her committed.

His mother, the Marchioness of Falconridge, now the dowager Marchioness, resided in a private lunatic asylum.

He doubted James Rose would have been so quick to sign the settlement papers if he'd known that. But Michael had never told a soul. Even when he used the carriage, the driver knew only the destination, not the reason behind the visit. As far as London was concerned, his mother simply preferred the country life. The truth of her circumstance was his burden to bear alone.

And he'd dealt with the burden by losing himself in a woman—her fragrance, her softness, her heat.

He thought of his wife, with her ample curves that would provide such solace. He remembered the enticing shadows he'd seen beneath her gossamer gown last night. How he would like to run his tongue over the tempting flesh . . .

He moaned low as carnal images caused his body to tighten, but he would go unsatisfied this day, this night. He would have to find another way to fight his demons until he earned her affection.

"Stop!" he called to the driver as they passed a jewelry shop.

As soon as the carriage rolled to a stop, Michael opened the door and stepped out. "Wait here, I shan't be long."

With sure strides through the bustling crowd, he made his way back to the jewelers'. He'd bought numerous gifts there for his mistress. For the first time, he wondered if she'd truly liked what he'd selected or if she'd only pretended. She seemed to favor pieces with lots of sparkles. He couldn't see his wife wearing anything he'd purchased for his mistress. His wife's tastes would be more subtle. Or at least he thought they would be. If he were wrong, then any gift at all would have the opposite affect of what he intended. Still, he opened the door and strode into the shop.

"Good afternoon, my lord. It's a pleasure to see you."

No doubt because his bills had been paid. Michael nodded at Potterton, the proprietor. "Good day, sir."

"I saw you were recently married. Congratulations."

"Thank you." Although he wasn't certain congratulations *were* in order. More like sympathies.

"Need a bit of fancy for your wife? We have several items which are deserving of the throat of a marchioness."

Michael thought of draping a necklace around Kate's throat, securing it from behind, pressing his lips to the nape of her neck, planting a kiss at the soft spot beneath her ear, inhaling her fragrance . . . yes, a necklace might do the trick.

Potterton showed him several necklaces that sparkled with diamonds, emeralds, or sapphires, but Michael didn't know her favorite color, so how the devil was he to know her preference in gems? He had a feeling she wouldn't be nearly as easy to please as his mistress, who'd been grateful for any trinket delivered. He remembered that Kate had worn pearls the day they married. Pearls. White. Was that her favorite color? Diamonds were the closest thing to white that he saw . . . or silver. Perhaps more pearls. Or a cameo.

"Do you see something you think she'd like, my lord?"

"Actually, I'm not here to make a purchase." He removed the glove from his right hand, removed the ring he wore on his little finger, and set it on the counter. "How much will you give me for the ring? It was my father's."

If Potterton was surprised by the request, he masked it well. He leaned forward and said in a low voice, "My lord, your debts here have been paid in full."

"I am well aware of that fact, but I have need of funds for something personal."

Potterton's brow went up slightly. "Ah, yes. I understand completely."

Michael doubted it. He was fairly certain the man thought he needed money for his mistress.

"Would you care to step into the backroom, my lord, for a little private, discreet business?"

After Potterton picked up the ring, Michael followed him into the back room. Potterton sat at a table, brought a loupe to his eye, and studied the ring. "Fine bit of craftsmanship here," he muttered. "But even with that, I could pay you only a few pounds." He laid it on the counter. "I'm certain it is worth far more to you than that."

It was. It was worth ten times, a hundred times that much.

"I'll take whatever you're willing to pay."

Now Potterton did look surprised. "As you wish, my lord."

Michael walked out of the shop feeling like a rich man. Although the amount was small, it was his, earned with the piercing of his heart. He planned to put it to good use. He climbed into the carriage. "Stop at the first confectioner's shop you see."

"Yes, my lord."

His driver urged the pair of horses forward. Michael sat back with satisfaction. His first purchase would be chocolates that he'd present to his wife tonight when he went to say good night. Chocolates didn't come in a variety of colors so he couldn't go wrong there. Perhaps if he purchased a large enough box—

"No, wait! Stop here!"

Michael was out of the carriage before it had come to a complete stop. He strode into the dressmaker's. A woman behind a counter smiled. "Good afternoon, sir."

"Good afternoon. I'm considering purchasing a gown for my wife, but I want something unusual as she is a most unusual woman." He smiled triumphantly, having decided his wife was not a woman who would fancy ordinary colors. No, she'd set a challenge for him knowing he would never guess the proper color. But if anyone knew all the varied colors that women liked, it would be a dressmaker. "Have you a listing of every *color* of fabric that is available?"

Chapter 7

❦

Sitting on the chaise longue in her bedchamber, Kate opened the largest box of chocolates she'd ever seen. Wearing his green silk dressing gown, her husband had come to say good night and brought with him this amazing selection of chocolates.

"I hardly know what to say," she said, looking up at him.

"Just so you know, I didn't use your funds to purchase them. I had a bit of money I'd set aside for a rainy day, and, as I feel I'm in the midst of a tempest, using it seemed appropriate."

"You do realize that your disgruntlement reduces my pleasure at receiving the gift."

Sighing deeply, he gripped the bedpost, and she could see him struggling. Finally, he looked up at her. She'd expected an attempt at a smile.

Instead, he fairly growled, "Plum."

She stared at him. Was he hungry? "Plum?"

"It's a color. Apparently the wrong color. Good night, then."

She watched in stunned fascination as he strode from the room, slamming the door in his wake.

She couldn't help herself. She laughed, nearly doubling over from the effort of holding the sound in. Did he honestly believe he simply needed to announce the right color to win her heart?

As her gaze fell on the box of chocolates, her humor abruptly fled. Know the right color and bring her chocolates. God, he was trying. She'd give him that. She hadn't truly expected him to try to win her favor. She'd expected him to simply be content with the money. How could she forget how much men wanted the bedding?

And he apparently wanted it quite desperately.

She opened her book and removed the letter that had been delivered to her that very afternoon. It was her first official letter since her marriage, addressed to *The Most Hon. The Marchioness of Falconridge.* Its contents made a great deal more sense now, she thought, as she removed the letter and read it again.

Madam,
I beg your forgiveness regarding my impertinence. However, I thought you would find it of interest that the Marquess paid me a visit this afternoon and exchanged his father's ring for a few pounds. I estimate its sentimental value to be considerably more. I shall hold it in my shop for forty-eight hours. Would your ladyship care to make an offer? I await your instructions.

I have the honor to remain,
Your Ladyship's obedient servant,
Thomas Potterton

She did indeed find his letter of interest. Why had Falconridge gone to the trouble to sell his father's ring? To purchase her chocolates?

How absurd.

How touching.

He'd not sold it to pay his debts, but he'd sold it for her. Or at least she assumed he had. Perhaps he hadn't. Perhaps he'd used the money for something else, although had he not just told her he'd used his own funds?

She rose from the chaise, crossed over to the writing desk, pulled out the chair, and sat. She removed a sheet of stationery, bearing a monogram with her new initials—a gift from Jenny so she'd never have an excuse not to write—and dipped her pen into the inkwell before applying it to the paper.

My dear sister,

As you know my husband and I leave for his ancestral home tomorrow. It seems I have some unfinished business in London I will not have an opportunity to complete before leaving, and so I must trust it to you. I will need you to pay a visit to a certain jeweler. His letter is enclosed with mine. Please purchase the ring he mentions at its sentimental value and hold it for me until I return to London. I trust you to keep this secret between us, as I cannot imagine what it must have cost my husband to part with something so valuable for so little. I cannot help but think there might be more to Falconridge than a man simply in want of

money. I'm actually looking forward to our jour-
ney together and the opportunity it will afford us
to get to know each other a bit better.

My love always,
Kate

* * *

She sat in the coach seething. Alone. Totally
alone. As though she was someone to be ashamed
of, someone not worthy of the courtesy of company.

While it was a well-sprung vehicle, it still jos-
tled too much for her to read or to stitch or to pen
a letter to her sister outlining her frustrations. So
she was left with nothing to do other than to gaze
out the window at the passing scenery and wish
it would pass much more quickly. Her husband,
with whom she'd hoped to become better acquainted, was leading the way, riding a gorgeous
black thoroughbred.

Kate wouldn't feel quite so neglected if it wasn't
for the raging downpour outside the carriage.
She'd seen the ominous black clouds billowing
earlier and rolling nearer, and she'd welcomed
their approach, thinking they would at least force
him inside. Instead, he'd thrown a cloak around
his shoulders, replaced his top hat with something
broader of brim and sturdier, and continued on.

Did he resent her so much he didn't want to be
within close proximity of her?

But he'd brought her chocolates . . . had that gesture been merely a ruse to get into her bed? Did

he think she'd be so grateful for the sweets she'd willingly slip beneath the sheets and invite him to join her? Did he not understand that as long as they remained distant, she would refuse him?

She knew he required more than money. He required an heir. Perhaps after she'd rebuffed him again last night, he'd decided he was in no hurry to acquire one.

Meanwhile, she was absolutely miserable. She didn't suffer loneliness well, and without the means to read, she was well and truly lonely. With a book, she could at least visit with people, even if it was vicariously, even if they didn't exist beyond someone's imagination. Here, she could do little more than twiddle her thumbs—and where was the entertainment in that?

It was her mother's answer to her squirming when she was younger. "Occupy your mind, twiddle your thumbs."

It hadn't worked then and it wasn't working now.

It was such a long, insufferable journey. She could at least have told her lady's maid to travel with her, but she was in the coach following, along with a valet she'd hired to see to her husband's needs and two footmen who would be available to carry things to and from the coaches as needed. She'd learned from her mother that one could never have too many servants, and while married gentlemen generally didn't have a valet, Kate certainly wasn't going to take responsibility for dressing her husband or seeing that his clothes were readied. She wondered if the hiring of additional servants had angered him. Or if he was simply not riding with her as a way to show his displeasure because she hadn't been more welcoming last night.

If Falconridge thought he was going to ignore her completely, he had another think coming. She should have brought Jenny, but she had balls she wanted to attend, dukes she wanted to ensnare. Yes, Kate had little doubt before the Season was over, Jenny would have a duke.

Perhaps Kate should have waited to marry until Jenny was snatched up. Then she could have found her own lord who would at least relish traveling with her. Only her heart had been so broken she couldn't envision trying to snag anyone's attention. She hadn't wanted anyone's attention.

Now she did, and he was out in the cold rain riding a damned horse.

She couldn't have been more grateful as evening drew near, and they made a proper stop at a tavern. They'd stopped twice throughout the day to rest or change the horses, she knew not which. The rain had continued to pour and because her husband was drenched, he'd merely passed a bundle of food through the window to her. The bread and cheese had tasted like sawdust. Even the wine hadn't helped either go down anymore smoothly.

The door to the coach opened. Her husband stood there with water dripping from the brim of his hat, his face damp with raindrops. How could he not be shivering? Before she made a move to alight, he said, "It would no doubt be best if I settled my account here before asking for rooms for the night."

"Oh, of course. How much?" she asked, reaching for her small bag. It was one of her favorites, made of seal leather and edged in silver.

He told her the amount and she stared at him. "You make a good many trips."

"I do."

As usual he was succinct and not very forthcoming. She handed him the money. "I have more in my trunk if we need it."

"Let's hope we're not set upon by highwaymen."

"Most don't take off with trunks."

"They do however take a gander inside for valuables."

"Could we discuss this later? I'm chilled."

"Of course. My apologies. Nesbitt is waiting with the umbrella." Falconridge held out his gloved hand and she slipped hers into his. She stepped down, and the newly hired valet quickly moved the umbrella into position, shielding her from the rain while everyone else suffered through its onslaught.

Once inside, she stood before the roaring fire in the front room while Falconridge talked with the proprietor. She caught a glimpse of the dining room, and it looked to be quite crowded. It was some minutes before Falconridge returned to her side.

"We're in luck. They have two bedchambers and a private dining room we may avail ourselves of. I, for one, would like to get dry before dinner. Is it agreeable with you for us to be served in half an hour?"

"If you'd shown more common sense you wouldn't need drying."

He blinked. "Pardon?"

She hated that she sounded like a petulant child. More, she hated that she'd looked so forward to traveling with him, and he'd disappointed her by preferring the company of his horse. She waved her hand dismissively. "Never mind. I want to freshen up as well."

He led her to the stairs and proceeded to follow her up them to the next floor. He opened a door.

"Your room. I shall be just next door, after I've spoken with the servants. They'll be up shortly with our luggage."

He left her there, so he could see to the other arrangements. She walked into the room, glanced at the four-poster bed, grateful that two rooms had been available. She wondered if he'd come see her tonight, wondered what color he might guess.

Wondered what she would do if he ever guessed the correct one.

He was damned miserable, hadn't been able to shed his clothes fast enough. He sat in front of the fire, a blanket draped over him, waiting for the warmth to seep into his bones. But as miserable as he'd been riding his horse in the rain, it was far better than sitting within the suffocating confines of the coach.

"You need to get something warm into you, my lord," Nesbitt said.

Michael grimaced as the sight of the cup of tea, but he was desperate enough to suffer through the swallowing of the brew. "Whiskey would have served just as well."

"Shall I fetch you some, then?"

"No, I told my wife half an hour. I didn't think it would take so long to get warm."

"You were out in it for some time, my lord."

He was unaccustomed to having a valet. While once he'd welcomed the assistance one offered, he'd grown accustomed to doing for himself. But his wife had insisted that a man of his stature should have a personal servant, and he'd not argued because it seemed they argued over every little thing. It was becoming quite tedious.

Fortunately, she'd not faulted him for paying for Obsidian to have extra oats and an extra rubdown. The gelding was a good horse, black as midnight.

Black. That was a color he'd never considered a woman favoring. It might be just the thing his somber wife preferred. He smiled.

"Feeling better, my lord."

"Indeed. Let's prepare me for dinner now, shall we?"

He was knocking on her door in record time, almost precisely half an hour on the dot from when he'd predicted dinner would be served. Her maid, Chloe, opened the door and curtsied.

"My lord, my lady prefers to have dinner in her room."

"Is she not feeling well?"

"I don't know, my lord."

"I'll have a word with her, then."

He edged past the maid, who seemed particularly jumpy. Perhaps she didn't fancy storms. He found his wife sitting in a chair on the far side of the room, reading.

"Are you unwell?" he asked, when she failed to even acknowledge his arrival.

"No, I simply prefer to eat in here."

"They've prepared the private dining room for our pleasure. Surely you don't expect me to dine alone?"

She did look up at him then, and he was surprised by the hurt he saw mirrored in her eyes.

"Why not? You expected me to travel alone."

He slammed his eyes closed. He'd not considered she'd take offense at his not traveling with her. A wife was a good deal more trouble than a mistress. He opened his eyes. "My apologies, madam. I don't usually travel in a coach. I prefer going by horse."

"Even in the rain?"

"Even in the rain."

"You might have caught your death."

"Yes, I think perhaps I did."

He watched as, miraculously, her hurt turned to concern. "Are you not feeling well, then?"

"I feel fine, but I would feel better if you would join me for dinner."

She shook her head. "I don't think you'd enjoy my company much. I don't suffer loneliness well, and I'm in a most disagreeable mood."

"It seems you would be more lonely in here than down there."

"Why do you care? We've never even had a true conversation."

"Even without conversation, I appreciate . . . your company." Dear God, she looked so bereft staring out the window, bereft like those who lived in the same residence as his mother. Was that how it began? With a sadness so profound that the mind sought escape into fantasy?

"I'm sorry, my lord, silent company isn't enough for me."

He wanted to kneel before her, take her hand, and comfort her. Instead, he said simply, "As you wish. I shall have a tray sent up. And I shall see you in the morning."

He walked toward the door, stopped beside the bed, and glanced over his shoulder, not certain why he took pleasure in the fact she was watching him. "Obsidian?"

He caught the barest hint of a smile before she turned away and shook her head. When he left the room, he took a sense of satisfaction with him.

Chapter 8

His wife ate breakfast in her room as well, stubborn chit. Michael had barely slept, worrying about her. He'd never planned to hurt her. It was only that she asked for more than he knew how to give.

Tugging on his gloves, he walked out of the tavern in time to see his wife being assisted into the coach. At least she'd not delay their departure.

The rain had ceased, the skies were gray, and dampness still clung to the air and ground. Michael walked to where his groom stood, holding Obsidian, ready and waiting. Michael never traveled without his groom or his trusted steed.

Obsidian nickered as he neared. Michael felt a pang of regret knowing he was going to disappoint the gelding, but he supposed that was better than disappointing his wife. He patted the thoroughbred's sleek neck while offering him an apple, which he hastily chomped.

"Unsaddle him, Andrew, and tether him to a coach. I'll be riding with the marchioness today."

His groomsman had trouble schooling his features so as not to look surprised. Michael knew the man was well aware that his lordship *never* rode in a coach, and he had little doubt he was going to receive a few stares from those familiar with his habits.

"As you wish, my lord."

It wasn't really what he wished, but what his wife wished. He patted his horse again. "See you later, old boy. Tomorrow I'll take you on a ride across the hills."

He strode to the first coach. The footman, a recent hire who obviously had expected him to follow the precedent he'd set the day before, was slow to open the door for him. Michael removed his hat, climbed inside, and sat across from his obviously startled wife. He took a small measure of satisfaction in her startlement.

"Here I am, madam. What is your pleasure?"

His wife stared at him as though she hardly knew what to make of him. Not that he blamed her. He hardly recognized his own behavior. He was accustomed to doing as he pleased, in seeking his own pleasure above all else. It was disconcerting to find himself bending so easily to her whims.

"I want you to be here because you want to be here," she stated, with chastisement reflected in her voice.

"Women are cunning and that is a convoluted line of reasoning. You wanted me to be here; I want to please you, and, therefore, I am here."

"But if you had your druthers?"

"I would be on my horse."

"I am perfectly fine with you choosing your horse over me."

"Devil take it! I'm not choosing the beast over you. I'm choosing my horse over the coach." He sighed, failing miserably at not showing his frustration. He was on the verge of getting blistering mad at her. "I don't want to argue, madam. You wanted me in the blasted coach, so now I'm in the blasted coach. Enjoy it."

"Your temper makes that quite impossible."

Before he could cut a scathing retort, the coach lurched forward. He closed his eyes and clenched his jaw momentarily. He could stop the coach in a heartbeat, step out, and be in the open. The coach would only seem to close in on him if he looked at the walls, floor, and ceiling. If he focused on something else so those objects were not in his vision . . .

He opened his eyes and narrowed his gaze on his wife, until she was all he saw, all that filled his vision. Her red hair pinned up beneath her hat, a gray hat trimmed with red velvet. It matched her gray traveling dress, which was also trimmed in red. She wore gray kid gloves and gray slippers. His gaze followed the line of her pearl buttons and he imagined loosening them and revealing the treasures they presently hid.

He wondered how long he'd have to endure not knowing the exact shape, texture, and hue of what lay beneath the cloth. He couldn't imagine that any aspect of her would be displeasing, and while he'd told his mother he didn't fancy the shade of Kate's hair, he couldn't deny he had an incredible urge to see it loose and flowing around her face, over her shoulders. He wanted to bury his face in the lustrous strands, fill his nostrils with the sweet scent. Hair he could easily escape. The confines of the coach—

He leaned out the window, yelled up, "Stop the coach!"

"What's wrong?" Kate asked, obviously worried, but he had no time to reassure her. He'd already broken into a sweat and his chest was tightening painfully—

He was out the door before the coach had been brought to a full stop. He landed in mud, slipped, and caught his balance. Taking in great draughts of air, he walked farther away from the conveyance. He wiped the beads of sweat from his brow. It was easy enough to stop the damned thing, easy enough to get out. It wasn't a trap. It wasn't inescapable. He had but to—

He heard a feminine screech. He spun around to discover his wife sprawled on the ground, Nesbitt, Andrew, and a footman rushing toward her. Somehow, in spite of the odds, Michael reached her first and crouched beside her.

"Good Lord, woman, what are you about?" he asked, as he took her hand, cupped her elbow, and helped her sit up.

"The way you leapt from the coach, I wanted to make sure you were all right," she said.

He hadn't been this close to her since they'd exchanged vows. She smelled of raspberries. He'd never known a woman to smell of raspberries. He wondered if she'd nibbled on them for breakfast. Her lips were slightly parted, her brow furrowed, her cheeks flaming a shade that almost matched her hair. He wanted to remove his gloves and touch that brightly colored cheek. He wanted to search through her hair and remove the pins that kept it anchored. She was sitting in the mud. Her being more disheveled only seemed appropriate. And yet as his thoughts wandered into dangerous territory, he couldn't imagine her welcoming the touches he longed to give, not here in the open, before servants.

"Why wouldn't I be all right?" he snapped, as much in frustration because she was denying him what he was beginning to so desperately want as irritation with her for behaving so unpredictably.

"Excuse me for caring, but you looked as though you were about to be ill."

Unexpectedly she shoved on his shoulder, hard enough to send him off-balance. He landed in the mud he'd so carefully avoided only moments earlier.

"Well, this is just jolly lovely," he ground out.

And she laughed. The most beautiful, joyous sound he'd ever heard. Her smile bright, her eyes sparkling. She covered her mouth with her cupped hands, and he wanted to beg her not to, not to deny him the sight of such happiness. He couldn't remember the last time he'd heard such joy. He was tempted to stand up and fall down again just to see if she'd laugh all the harder at his antics.

"You think it funny, madam, that we have hours yet to travel and we shall be doing so in mucked up clothing?"

Shaking her head, she bent forward, pressing her forehead to her upraised knees, her shoulders quaking with her mirth. "I'm sorry," she said through her laughter, but she didn't sound at all apologetic. "It's just . . ."

When she looked up at him, she had tears rolling down her cheeks. "You looked so stunned. You have to admit it's funny. I mean, here we are, in the mud on the side of the road . . ." She wiped at her tears with the edge of a muddied gloved hand, smearing—

"You're making a mess of yourself," he said, reaching out, swiping at her face, only to worsen the damage done. Looking at his hand, he realized it was equally muddy. Damnation!

She took a deep breath, sighed, and released one last giggle, before clearing her throat. "Surely there's a village nearby where we could change clothes. Or we could return to the tavern—"

"And how do we explain our state of dishevelment?"

"You're a lord. You shouldn't have to explain anything."

Except to her. He was going to have to explain every damned aspect of his life to her in order that she continually release the funds he needed.

And if he told her about his mother before their marriage was consummated, would she be so appalled that she'd demand the annulment she so blithely referred to on their wedding night?

He looked back the way they'd come. Concentrating on her in the coach had apparently kept him distracted longer than he'd realized. It appeared they'd traveled a good distance already, and quite honestly, he had no desire to travel back. "There's a village not too far up ahead," he said. "We'll make for it."

"Could we walk for a while?" she asked. "Until we've dried off a bit?"

"Do you have any idea how far we have to travel?"

"Not really. But will half an hour truly make so much difference?"

In the end, Falconridge's valet and Kate's maid brought blankets over and did their best to remove as much of the mud as possible. Kate considered asking them to find something in the trunks she could change into with the minimum amount of fuss, but she didn't think slipping behind the trees lining the side of the road would provide adequate cover for changing clothes. Besides, she'd no doubt only serve to get another outfit muddy.

She and Falconridge walked behind the last coach, so they could avoid the risk of being trampled. It was not as muddy along this stretch of road. The driver had apparently simply chosen a very poor place to pull to a halt when her husband had yelled for him to stop. So perhaps it was Falconridge who was responsible for the mishap.

She still couldn't believe how much it had tickled her to see the astonishment on Falconridge's face when he'd landed in the mud. She'd thought for a moment he'd actually looked amused, that he, too, might laugh. She couldn't help but wonder what his laughter might sound like. Deep, she decided, a rumble as mesmerizing as his voice.

"Why did you get out of the coach so fast earlier?" she asked, quietly. "It was almost as though you were trying to escape me."

She watched as his jaw tightened, his eyes narrowed. Obviously he didn't like her prying but if they didn't ask each other questions, how would they ever learn about each other? She could only observe so much, and he had a history, a past, that had made him the sort of man he was. He wasn't cold, but he was more distant than she would have liked. In a way, she supposed with her questions, she was attempting to build a bridge.

"Not you," he finally said, his voice sounding as though he'd pushed up those two little words from the depth of his soul.

"What then?" she asked.

"I'm not certain I've ever known as inquisitive a woman as you."

"It's a simple enough question. Don't view it as my prying. View it as my having an interest in you. I'm trying to understand—"

"There's nothing to understand. If you *must*

know, I don't relish traveling within the confines of a coach."

"That was more than dislike—"

He spun around and glared at her. "I do not suffer confinement well. I don't know how to explain it any clearer than that."

"That's the reason you rode your horse yesterday."

"Yes."

"Why didn't you simply explain your reasons to me last night—"

"My inability to control my reaction to confinement is not something of which I'm particularly proud."

"Well, if you'd said something, we wouldn't now be traveling covered in mud."

His gaze shifted from irritation to intense wonder. "Nor might I have ever heard your laughter. It was quite mesmerizing."

He looked as though he wanted to take her into his arms, kiss her unmercifully, and draw her laughter into his soul.

"Do you ever laugh?" she asked, uncomfortable with the thoughts bombarding her.

He looked to the sky as though he'd find the answer there. "I can't remember the last time I did. A shame, that." He turned his attention back to her. "Why would sitting in mud cause you to laugh?"

"It just struck me as funny—the proper marquess and his marchioness rolling about in the mud—"

"We weren't rolling."

"It might have been fun, though, to do it."

"It might at that, especially if we weren't encumbered by clothing." His eyes darkened, and she wondered why he had to turn the most innocent of suggestions into carnal desires.

She shook her head in an effort to rid herself of images of them nude and cavorting in muck, the length of their bodies, slipping and sliding—

She cleared her throat and thought to get the conversation back on track. "I don't know that I was really laughing about the mud. I think I just needed to laugh, to release the tension that's been building ever since I walked into the church."

"I know of more satisfactory ways to release tension. I could share them with you tonight."

Based on the intense heat that suddenly lit his gaze, she didn't think he was offering to share humorous tales with her.

"They're leaving us behind," she said, suddenly experiencing her own warmth.

She began walking, quickening her pace, trying to outdistance her unexpected desire.

"I take it you find fault with my suggestion," he said, his long legs making it possible for him to easily catch up with her.

"Quite honestly, I don't see us progressing to that point anytime soon."

"Unless I suddenly transform into Lord Bertram. I always thought he resembled a startled fish."

She erupted in laughter at the image, before scowling at him. "Don't be cruel."

"If you're so enamored of him, why didn't you marry him?"

"He didn't ask." Plus he was a viscount and her mother had forbid her daughters to settle for any rank lower than marquess.

"Did you want to marry him?"

"I hadn't really considered him as a suitor."

"You didn't attend many balls."

She peered at him. "You noticed?"

"Of course. I *was* besotted, after all."

"Now you're teasing me, and cruelly at that."

She expected him to apologize. Instead he said quietly, "I did notice." As though upon further reflection, he not only realized he had, but was surprised by the discovery.

He glanced over at her as though trying to decipher a rather complex mathematical problem. "You're not the social butterfly your sister is."

"I'm not nearly as pretty or popular."

His brow creased to the point it looked almost painful. "I can't speak to your popularity, but you're equally as attractive as she."

She averted her gaze, not trying to be coy or flirtatious, but unable to stop herself from saying, "You're simply being kind."

"Have you failed to notice that being kind is not in my repertoire of usual behavior?"

She peered over at him. Why was he so insistent on not appearing kindly? Had he once been rebuffed? Was there less chance of disappointment if he kept the distance between them?

"Does your mother live at your country estate?" she asked.

"No."

She forced herself not to growl at his succinctness. "Where does she live?"

"The edge of London."

"You told my mother yours wasn't in London."

"She's not *in* London. She's at its edge."

"That's hardly a significant distinction."

"Still, it is a distinction."

"Should we have not visited her before we left?"

"She prefers her solitude."

"Because of her illness?"

"Do you ride?" he asked quite suddenly, as though the inquiry had unexpectedly popped into his head. And she realized he didn't wish to discuss his mother, that it was a painful topic. Not that she blamed him, nor would she push the subject. She could only imagine how difficult it would be to have an ailing parent.

"As a matter of fact, I do."

"I have a gentle mare at the estate. Perhaps you'll take a fancy to her."

"How did you manage to keep your horses?"

"By placing myself in further debt. I sold off all except those I couldn't bear to part with."

"You'd not struck me as a man who would be sentimental toward animals."

"Sentiment did not play into my decision. I

kept the best of the lot. They provided the means by which to transport myself from one place to another."

And yet, she knew he'd paid for extra care to be given to his horse last night. And she'd seen him patting and talking to it earlier. Why did he insist on portraying himself as so uncaring?

"Tell me about your estate," she said.

"You'll see it soon enough."

"If you won't discuss yourself, your estate, or the arts, what should we discuss? The dreary weather?"

"I'd rather discuss you."

She should have known better than to feel a measure of pleasure and satisfaction at his choice of topics.

Because in the next instant, he gave her a devastatingly handsome and seductive smile and asked, "What's your favorite color?"

She couldn't help herself. She burst out laughing. Perhaps she should simply tell him and be done with it. Apparently he wasn't going to take interest in anything else until his curiosity was satisfied in that regard. And she couldn't deny that it did please her that he was so thoroughly interested.

But in the end, she decided not to make things easy for him, because she was rather enjoying the pursuit, and she was beginning to suspect he was much more skilled at it than he let on.

Chapter 9

"**W**elcome to Raybourne."

It was nearly dark when they finally arrived. Kate was grateful they'd had the opportunity to change clothes at the first tavern they spotted in the first village they encountered. She'd graciously allowed that Falconridge was more than welcome to ride his horse, but he'd chosen instead to journey in the coach with her. Whether he'd made his decision as a means to please her or himself no longer mattered. She'd used the time to acquaint him with her family and her youth. She knew she had a gift for telling a story, no doubt a natural extension of her spending a good deal of time reading. He'd actually seemed interested in her tales of Jenny and Jeremy's mischief, or perhaps by concentrating on her words, he discovered he no longer felt a need to leap out of the coach. What a complicated man her husband was turning out to be.

"What is it with the British inclination to give their residences names?" she asked now, standing on the cobbled drive, wishing they'd arrived while adequate light remained instead of when the shadows gave an ominous gloom to the place. Torches had been lit along the drive and at the top of the steps, obviously held in place there with sconces, like some sort of medieval dwelling.

"We have too many residences. How else are we to keep them straight?"

She glanced at her husband. "I mean, do you even know who Raybourne was?"

"The builder." He arched a brow. "And I believe the lover of the first marchioness. If legend is to be believed."

Because he sounded as though he did believe it and, more, found it a romantic notion, she felt compelled to say, "I don't condone married people taking lovers. I'll warn you now that I'll cut off more than your funds if you ever do."

A heavy silence stretched between them.

"Are you threatening me with bodily injury?" he fairly purred, almost in a challenge.

"I'm simply stating my position on the practice of taking lovers." She hated that even the thought of him with another woman caused such unexplained jealousy. She sighed. "Let's not ruin what had turned into a rather pleasant afternoon by belaboring the point. Besides, I'm very anxious to see your home."

"I'm not sure this monstrosity qualifies as a home. That word creates the image of something far quainter. It's difficult to tell in the dimming light, but the gardens have been let go."

"And here I was hoping they'd been designed on purpose to resemble a jungle."

He chuckled. "Are you attempting to make the best of an unfortunate situation?"

"Surely, not everything has been let go."

"Unfortunately, for the most part, yes. I had no need to keep up appearances here as no one visits me at this residence. The staff is too small to adequately see to it and most of the residence has been closed off as it's never used. There seemed little point in suffering through the expense of keeping it maintained."

"I suppose we'll change all that now."

"If it pleases you." He extended his elbow. "Allow me the honor of introducing you to your new *home*."

He escorted her up the stone steps. No footman stood at attention to open the door. As a matter of fact, the servants they had brought lingered by the coaches as though they'd been given orders to wait until the marquess ensured all was in order.

As he opened the door, Kate caught sight of flickering shadows beyond the huge archway. He led her inside where candles on exquisite chandeliers provided dim lighting for the entryway.

She knew it had been ten years since electric lights had begun being used in various buildings throughout London. She'd also heard of a lord who'd installed a private electric generating plant at his own country estate. It had been quite costly, and while she doubted her husband had ever been in a position to indulge in modern conveniences, she couldn't deny that she was disappointed at the prospect of living by candlelight.

"Am I to assume you have neither electric nor gas lighting here?" she asked.

"Unfortunately, your assumption is correct."

"Am I also correct in deducing that each sentence you utter from this moment on is going to begin with *unfortunately*?"

He grinned at her. Not his usual seductive grin, but a smile with which she was more comfortable. "Unfortunately."

He held her gaze, and she realized that he belonged here, in what at first glance she could only describe as a palace. Huge, cavernous, and yet she could tell that it exhibited exquisite craftsmanship. The walls visible to her housed enormous paintings, some she recognized as being created by the hand of masters. Porcelain, gold, and silver figurines and statuettes lent their beauty to welcoming guests. Obviously, at one time, this family possessed wealth that rivaled that of her own. How difficult it must have been to have fallen from such great heights.

She heard light footsteps coming from a hallway and a man who looked as though he may have served the first marquess appeared.

"My lord."

"Lady Falconridge, allow me to introduce Gresham. He's been the estate's butler for some years," her husband said.

Since the turn of the century by the looks of him, Kate thought.

Gresham bowed. "My lady, 'tis an honor to be at your service."

"Thank you, Gresham. I'm quite pleased to be here."

"If it pleases you, I'll assemble the staff for introductions and then see that dinner is made ready."

Kate nodded. "It would please me very much."

It didn't take long to be introduced to the half dozen staff members. Afterward, Falconridge suggested taking Kate on a tour of the main rooms, while the newer servants were bringing in their luggage and preparing their bedchambers.

Falconridge escorted her into the great hall, an enormous room with paneled walls and elaborate molding along and over the ceiling.

"This room has changed little since fifteen eighty," Falconridge said.

"The craftsmanship is exquisite." Kate couldn't help but be impressed, walking through the room, admiring the intricate detail. Someone had put a great deal of love into the workmanship. She looked over her shoulder at Falconridge. "Is this Raybourne's work?"

"Indeed."

"His care with the construction was his gift to the first marchioness," she mused.

"His influence is difficult to overlook."

"He must have known the marchioness very well to have been so confident that he could please her with his creation."

"I suspect he knew her favorite color."

Kate smiled. "I suspect he did."

They dined in the small dining room, rather than the larger one or the state one, which was used when royalty visited. The smaller room was much more intimate, with a table that sat only six, and while Kate sat at one end and her husband at the other, they weren't nearly as far apart here as they'd been in London.

Kate sliced into her baked chicken. "I assume these are portraits of your family."

Falconridge lifted his goblet and took a sip of wine. "Above the fireplace is the first marchioness, painted shortly after she was married."

Kate studied the fair-haired woman. "She wasn't very old."

"I would have to check in the family Bible, but I believe she'd just seen her fifteenth year."

"She wasn't far removed from being a child."

"Over my shoulder is the first marquess, his portrait also done shortly after they were married."

Kate stared at the picture, then looked at her husband, who seemed to be studying her, waiting for her reaction. "You mean the old man?"

Falconridge swirled the wine in his glass as though he were suddenly very pleased by something. "Fifty years her senior."

"Oh, my Lord. Why would she marry someone so much older?"

"Two reasons. She wished to be a marchioness . . . and her mother wished her to be a marchioness. So you have something in common with her."

Kate found herself empathizing with a girl she didn't know.

"Raybourne was not so old," Falconridge continued. "There are some in the family who believe my ancestor hired Raybourne specifically to provide entertainment for his young wife. The first marquess had his heir and his spare . . . and it is said he loved his wife and wished nothing more than for her to be happy. In that regard, he and I are much alike."

"You don't love me."

"No, but I wish nothing more than for you to be happy. Following dinner, I shall share with you a room that will please you beyond measure."

"Oh, my word," Kate said softly.

Michael was pleased by her reaction. His mother had once been a voracious reader, much like Kate. This room had been her favorite, the place where the family gathered in the evenings when they were in residence. "The Red Library. Obviously it takes its name from the coloring on the walls."

Laughing Kate looked over at him. "Not only do you give your residence a name, but you also name the rooms?"

He shrugged. "When there are so many, how else can you determine where to meet?"

"You could just say, 'Meet me in the library.'"

"We have three libraries here."

She faced him completely. "Three? Why didn't you show them to me earlier?"

"The other two are farther back, closed up, and need a good bit of dusting I suspect. You'll no doubt want to make them habitable as soon as possible."

"How many books?"

"The total within all three libraries comes close to two thousand."

"This is absolutely wonderful." She glanced around. "But we must get proper lighting in this house."

"Unfortunately, plumbing as well. Water is still carried upstairs."

"It's almost archaic, isn't it?"

He gave her a self-deprecating smile. "Unfortunately."

"I don't really feel it's unfortunate."

"Don't you?"

"No. I"—she lifted her shoulders as though suddenly uncomfortable with what she was about to say. She touched a figurine on a table, ran her finger along the back of a chair. "There's so much that needs to be done that it gives me a purpose. Until I married you, the only purpose in my life was to be a good daughter. I mean, I noticed wall coverings and draperies that need to be replaced and I know I have the means to replace them, to make a difference."

"Is that how you want to be remembered? For wall coverings and drapery selections?"

"I want to be remembered for making a difference. Making improvements to your residences is a start."

Her voice had become clipped. Dammit. He'd somehow managed to hurt her feelings.

"And what of you? What do you want to be remembered for?" she asked tartly.

He slowly shook his head. "I just want to be remembered."

Chapter 10

Chartreuse.

What the devil did that color look like? Michael sat before the fireplace in the sitting area of his bedchamber, studying the damned list that the seamstress had given him. He'd felt a tad guilty implying that he was considering purchasing a gown when his soul purpose in entering her shop had been to acquire a list of colors. The very last thing his wife needed was another gown.

It had begun raining again, and a chill permeated the air. Perfect weather for snuggling up against a warm body beneath a layer of blankets, although he wasn't certain why he thought that. He'd never snuggled and certainly not beneath a suffocating layer of blankets. Yet, he couldn't deny that the steady drumbeat of water slashing against the pane, the sporadic lightning, occasional thunder . . . it all begged for intimacy.

He just had to determine her favorite color. The hell of it was, there were so damned many. A good many of which he'd never heard of before. Lord, but she'd set him an impossible task. Her clothing was no indication as she'd not yet worn something the same color.

Perhaps her favorite color was something mundane, like brown. No, he couldn't envision that. Not a woman who smelled as enticing as she did. Even now, hours after arriving at his ancestral home, her sweet scent surrounded him.

Her nearness had made the journey in the coach bearable. She was well-read, intelligent, interesting. He'd never considered that a woman was useful for much more than overseeing the household, serving as a decoration for one's arm, and providing a willing body upon which a man could sate his lust. But Kate was more than that. As her discussion with Giddens had demonstrated, she had a keen understanding of figures. Michael could envision her managing a bank, informing investors, holding her own during any disagreements. She was unlike any woman he'd encountered before. She had a backbone of steel, and yet, she possessed an inner softness.

Throughout the day and evening, it had flickered toward him, every now and then. A gentle smile, a kind word, a dream revealed. Then she'd rein it all back in as though he were undeserving. He'd not yet earned the trust for sharing intimacies. For revealing everything about her that had begun to intrigue him.

Not that he could blame her. He'd hardly shared anything with her.

They were strangers, and until recently, he'd thought it would be enough for him. Certainly, he'd never carried on a conversation with his mistress. Her sole purpose had been to provide him with pleasure.

Yet he couldn't deny that riding in the coach with Kate had been . . . dare he acknowledge it?

Pleasurable.

In a way he'd never before experienced.

She was a mystery, and he found himself wanting to unlock the puzzle of Kate.

He flicked the corner of the paper. Perhaps he should simply write each color on a scrap of paper, put them all in his hat, and draw them out one at a time. He'd no doubt have as much of a chance discerning her favorite color by doing that as he was by studying the list. Whatever color chartreuse was, it sounded Kate-ish.

Not simple. Not easily deciphered. A mystery. Yes, that was the color he'd spring on her tonight. If nothing else, he'd be giving notice he'd deduced that the plain colors—red, blue, green, yellow— would hold no fascination for her. Perhaps that would be enough to win her over.

He could always hope. Then he could put this courtship business aside and concentrate on persuading her that their plans for the future should include a good deal more than wall coverings and draperies. He could reveal his plans, his hopes without fear that she'd immediately seek an annulment.

But first things first. Cementing their arrangement.

He set the paper on the table beside the sofa

and stood. He tightened the sash on his dressing gown, combed his fingers through his hair. Why did he feel as though he were on the brink of battle? Because she had defined their relationship as one of opponents. He wanted what she would not grant willingly without concessions.

So be it.

Chartreuse.

He rapped on the door separating their bedchambers. When he heard nothing, he opened the door, peered inside. The bed had been turned down. Inviting. Incredibly inviting. He walked farther into the room, expecting to see her sitting on the chaise longue she'd had the servants move into the room earlier. But its only occupant was her book.

He wasn't a man who normally worried over things, and yet, he knew it was easy enough for someone to become lost in this monstrous house. It had happened to his mother often enough. And Kate was not yet familiar with the maze of corridors.

As he turned, he caught sight of the door to the bathing room. It stood ajar. But surely it was too late for a bath. Yet he could see light flickering from within the room.

Yes, she was probably in there. Preparing for bed. He should stand here and wait. Or perhaps leave.

Instead he found himself walking toward temptation. He had the right. She was his wife.

But as he gazed into the room, as he watched

his wife, with the flames of several candles creating wavering light, he couldn't help but think it might have been better not to know exactly what she was denying him.

She'd piled her hair on top of her head. Not in some sort of stylish coiffure. But in a manner that more closely resembled the untidiness of a bird's nest, and yet it was so incredibly enticing. Damp, springy tendrils fell along her neck, around her face.

Not that he was looking directly at her face. Her back was to him, as she stood in the copper hip tub. And what a lovely back it was. Her backside was well-rounded, and it was all he could do not to groan as she bent over and soaked a cloth in the water circling her calves. Straightening, she dropped her head back, lifted her arms, and created a waterfall that rained down over her sleek body. His gaze shifted to the mirror and he watched as the droplets rolled along her curves, slid into her valleys, only to tumble back down into the water. Her eyes were closed, her lips parted, as though she were in ecstasy, and he wondered if she were imagining a lover's hands caressing her glistening skin where the drops continued to fall.

She opened her eyes. They widened slightly, no doubt at his reflection now clearly visible in the mirror, and he wondered when he'd moved farther into the room.

He knew women who might have screamed at the unexpected appearance of a man in the mirror before them, who might have scrambled to cover themselves. But she did little more than meet his gaze, her hands clutching the wet cloth between her breasts, pushing them up, reshaping them as he longed to. It was obvious her breath had quickened.

She was magnificent standing there, defying him, challenging him. Proud in her stance. Unafraid.

Everything within him tightened to the point of pain. Everything within him yearned to reach out, to touch her, to take her within his arms.

He didn't know if he'd ever wanted any woman as much as he wanted her at that precise moment. He didn't want to be the first to look away, but if he didn't, he would take her. There, in the bathing chamber. Tonight. That very moment.

He spun on his heel and stormed from the room, before he did something that would cause him to lose all he'd given up his pride to obtain.

Kate sank into the tub, trembling uncontrollably. She'd never in her life been witness to such . . . hunger. It had thrilled, excited, and terrified her all at once.

She'd fully expected him to charge across the room, take her in his arms, and ravish her unmercifully. The most frightening aspect of all was that she doubted she would have protested.

Dear Lord, to think he could stir her desires with only a heated look. No, it was more than a look. It was as though he'd captured her, as though he'd held her hostage. She'd been able to do little more than remain standing and allow him to have his fill of her.

She buried her face in her hands, but it did no good. She could still see Falconridge's gaze traveling the length of her body. Oh, how she'd almost turned to face him. How she'd almost dared him to look, dared him to touch. But he'd appeared to be a man standing on the precipice of desire.

That he'd walked away astounded her. Not only because he'd turned aside his yearning for her, but because she was fairly wishing that he hadn't. What would it be like to be touched by a man who gazed at her with such intensity, who looked at her as though he would die if he didn't possess her?

Even Wesley had never looked at her like that.

Would the passion generated between her and Falconridge be enough to make her no longer desire love?

With a shaking hand, she reached for the towel, stood, and began to dry herself. When had her skin become so sensitive to touch? How could his gaze alone cause her to reach such awareness? She thought she might ignite into flames.

When she was dry, she slipped her nightgown over her head. Her toes curled against the floor with the sensation of the cloth whispering along her flesh. She felt a tightness coil between her thighs. She needed release, but possessed too much pride to ask it of her husband—a man she'd denied for want of something greater than passion.

And now she was suffering because of it.

She peered into the bedroom, grateful, as well as disappointed, to discover her husband wasn't about. She darted a quick glance at the bed, imagined him there—

Shook her head. No, she wouldn't think of what might happen between them at some point.

She sat on the sofa, pressed herself into the corner, brought her legs up, and hugged them tightly. She'd decided to prepare her own bath, dismissing Chloe earlier, because her maid had worked so hard unpacking all of her trunks, putting away her things. Preparing herself for bed had seemed a small enough matter after the tall footmen Jenny had encouraged her to hire had carried up the heated water.

She'd certainly not expected Falconridge to walk in on her. And now her mind was filled with all sorts of carnal images.

How was it that she could even contemplate allowing into her bed a man she didn't love?

But considering it, she was.

Urging Obsidian on, Michael rode at a reckless pace across the rolling hills. A madman. With his cloak billowing out behind him and the rain slashing at his face and shoulders. He'd not bothered with a hat. He'd barely bothered with his clothes. Trousers, boots, a shirt more unbuttoned than buttoned, and a cloak.

He'd needed to distance himself from his luscious wife. He wanted to bury himself deeply within her. He wanted to become lost to passion, his troubles set upon a distant shore. He wanted to be free of the burdens that plagued him.

Damnation, but he should have insisted on Jenny. He should have stood his ground, instead of settling for a woman who could do little more than satisfy his financial needs.

Bringing Obsidian to a halt at the crest of a hill, Michael dismounted and with the wind buffeting him, he stared out at his land, his legacy, barely visible in the moonlight.

She wanted love, damn her.

And yet she'd stood there, enticing him with her curves, with her dips, and hollows. Growling, he dropped his head back and welcomed the rain pounding at him. Felt the drops gliding over his flesh, imagined them gliding over hers.

She tormented him with what he could not possess. He was a fool to think flowers, chocolates, and citing her favorite color would earn him a place in her bed. He should simply insist, demand his husbandly rights . . .

But dear God, the thought of her willingly turning to him, holding out her hand, beckoning him . . . wanting him as much as he desired her . . .

And he'd begun to desire her as much as he desired the money that came with her, money for which he had to beg her favor.

He lowered his head. He wanted her body, he wanted her money. She wanted his love. Their relationship was unbalanced. She'd been dictating the terms. He'd been trying to please her. Perhaps it was time he began playing by his rules. He didn't have to earn her love.

He simply needed to entice her with something she desired more.

Kate tossed and turned for what had seemed hours. She told herself it was the thunderous storm crashing outside, but the truth was, she feared it was the storm raging inside her body as it sought surcease. It had been so very long since she'd felt these stirrings—if she'd ever truly felt them this intensely.

The first time Wesley had kissed her, her body had grown as warm as an oven baking bread. But she'd never felt that heat from something as distant as a . . . look. She was tempted to invite Falconridge into her bed, to risk his anger when he discovered the truth—

She threw back the covers and scrambled out of bed. She wouldn't compromise her integrity or her belief that a woman should only welcome into her body a man whom she loved or at the very least a man who loved her. She wouldn't let her flesh have control over her heart.

She snatched up her wrapper from where she'd left it earlier at the foot of the bed and drew it around herself. There was plenty to occupy her within this household, to keep her mind from wandering down dangerous paths. Nothing dictated she only look over matters during the daylight hours. In truth, looking over the books in the middle of the night would ensure she had no disruptions.

In her youth, she'd fallen asleep many a night while sitting on her father's lap, watching in fascination as he manipulated numbers and figures until he made sense of them. For her, dealing with numbers served as effectively as any bedtime story or glass of warm milk. They forced her to concentrate as nothing else did. She could become lost in them, until eventually dealing with them would wear her down and she'd sleep the slumber of the dead.

Based on the manner in which the residence had been kept, she could only deduce that the books would be equally in shambles and need to be set right. Since sleep eluded her, she might as well get started on them.

Taking the lamp, she stepped into the dark hallway. She cast a quick glance at the door which led into her husband's chambers. No light spilled forth from beneath it. Damn him for finding sleep so easily. Damn him for disturbing her so easily. Damn him for . . .

Lord, she could stand there all night cursing him to perdition and she'd accomplish nothing. What she should do was march into his room and stare *at him* . . .

Only she feared if she looked at him as he did her, he'd not tremble as she had. He'd merely draw back the blankets and invite her in.

She had an unsettling feeling she'd eagerly accept the invitation.

She spun on her bare heel and hurried sound-lessly down the stairs, one hand gliding over the banister while the other held the lamp aloft to guide her steps. The house was eerily quiet, which made the rampaging storm seem that much more sinister.

And cold, the house was so cold. As though it had never known warmth. As though it had never known love. She couldn't imagine delightful laughter echoing along the hallways. She imagined this house always as quiet, as ominous as it was now.

She staggered to a stop at the bottom of the stairs, considered returning to the sanctuary of her room, but she was so tired of retreating, and she'd been retreating ever since Wesley had been torn from her life.

Deep within her heart, she knew her parents had done what they'd thought was best for her. They loved her. She'd never questioned that. But how was it that they failed to understand her needs when it came to men? All she wanted was to be adored—for herself. Perhaps it made her shallow, selfish but she knew young men had always looked at her calculatingly . . . all except Wesley, who'd not even realized she was wealthy until he'd proposed.

Wesley had wanted her, not her money. The same certainly couldn't be said of Falconridge.

And for good measure, she cursed him again before continuing on to the study. He'd shown her the room earlier and waved it off as though it were of no consequence. Little wonder the man found himself in financial straits. He obviously spent far too much time in bedchambers and not enough time scouring over his ledgers.

She didn't like the prick of jealousy she felt over the thought of him in bedchambers. It was actually more than a prick. It was more like a stab, a stab accompanied by anger. Dear Lord, if these emotions swelled *within her*, what might her husband feel with the knowledge that his wife had entertained a man . . .

If only he'd come to see her before their wedding day . . . if only she'd not hidden away . . . if only her parents had never interfered . . .

She opened the door to the study and the musty scent of abandonment puffed out into the hallway. Evidence lingered everywhere testifying to the fact Falconridge cared so little about this residence. So why were they here? To put things to rights, obviously.

But what sort of man would allow it to come to this at all? And he'd certainly not done without in London.

This room, she decided, would be aptly named The Nothing Room. It was large but sparsely decorated. The desk, the chair behind it, two chairs angled before it. An enormous table in front of the window. Beside it was a copper bucket housing scrolls of parchment. She crossed the room to the desk and set the lamp near the corner, where it only served to illuminate the dusty surface. Behind the desk were shelves where ledgers served as anchors for spider webs. Fortunately, those horrid creatures appeared to have abandoned the room as well.

Kate reached for a ledger, stirring a ball of motes. She sneezed, rubbed her itching nose, and put the ledger back. She should get a cloth and wipe away the evidence of abandonment. She released a deep sigh. She needed an army of servants to get everything squared away.

One step at a time. She'd get a rag, wipe down the desk, then the ledgers, and then she'd set to work. She'd not be discouraged. Instead she would embrace the challenge. Surely, it would keep her from thinking of her husband.

She lifted the lamp and turned toward the door. The light struck the nearby table and its gleaming surface.

Gleaming? Was there actually a portion of this room that didn't appear neglected?

She walked over to the table. It seemed ordinary enough. Except for the can that had once contained beans and now housed an assortment of pencils and various rulers. What was this table used for? Did Falconridge write here? No, more likely, he drew.

Was her husband an artist?

She was surprised by the flicker of excitement at the prospect. That talent might explain his moodiness. Weren't creative sorts generally more melancholy than most?

Was he desperate for her money so he could establish an art gallery? What fun that would be! She loved the arts.

She shifted her attention to the rolled parchments sitting in the copper bucket. She reached for one and immediately drew back her hand. These were possibly his drawings, and he'd not elected to share them with her.

She should wait for an invitation. Tomorrow, she might innocently mention how much she'd enjoyed touring the National Art Gallery. And from there, he *might* offer to show her his drawings. Or not. Most likely not.

To hell with waiting for an invitation. Patience had never been her strong suit.

She lifted out a scroll, pulled the string forming the bow that held it secure, and slowly unrolled it across the table. It wasn't art. Not really. But it *was* a drawing. An outline. Of a building. A cottage. Extremely detailed with numbers carefully written that seemed to indicate measurements. She could hardly fathom the amount of time and patience it had taken to draw something this exact, this precise.

It was almost as though he had plans to build—

"What the devil do you think you're doing?"

Kate spun around. Her husband stood there, as dark as the tempest rampaging beyond the walls. His wet hair curled, no semblance of civility to it at all, which seemed appropriate since he hardly appeared civilized.

Her heart pounded so hard she was surprised she could still hear the distant thunder. Her mouth had grown dry, her throat felt as though she might strangle.

He strode across the room, fury in every step, until he stood so close she could see droplets of water on his eyelashes, a dampness to his skin. He didn't carry the scent of a man who'd been bathing. Rather he smelled like wet leather and horse—

"Answer me, woman, what are you doing?"

Answer him? The arrogant man. Kate Rose no longer answered to anyone. She'd paid a high price for that freedom. She had no plans to take it for granted now.

"Were you out in the rain?" she asked.

"Not that it is any of your concern, but yes. I went riding."

"What is it with you and riding in the rain?"

"It was either ride Obsidian in the rain or ride *you* in the bathing room—"

The crack of her palm against his cheek echoed through the room.

"How dare you! How dare you be so crude when speaking of me, your wife. I daresay you shall spend a good deal of your life riding your horse as I doubt a time will ever come when I shall harbor enough affection for you to allow you to ride *me*."

His eyes darkened, his breathing grew more harsh, his jaw tightened. "How is it that I want you at every turn? How is it that a woman with so much fire would choose love over passion?"

"I'm not choosing love over passion. I'm choosing love *before* passion."

Raking his hands through his hair, he dropped his head back. "I swear before God, you shall be the death of me."

Of all the words he could have said at that moment, those were the very last she'd expected. She despised that he could prick her anger and her curiosity in equal measures. "Why?" she heard herself asking when she'd have rather held her tongue.

Shaking his head, he lowered his gaze to her. "You wouldn't understand."

As though he'd lost whatever fight had been in him, he reached past her and began rolling up the parchment she'd spread over the table. "These are personal. They don't concern you. I would ask that you leave them be."

"Do they represent buildings you'd like to have built?"

"Some do. Some are simply a . . . fool's fancy."

"I'm surprised you had the funds to hire an architect. Or will I find myself paying for his services in the morning when I settle accounts?"

"You'll not find yourself paying for these pitiful efforts." Keeping his back to her, he dropped the scroll into the bucket. "I believe we're done here."

"I don't think they're pitiful. From what I saw they were very well done. I wouldn't mind looking at all of them."

He swung his head around, studying her as though he doubted her sincerity.

"Perhaps another time, madam. In case you've not noticed, it is well into the middle of the night. Any sensible person would be abed."

She angled her chin, surprised by the sting caused by his refusal to share them now. "I'm not known for being sensible. Case in point, I married you."

With that, she spun on her heel and marched from the room. She couldn't say why the sound of his low chuckle following in her wake pleased her.

She only knew that it did. That in some way, it signaled a small victory.

Chapter 11

Michael was not particularly skilled at reading women's moods, but he had no doubt that his wife was still royally miffed at him. Not that he blamed her. It was not his habit to be deliberately crude with the fairer sex, and yet his frustrations had gotten the better of him last night. He'd been wet, cold, and the fact that she'd been in his private sanctuary, looking at his unschooled efforts, had not set well with him.

And so he'd lashed out, unforgivably so. Even then, she'd stood her ground, tossing his words back at him as though she were accustomed to spouting crudities when he doubted she had a clear understanding of exactly what he'd had in mind when he spoke of riding her.

Unfortunately that morning, she'd not joined him for breakfast. Rather she'd had a tray delivered to her bedchamber. He'd actually missed her company, suffered through a moment of loneliness before reminding himself that being alone was a natural state for him and something with which he was well familiar. She'd sent her maid down to inform him she would be looking over the accounts this morning. He'd sent a footman up to announce the arrival of Michael's steward, Mr. Swithin.

He wondered how long they'd play this game of cat and mouse, each effectively ignoring the other.

He'd been standing beside the desk talking with Swithin when his wife had waltzed into the room wearing a pale pink dress with cherry-colored silk stripes running its length. Velvety loops of ribbon decorated the sleeves and the sides of the under-skirt, visible where the upper skirt was gathered up. Strangely, in spite of the various decorations, the entire attire had a very no-nonsense quality to it. Perhaps it was because below her chin, the only skin visible was that of her hands.

Yet, still he found her enticing. She'd given Michael a very succinct greeting before settling behind the desk and getting down to business with Swithin.

As much as Michael loathed his wife prying into the details of his estate, he couldn't deny he was fascinated watching her. His steward sat in a large leather chair across from her, answering her insightful questions about the management of the house, the grounds, the stables, monies spent and the dwindling income from farming.

Kate looked at Michael and said, "Surely, you saw the need to replace what you were no longer gaining."

"We did. Unfortunately, we made some unwise investments."

"The problem with investing is that one must always be able to withstand the loss if the risk doesn't pay off."

"So I learned."

She turned her attention back to Swithin, while Michael focused on her. Last night, he'd almost told her about his sketches, about the buildings he did want to bring to reality. But seeing her in her nightclothes had reminded him of seeing her *out* of them, and he'd only wanted to be rid of her presence, before he decided his need for her outweighed her need for affection.

For most of his life, his parents had been absent. He'd been cared for by a strict nanny and even stricter governess. Going away to school had been a godsend.

He was striving to be patient with Kate, to give her the time she wanted to grow accustomed to him as her husband, because he identified with her desire to be wanted for more than her money. Ironically, he understood too well what it was to be wanted for something other than oneself. He'd never been a son. He'd always been the heir.

He had no memory of being hugged until he'd bedded his first woman. He'd been at Ravensley's estate when the daughter of the old man's valet had taken it upon herself to introduce them all to the ways of the flesh. She'd been a lovely, caring lass who hadn't ridiculed him or told the others that he'd wept in her arms.

He'd had many women since, but it was always business, and as a result, the encounters were usually impersonal. He'd stopped longing for the tender touches. Even his mistress had been as cold as the gems he'd given her. For whatever reason, he seemed to lack the ability to warm a woman's heart toward him.

Now his wife insisted he make her care for him. Baubles and trinkets weren't the answer. Even doing things that she wanted didn't seem to please her. She wanted him to know—without her saying—exactly what she wanted. She asked the impossible.

"My lord?"

He was snatched from his reverie to find his wife looking at him expectantly, as though she wanted something from him. No doubt, whatever it was, it wasn't what he wanted to give.

"You have eight thousand acres of land here."

He arched a brow. "I am more than familiar with what I have and what I have not."

"Your income—"

"I am acutely aware of my income. It is sadly lacking in what is needed to sustain the estates or my London residence—as Mr. Swithin's books will sadly prove."

She looked at him, looked at Mr. Swithin. "I want to study these more closely at my leisure."

"Of course, my lady," Swithin said.

"In the meantime, I will, naturally, approve the payment of these debts."

"Thank you, my lady."

She looked back at Michael. "Mr. Swithin has

done an exceptional job of overseeing your estate."

"Of course he has. I don't hire the incompetent."

"Did you wish to recommend an additional payment amount for him?"

She was tossing him a crumb, to give the appearance he still had some say in matters. He didn't know whether to be furious or grateful. In the end, he decided to toss the crumb back. "You're the expert in financial matters. I leave the amount to your discretion."

She seemed surprised, but pleased, and turned her attention back to Swithin. Michael wondered if Albert had felt this useless married to a queen who held power over the whole of England and a good part of the world. Michael had decided last night that he needed to shift tactics. And here he was still feeling as though he were groveling.

Swithin took his leave, more than happy with the turn in his lordship's fortunes. Michael watched as Kate continued to scour through the ledgers.

"What are you searching for?" he asked.

"It's just inconceivable to me that the state of your affairs could have gotten so out of hand."

He walked over to the desk, stood behind her, reached around, and closed the ledger. "You won't find the answer there."

"Well, if it's not in the ledger, I'll never find the answer, since you won't tell me."

She had her hair pinned up, with stray wisps curling along the back of her neck. He trailed his bare finger along the thin line of bare skin just above her collar, felt her shiver with his touch. She wasn't as immune to his attentions as she pretended.

He leaned nearer. She still smelled of raspberries. "Let's go for a ride."

"Do you have any idea how much work needs to be done here?"

"You can make wiser decisions if you see all of the estate. I want to show it to you. You can ride the mare, I'll ride the gelding. No enclosures, no chance of mud."

"In England, there is always a chance of mud."

"Aren't you the least bit curious about all you've acquired through marriage or are you simply afraid?"

She jerked her head around, which brought her mouth incredibly close to his. "What would I fear?"

"That if you are in my close company long enough you might come to want me as much as I want you."

"For me, without affection, there can be no *want*."

Ah, yes, she was still royally miffed. Or maybe he'd simply hurt her feelings by being so callous about something which she obviously highly prized. He was going to take her virginity, and that realization no doubt terrified her. Perhaps if he thought of her as a horse that needed to be gentled . . .

He crouched beside her. It was as close to begging as he would come. "I owe you an apology for my words in here last night. My choices were to offend you or attempt to seduce you. Quite honestly, I wasn't in a frame of mind to meekly accept another rejection."

"Meaning what? You would have forced yourself on me?"

He bowed his head. He couldn't win with her. "Most women would be pleased beyond measure that their husbands wanted them as I want you."

"It is only the physical—"

He brought his head up. "What is wrong with that?"

"I need more."

"And I'm trying to give it to you." He reined in his temper. "Kate, from the moment you married me, you've seen nothing but the tragedy of my life. The mounting debt, the residences in disrepair. Let me show you one corner of my world that I believe makes everything else worth it."

She narrowed her eyes in suspicion. "You're actually going to willingly share something with me?"

"I am."

"And it requires an outing?"

"It does."

She pressed her lips together.

"I promise no crude comments," he offered.

She peered at him. "We always seem to be at odds."

"Not always. Yesterday, for example, we had several very pleasant moments."

Sighing, she nodded. "I'll accompany you on an outing."

"Do try to sound a bit more enthusiastic, unless it's your intent to ruin my good humor."

"This is you in a good humor? It very much resembles you in a bad humor."

"Your eyes are changing shade. They were a sort of green, but now they're going to blue."

"Don't be ridiculous. My eyes don't change color, except with my clothing. They sometimes reflect the color of the cloth."

"Perhaps." But he thought he might be managing to improve her disposition. He wished he'd developed a skill for effectively teasing a lady. But if need be, to make her laugh, he supposed he could always seek out mud.

"I assume you have a riding habit," he said.

She laughed lightly, her breath skimming over his cheek. "More than one."

"Then I shall see that the horses are readied while you see to yourself." His body tightened as the tip of her tongue touched her upper lip. He thought her breathing might be growing as labored as his. He watched her throat work as she swallowed.

"I need room so I can stand," she said, her low voice carrying a sensual rasp.

His lower body reacted with a fierceness that made it nearly impossible to stand back up, but he somehow managed to do so, moving behind the chair and pulling it out so his reaction to her wasn't visible.

She rose gracefully from the chair and took two steps before turning back to him. "Thank you for the apology, and more, for trusting my discretion regarding the additional amount."

"No need to thank me for what in a short time you've effectively earned. Your father alerted me to your financial acumen. I'm quite impressed to see it at work."

She blushed. "I should go change before I thank you again."

He watched her leave the room with a definite spring in her step he'd not seen before. It seemed he'd somehow managed to please her. Imagine that.

"What sort of investments did you make?" Kate asked.

They'd ridden sedately over the land for less than half an hour before he'd led her over a rise and into what she could only describe as a shallow valley where wildflowers bloomed in abundance in the clearing before it gave way to the woods. At a small pond, she'd spotted a deer drinking before it dashed off between the towering trees. Birds twittered in the boughs and a gentle breeze wafted through the leaves. Here was a touch of heaven.

Her husband had surprised her by spreading a blanket on the ground and carefully unrolling another blanket to reveal offerings for a picnic—cheese, bread, wine, and raspberries. She wondered if the fruit had been selected on purpose.

Surely not. It was no doubt coincidence that their choices included her favorite berry. She watched him now as he uncorked the red wine.

"I believe the first investment was named Lucky Lad. Failed to live up to his nomenclature." He poured the wine into two crystal goblets. She was amazed they hadn't cracked on the journey.

"What was wrong with him?" she asked.

"Couldn't race worth a fig."

"You bought a racing horse?"

"No, I bet on one." He handed her a goblet.

"Your investment was to bet on a race?" she asked incredulously.

He gave her a self-deprecating smile. "It seemed an expeditious and easy way to change my fortune. Which it did. Just not in the direction I'd hoped." He clinked his glass against hers. "Here's to wiser investments in the future."

She peered over the rim of her glass. "I think any investment would be wiser than that." She drank a sip, trying not to notice the way his fawn-colored breeches pulled across his thighs. He was sitting with one knee raised, his wrist resting on it lightly, his hand slowly swirling his glass of wine.

"You said the horse was your first investment. What was the second?"

"Shooting Star, who managed to fade to the back of the race the same way a star fades at dawn."

"How many times did it take you to learn your lesson?"

"Not sure I've learned yet. Perhaps next year we'll go to Ascot."

"I'm not betting on a horse."

"But we can afford to lose now. Wasn't that your requirement?"

She shook her head, trying to appear uninterested, but she was intrigued by the thought of going to the races with him. "If we go, I shall select the horse."

"Have you a knack for it?"

"We won't know until I try."

"You've never bet on a horse?"

"I've never gambled at all."

"It's a way to make an abundance of money quickly."

"It's also a way to lose it. I don't trust schemes that promise quick riches. There is always some hidden trap."

"I can't argue with that," he mumbled before taking a sip of his wine.

Gazing at him was certainly no hardship. The breeze had begun to toy with his hair just as it toyed with the trees. She had an urge to run her fingers through his dark strands, but touching him would no doubt give him leave to touch her, and after last night, she suspected he'd like to do more than play with her hair. Best to keep the conversation off personal matters.

"Surely with as much land as you have, you could sell some of it," she said.

He swung his head around to study her. "It's

all entailed. I'm forbidden to sell it. I can lease it for farming. But there is no money in agriculture these days. Not for us. We can import it from you Americans cheaper than we can grow it. Since the title and its responsibilities fell to me, I've lost almost all my tenants. And who can blame them for going to the cities where more opportunity and a better life awaits them?"

"But surely there is something you can do with this land that would bring in more income. You could build a factory—"

He grimaced. "Even if I could, which I cannot because of restrictions placed on the deed, I wouldn't entertain such a notion. It's part of the reason that I invited you to take a ride with me. I want you to see what you gain through marriage to me. This land's purpose is the same as a woman's—to be beautiful and appreciated. Look around you, Kate. There is poetry in the land."

He'd never given her beautiful words or recited poetry to her, but surely a man who saw such beauty in the land held poetry in his soul.

"Is this where you rode to last night?"

"Eventually, once I got the fire out of my blood." Reaching out, he trailed his bare finger along her bare hand. They'd taken off their gloves to eat and yet the cheese and bread remained untouched. "Do you often give yourself a bath?"

She could see from the intensity of his gaze that he was remembering exactly what he'd seen last night. She'd deliberately chosen clothes to wear today that left very little skin exposed. She felt her cheeks warm and hoped her blush wasn't visible.

"Chloe worked so hard to get everything un-packed that I didn't wish to bother her with a bath. I had footmen bring up hot water, but I'm fully ca-pable of washing myself." She cleared her throat. "I think the first thing we should do is modernize your plumbing."

He grinned at her. "Nothing wrong with *my* plumbing, I assure you."

She grew even warmer. "The plumbing in your house, you dolt."

He chuckled low and she almost felt the vi-brations travel through his hand into hers. She thought about moving hers from beneath his fin-ger but it felt so lovely—the slow, sensual circles that he was drawing on her skin.

"You have so much fire within you that it's little wonder your hair is so incredibly red," he said.

"I've always hated the shade of my hair."

"I rather like it. It's not common."

Now it was her turn to laugh. "No, it's not." She wanted to turn the discussion away from her and back to him. "You'd not struck me as a man who'd appreciate the beauty of the countryside."

"I appreciate beauty in all its forms." His gaze traveled slowly over her face, lingered on her lips. "Most especially when it's associated with a woman."

She felt a wet drop splash against her nose, jerked her head back, and was hit with a droplet of rain in her eye. "Oh, no, it's going to rain." She'd not even noticed the clouds moving in.

"Come on."

After helping her to her feet, he grabbed her hand, but instead of leading her toward the horses, he urged her toward a tree.

"Where are we going?" she asked.

"It's probably only a quick afternoon shower. The boughs of the tree are thick enough to lessen the impact of the downpour."

And it was a downpour. He'd barely gotten her back against the tree when the rain hit. He stood so close, his arms raised and pressed against the trunk of the tree, hemming her in. She dared not move. Instead she studied the perfection of his burgundy silk cravat, a color that matched her riding habit, wondering that he would dress almost formal for such an informal outing. Almost as though he felt a need to impress her.

He was so near she could feel the warmth radiating from his body. He bowed his head slightly and said in a low voice near her ear, "Chartreuse?"

She furrowed her brow. "What's chartreuse?"

"The wrong color." His lips skimmed against the outer shell of her ear. "Burgundy?"

She slid her eyes closed. "No."

He lowered his right hand until he could skim his thumb along her jaw. "Brown?"

"No."

She felt his hand beneath her chin, movement against her buttons, and her collar loosening around her neck.

"Blue?"

"No."

She felt his lips pressed against the sensitive skin below her ear and her breathing became small pants.

"Yellow?" he rasped, and it sounded as though he was having as much difficulty drawing a breath as she.

"No."

She felt a need to weep, a need she didn't understand. Desire swirled through her. Hot and fierce. Running his tongue along her skin, he nestled his lips up against her throat.

"Purple?" Somehow his mouth reached her collarbone. "Pink?" His sturdy leg pressed between her thighs. "White?" His hand cradled her breast, his thumb stroked across her hardened nipple.

"No." The sensations were building. "No." His hand, his mouth, his thigh. "No!" Her body tightened and coiled and tiny shivers of pleasure were coursing through her as she instinctually pressed more firmly against his thigh, felt her legs become as insubstantial as jam, and clutched his shoulders to remain standing. Oh, dear Lord, she'd never experienced anything this intense with so little effort.

"A little death?" he murmured. "Tell me your favorite color and tonight I shall gift you with a good deal more than that."

"No!" She shoved on him, putting enough distance between them to edge past him and dart out into the rain.

"Kate! Kate, wait!"

She felt his arms come around her and fought

against him until he released her. She faced him. "How could you do that to me? Outdoors! Where anyone could see! You had no right to make my body do that. I didn't give you permission."

"I don't need your damned permission. I'm your husband!"

She shook her head frantically. If he took such liberties in broad daylight, what would he do when darkness provided cover for more wicked things? "I don't want that from you. I'm not ready."

He turned away from her. Bowed his head. She watched his hands fist at his sides, as he struggled to regain control of his temper . . . or perhaps he was contemplating murder. How could something as innocent as a picnic, something as carefree as escaping the rain turn into something so sensuous? She'd never reacted so strongly to nothing more than the nearness of a man. The power Falconridge held over her body terrified her.

When he once again faced her, she could read nothing in his expression, nothing in his eyes.

"Forgive me. I forget you're innocent when it comes to passion. Your reaction to my touch . . . is nothing to be ashamed of."

"You don't know how vulnerable, how . . ."— she swallowed hard—"please don't ask it of me before I'm more comfortable with you."

"Before you hold affection for me."

His words were spoken as a statement, not on inquiry. She nodded slightly.

"As you wish."

His words were spoken succinctly, flatly, with

no emotion whatsoever. And while she was certain she'd gained a reprieve, she feared she may have lost something she might not have even realized she'd gained.

That night they ate dinner in silence. He bid her good night at the door to her bedchamber. After Chloe prepared her for bed, Kate sat by the window until long past midnight, waiting for him to come in and announce a color.

He never came.

Chapter 12

Michael had always considered American women to be spoiled, pampered. The Rose sisters, especially, he'd delegated to that category. After all, they'd grown up surrounded by an exorbitant amount of wealth that he could only imagine, and while a portion of it was now at his disposal, he'd never forget the ease with which James Rose had spit out the amount he was willing to pay for Michael's title as though it was nothing more than pocket change.

But Kate Rose Tremayne threw herself into the task of setting Raybourne right as though she'd made a wager with the devil himself and her failure would result in the forfeiture of her soul.

In the evenings, in the library, rather than reading, she sat at the desk and scribbled her plans for the next day on one piece of paper after another. She was so absorbed in her efforts that he doubted she'd have heard him if he'd *yelled* a color in her direction. Not that he'd tossed any her way since their encounter at the pond.

The first morning, they went to the nearby village where she hired a half dozen women whose job was to beat the dust out of the draperies and rugs that the London servants brought outside. He'd never seen so much dusting, scrubbing, and polishing in his entire life. Kate's first priority had been the essential rooms: their bedchambers, dining rooms, parlors, kitchen. Rooms were aired out. Men from the village were hired to wash windows.

He'd caught her more than once with a smudge of something or other across her cheek or her chin . . . once on the tip of her nose. A mark that he yearned to replace with a kiss.

He didn't want to press her for what she was not yet ready to give, but not having her was torment, especially at night when he envisioned her lying in bed, or worse preparing for bed with water caressing her flesh as he longed to.

So he rode over the hills at midnight or came to his study where he could pour his efforts into something else that brought him pleasure since his wife was intent on not providing him with any.

That harsh assessment wasn't entirely true. He took pleasure in her company as spare as it was. During meals, when she had questions about his lands, when she sought his advice about the arrangement of furniture as though it mattered at all whether the largest portrait was on the south wall or the north, whether a chair was set to the right or left of a sofa. Would this small table not be better placed here?

"Do what you pleases you," he'd finally said, only to have her give him a wounded look that had forced him to apologize—for God only knew what transgression—and he'd spent the next four hours of his life pushing furniture around. They needed more footmen, they needed more servants, they needed to return to London.

Kate waited for Michael every night. Some nights she heard his footsteps as he paced in his bedchamber. Other nights, she watched him gallop his horse over the moon-drenched rolling hills.

Sometimes she considered inviting him into her bed, suffering the consequences once he learned the truth. Perhaps it wouldn't matter to him. Sometimes she contemplated confronting him, telling him everything.

And sometimes she wanted nothing more than to return to London.

Tonight she was restless, unable to sleep. She hadn't seen her husband galloping across the hills, but she knew he wasn't in his room. She'd pressed her ear to the door trying to catch the sound of his snoring or his bed creaking as he rolled over. Or his frequent pacing. But she heard nothing at all. Just an unnatural stillness, so she was fairly certain he wasn't there.

As she walked through the manor on her way to the study to look over more ledgers in an attempt to force herself to sleep, she ran through her mind everything she needed to accomplish when they returned to London. She needed to hire additional servants. She needed to make a list of repairs and enhancements she wanted done. They needed supplies that couldn't necessarily be provided by the tradesmen in the village. So many things to consider, so many decisions to be made.

She walked into the study, only to discover her husband there, bent over the large table, drawing lines on a piece of paper, so absorbed in his endeavors he obviously didn't hear her approach. But she recognized the drawing beneath his hands. It was the small cottage she'd seen before.

"*You're* the architect," she said quietly, awed.

He spun around. She wasn't surprised to see that he wasn't pleased by her discovery, but then his glare had also ceased to intimidate her.

"It is rude to sneak up on a person," he said.

"I hardly sneaked." She eased closer to the table. "Why didn't you admit these efforts were yours?"

"They're personal, a distraction from troubles."

She looked up at him. "Like my reading?"

He gave a brusque nod.

"Have you ever had any of these built?"

"No, but this one"—he pointed toward the table—"this one is special. I would like to hire a builder and have it built near the pond where I took you the other day."

"Why?"

"Must I justify every expense?"

"No, of course not."

Clearly agitated, he began rolling up the paper. "I should like to hire a builder when we return to London."

"I'll want to look over his costs, of course."

His jaw clenched. "Of course."

"Not because I don't trust your judgment, but I need the figures so I can determine a proper budget for handling all our expenses."

He gave her a look of incredulity. "Are you unfamiliar with exactly how much your father gave us?"

"Are you unfamiliar with how much work needs to be done?"

"We could never spend all that we've been given."

"You would be surprised, my lord. And I don't want to just spend it. I want to find a way to increase it."

Studying her, he hitched a hip onto the corner of the table. "A gentleman does *not* work."

"I've always considered my father a gentleman and he works."

"Then allow me to rephrase: *Nobility* does not work."

"I'm not referring to toiling in the fields. I'm talking about putting your mind to work, taking your strong suits and putting them to work." She shook her head, frustrated by her inability to explain. "You understand responsibility . . . and duty."

"Of course."

"Not everyone does. There are institutions—

banks, hospitals, prisons—that need someone to guide them."

He shook his head.

"My father raised me to believe that when you have an abundance of money you have an obligation to put it to good works."

"Charity."

"Not necessarily. Let's say you purchase a building. You have, in essence, given income to the owner of that building. If you then hire people to work in the building, then you're giving them an income, a means to support themselves."

"What are their jobs?"

"Well, I don't know. It depends what interests you."

"You interest me."

He slid off the table, and Kate was certain that he was going to approach her, touch her, kiss her. "I believe we should open a paint shop."

"A paint shop?" she asked, staring at him. She'd never considered where paint came from.

"Indeed. We shall only sell paint and we shall only sell it in your favorite color. I'll need to know what it is before I can begin the venture."

Shaking her head, she laughed. "Is bedding me all you think about?"

"No, sometimes I think about bathing you."

Her laughter ceased abruptly as that image took hold. It hadn't helped that his voice had deepened as he said it and little shivers had danced along her spine. "I was serious about us finding something to do with our money so what we spend is returned to us. You should speak with my father about investments. That won't require that you work." She nodded toward the scroll on the table. "Perhaps you can do something with the buildings you've drawn."

That suggestion seemed to take him aback. "Why would anyone have an interest in my pitiful drawings?"

"Because you have the money to build them whether or not anyone is interested."

After their midnight encounter in the study, the tension that had been between them eased somewhat, but not completely. Falconridge had begun to come to her bedchamber again—only to announce a color before bidding her good night. And Kate found herself longing to know him better.

A few nights later, during dinner, she announced, "I received a letter from my sister. Jenny. She is hosting a ball later in the week. A costume ball. I wish to return to London so we might attend."

Kate watched as Falconridge's jaw clenched, and she knew without him saying anything that he didn't fancy costume balls. In the past week, she'd learned he wasn't a man who filled his life with gaiety. To her surprise, he preferred not being noticed, although he was quite adept at taking care of the estate. They discussed all aspects and his knowledge impressed her. He wasn't quite the idle nobleman he let on to being.

"If it pleases you," he finally said.

A bit of the devil took hold of her. "I believe we'll go as Helen of Troy and Ulysses."

She thought her husband was going to be unable to digest his veal.

"Surely, you don't expect me to actually don a costume?"

"Of course, I do. That's the whole purpose of a costume ball. Perhaps Cleopatra and Cesar."

"Perhaps we shan't go."

"Perhaps I shall stop dispensing money."

He wrapped his hand around the stem of his wineglass, and she suspected he might like to wrap it around her throat. "Costumes are a frivolous waste of money, having an item sewn that will be worn only once."

"Following that logic, most of my wardrobe is a frivolous waste of money since I never wear a gown more than once."

He narrowed his eyes. "I'd heard that Americans spent a fortune on their wardrobe. Thousands—"

"Twenty to be exact."

"Pounds?"

"Dollars. Perhaps Pocahontas and Captain John Smith. That would be fun, don't you think?"

"Honestly, I think it will be hell. Why don't I go as an English aristocrat, and you go as his wife?"

"So boring to go as we are. Have you no fantasies of being something other than what you are?"

"Trust me, madam, I don't believe you want my fantasies voiced aloud."

"Don't be so secretive. Share them. Do you dream of being a pirate? A cowboy perhaps? A soldier? Come on. Do confess and I'll see that you're costumed appropriately."

He lifted his wineglass, studied the wine as though it held his fantasies. Then he shifted his gaze over to her, and her breath caught before he ever spoke.

"Your lover," he finally said, his voice low and seductive. "That would require I attend the ball without a stitch of clothing."

She felt her face warm at the thought of him bared, and suddenly she was quite terrified. Nude? Completely nude? Why would he have to remove all his clothing to be her lover? Wesley had never gone to such extremes.

Glancing down at her plate, she poked her fork into a pea. "Perhaps we should go as the Prince and Princess of Wales."

"Are you certain? Going as lovers has a certain appeal."

He was mocking her. She wished she could rattle him as easily as he oftentimes rattled her. She looked up, met his gaze. "I shall consider it."

Chapter 13

"**O**h, Guinevere! What fun, Kate!" Jenny said. "What of your marquess? Is he coming as Arthur or Lancelot?"

Kate and Falconridge had arrived in London the night before, so Kate could spend the afternoon visiting with her sister and helping her prepare for the night's activities. They'd spent hours instructing servants in the decorating of the ballroom.

"I think he's going to come as himself," Kate said.

"Where's the fun in that?"

They were in the Jenny's bedchamber, putting the final touches on their costumes. Falconridge would join her there at her parents' residence sometime this evening. It wasn't unusual for husbands and wives to arrive separately. Still, Kate was surprised by how much it bothered her that they wouldn't arrive together, arm in arm. This was after all their first social appearance since their wedding day. What sort of message would they be sending? Would people think the blossom on the rose of their love had wilted? That the marquess had found marriage to her not to be to his liking? And why did she care what anyone thought?

"I'm discovering that *fun* is not something with which my husband is intimately familiar."

"Oh, my goodness." Jenny took her arm, turned her so they faced each other. "Are you so terribly unhappy?"

"I'm not really unhappy. I'm just not happy."

"Tell me everything."

"Nothing to tell really. He's not awful, he just seems to have so little interest in me. We share our meals together, but our conversations are of nothing important. Every night he comes into my bedchamber and announces a color. I shake my head and he bids me good night."

"What?"

She released a frustrated sigh and explained about her first night as Falconridge's wife.

Jenny laughed, incredulous. "When you said you'd been pleased—"

Kate shrugged. "I didn't want to admit that I'd turned him away."

"And he thinks if he simply announces your favorite color, you'll fall into his arms?"

"Apparently."

Jenny laughed all the harder. "Oh, this is rich."

"No, it's not. It's pathetic." Kate released a bubble of laughter. "He announces colors I've never heard of."

"At least you have to give him credit for trying."

Kate abruptly ended her laughter. "Do I? Should I?"

"I think it's terribly sweet."

Sweet was not a word she'd ever associated with Falconridge.

"He's looking for a quick path to my bed."

"Considering how handsome he is, I think I'd drop rose petals along the way to ensure he doesn't get lost."

"Passion isn't enough for me, Jenny. I've known love. I desperately want it again."

"You can't force it, Kate. Besides, if you let him in your bed perhaps affection will develop more quickly."

"I can't imagine physical intimacy when the heart is but an observer."

"You read far too many romance stories. They're not real, Kate."

"Well, they should be. A woman deserves a man's undying devotion."

"I believe we've had this argument before."

"And I always win."

"You do not!"

Kate smiled. She always felt so much better after spending time with Jenny. "Were you able to get to the jewelers for me?"

"Oh, yes." Jenny popped up and went to her jewelry box. "It doesn't have the family crest or anything on it." She handed the ring to Kate.

It was a heavy ring that looked as though the gold had been braided into it. In some places it was worn and Kate wondered how many of his ancestors had rubbed their fingers over it.

"Won't he be surprised when you give it back to him?"

"I'm not sure I will."

"Why ever not?"

"I'm not certain he'd want me to know that he sold it. He has a great deal of pride, perhaps too much. I'll have to wait until our relationship is such that he won't be offended that I not only know what he did but that I took it upon myself to reclaim it."

"Marriage sounds like a complicated thing."

"You'll discover it all soon enough. How are things with your duke?"

"He's coming as Sir Walter Raleigh. Shall I let him sweep me off my feet?"

"Do you ever hear from Ravensley?"

"I don't want to talk about him."

"That's hardly an answer."

"He won't be here tonight so it doesn't matter. Jeremy is coming as a Wall Street banker. He's almost as boring as your husband."

"I suppose it would be more interesting if my costume were that of a banker."

"You could be a banker for real, considering the terms Father agreed to."

"Oh, Jenny. Where would I find the time? You have no idea the amount of work involved in overseeing the estate of an aristocrat. Do you know we have special rooms and china to be used only when royalty visits? Can you imagine the queen sitting at my dining table?"

"I daresay Mother would have it written up in the *New York Times*. She'd be the talk of the city."

"It would please her, wouldn't it?"

"Beyond measure."

"I'm surprised Mother and Father went to the seaside again. They were there only a few weeks ago."

"I'm not sure she's well, Kate."

Kate felt her heart lurch. "What do you mean?"

She watched, stunned, as tears welled in Jenny's eyes. "Father has been pressing me to accept the duke's offer of marriage. It's not like him to be so anxious to be rid of us. He wants me married before summer's end."

"Mother doesn't look ill."

Smiling, Jenny wiped the tears from her eyes. "Perhaps I'm wrong then. Let's hope so, shall we? Now, come along. I don't want to be melancholy tonight. I want to have fun. That's the reason I'm dressed as a harem girl. Now I just have to find my sultan."

"I'm having a difficult time believing you invited Hawkhurst's sister," Kate said. A good many of the guests had arrived. Once the music began playing, Jenny had dispensed with greeting guests and had begun dancing with one gentleman after another. She'd finally decided to sit one out so she could visit with Kate.

"Jeremy asked me to include her," Jenny said.

"That's interesting. Do you think he fancies her?"

"It's difficult to tell with Jeremy, but since Caroline has a questionable origin, Mother will never approve of her."

"It would be refreshing if one of us married whom we wanted without worrying about Mother's approval."

"I doubt it'll be me. I'll let Jeremy know that we've elected him to be the rebellious child."

"Who is the guest wearing the mask?" Kate asked. It was difficult to tell much about him because he wore a hooded cape pulled up over his head so she couldn't tell his hair's color.

"Dumas's man in the iron mask, perhaps."

"I don't recall seeing him when we were greeting guests."

"He must have slipped in after the dancing began. Obviously he didn't read his invitation closely enough as I specifically indicated it was a costume ball not a masked ball. I like to see who I'm dancing with. Perhaps he's your husband."

"No, he doesn't move with the grace of Falconridge. I'm beginning to think he's not coming."

"Have a little faith, Kate. He'll be here." Looking away from Kate, Jenny smiled. "Speak of the devil, although I thought you said he wasn't coming in costume."

"He's not."

"Interesting. So chain mail is his usual attire? Around the house and around town? To bed as well? Oh, that's right. You don't know yet . . ."

Kate jerked around to confront her sister and ask what in the world she was babbling about, but the words froze on the tip of her tongue at the sight of the tall, broad-shouldered man descending the stairs into the ballroom with all the pride and noble bearing of a king. Kate didn't know all the proper terms for a warrior's clothing. The chain mail was visible on his arms, its hood gathered around his neck. A white tunic with a red cross covered his upper body. He wore tight britches and gleaming black boots. Kate didn't think his outfit was an authentic rendering of a knight's costume, but it was close enough to please her.

"You know, Kate, I could be completely wrong, but it certainly looks like a costume to me," Jenny prodded.

"Will you be quiet?"

"He's really quite remarkable, isn't he? I can't believe you aren't welcoming him into your bed."

"Will you please hold your tongue?" Kate's voice was raspy, and she sounded breathless. Seeing Falconridge dressed like a warrior was almost as unnerving as having him watch her bathe. Not to mention he'd gone to an inordinate amount of trouble—her husband who abhorred costume balls.

He came to a stop before them and bowed slightly toward Jenny. "Miss Rose."

"We're related now. You may call me Jenny."

He nodded as though he were having as difficult a time speaking as Kate was. He shifted his attention to her. "Must you stare as though you've never seen me before?"

"I thought you weren't going to wear a costume."

"I thought you wished for me to."

"Well, I did, but you seemed to detest the very idea."

"What I detest is not of consequence."

"So you don't wish to be in costume?"

"Of course, I don't wish to be in costume—must we continue along this path of conversation that will only serve to prick your anger?"

"Of course, we're free to change topics, but, pray tell, who exactly are you?" Jenny asked.

Falconridge seemed even more disgruntled. "Arthur or Lancelot, whichever my lady wishes."

Jenny seemed far too pleased. Kate was baffled. She never told him which costume she finally decided to wear. "How did you know—"

"Your maid. I thought to wear armor but to dance in it would be impossible. I daresay it will be difficult enough as is."

"I suggest you find out, my lord," Jenny said. "A waltz is about to begin. Are you in need of a partner?"

Kate felt an unexpected spark of jealousy. Was Jenny flirting with her husband?

Falconridge looked at Kate, a quick flicker of doubt in his eyes. "Is your dance card already filled?"

Suddenly she found herself very pleased that he'd gone to such trouble for her. He was trying, bless him. He was trying. Whatever she wanted, he seemed willing to do. Smiling, she shook her head. "Of course not."

"Then will you do me the honor—"

"Yes," she said quickly, not needing him to finish. "I've never danced with a king."

"'Tis only pretend, my lady."

"Sometimes that's more than enough."

With a slight bow, he extended his arm. She placed her hand on it and allowed him to lead her on to the dance floor.

"Is the chain mail heavy?" she asked.

"Not too bad."

She had a feeling he wouldn't tell her if it was. "Wherever did you find the costume?"

"In an old trunk. I remembered my father once dressing up for a ball . . . it seems rather silly to me."

"I love costume balls. We have Nelson and Wellington, a couple of Caesars . . . Wouldn't you have felt self-conscious not wearing a costume, when everyone else is?"

"As I descended the stairs, I noticed young Jeremy Rose isn't dressed in a costume," he said, sounded disgruntled, avoiding her question.

"He's an investment banker."

He scowled. "Perhaps I should have come as a duke."

"I like that you came as Arthur . . . or Lancelot." She tilted her head and smiled. "I think the ninth dance is a waltz. I think I should like to dance it with Lancelot."

"If it pleases you."

"It would immensely."

He smiled warmly at her, clearly taking satisfaction in her words, and she thought tonight she might do a good deal more than dance with him.

She might tell him her favorite color.

The dance ended much too soon. It surprised her that she was so sorry to see him leaving her after he escorted her from the dance floor with the promise of returning for the ninth dance. She didn't know why husbands and wives didn't spend more time together at affairs such as this, why there was a reason to socialize with others. It was quite bothersome to be required to mingle when all she wanted to do was find a quiet corner, away from the revelry, a quiet corner that included her husband. The more she came to know him, the more she wanted to know him.

Next she danced with her brother.

"I can't believe you're so unimaginative," she chastised.

Jeremy smiled, the smile of a man who is not easily intimidated. "We're a little old to be playing dress-up."

"We're never too old to have fun."

"A lady's fun could be a man's torment."

She scowled. "Lord, but you're as bad as Falconridge."

"How is marriage, dear sister?"

She shrugged. "I'm growing accustomed to it."

"Does he treat you well?"

There was a seriousness to Jeremy's expression

that surprised her. He was eight years her senior. He had a casual, carefree mien, and yet she suspected he also possessed the ruthlessness and cunning that had made her father such a success in the business world.

"And what if he doesn't?" she asked.

"In Father's absence, he would answer to me."

She knew he was terribly protective of women. He'd been Louisa's champion when Hawkhurst had compromised her.

"And what would you do? Punch him as you did Hawkhurst?"

"If necessary."

"I wonder if he'd fight back," she mused aloud.

"Would you want him to?"

"Sometimes . . ." She shook her head. How to explain? "Sometimes I wish he'd just tell me to go to the devil. I can be difficult and he only grits his teeth. Everything is done for my pleasure."

"I thought that's what women wanted."

"Quite honestly, I'm not sure what I want anymore." She sighed. "So Jenny tells me you insisted she invite Caroline."

"Poor girl isn't invited to many parties. Most see her as a curiosity."

"And what do you see her as?"

"Intriguing."

"Mother would never approve of your association with her."

"I'm not going to marry her, Kate."

"Who are you going to marry?"

"I've not given it any thought."

While females thought of little else once they were old enough to realize they were expected to marry—and marry well. Men had such easy lives.

"I hope you're cursed with a dozen daughters so you have to give marriage a great deal of thought in later years."

Jeremy laughed, his smile bright. "I plan to marry a woman with the good sense to give me sons. I suspect your husband is hoping the same thing."

"It's not a hope but a requirement among the aristocracy. They're a rather demanding lot when it comes to their heirs."

"You know wagers are going about as to when your first child will make an appearance."

"So I heard," she said, not bothering to disguise her disgust with that ridiculous practice.

"I put my money on ten months. Is it going to pay off for me?"

She very nearly stopped dancing. "I can't believe you did that!"

"I believe in taking advantage of opportunity. Besides, it gave notice that my sister wasn't marrying under scandalous circumstances."

"So you're my champion?"

"Do you ever doubt it?"

She shook her head. "But there is a fine line between being a champion and being meddlesome."

"He wasn't good enough for you, Kate."

She narrowed her eyes at him. She wasn't going to discuss Wesley, not tonight, not ever again.

"Tell me true, you're happy with Falconridge, aren't you?"

"I'm content."

Unlike her dance with Falconridge, she was grateful when her dance with Jeremy ended, so she didn't have to answer his probing questions. Even if they were asked with the greatest of intentions, they only served to make her question her acceptability as a wife.

She wanted what every woman wanted: to be loved, cherished, appreciated.

Would her husband ever love her? Would she ever love him? Was she beginning to have a fondness for him?

Those questions circled her mind as she danced with the Duke of Pemburton, the man her mother wanted Jenny to marry. She'd expected Pemburton to pepper her with questions about Jenny, but instead he simply smiled, apparently confident he had Jenny's hand already firmly nestled in his. He was incredibly distinguished, but not very exciting, almost cold, and she wondered if he'd be able to deliver the passion that Jenny so desperately wanted.

During the eighth dance, she stood near the open doors that led on to the gardens, allowing the cool night breeze to waft enticingly over her warm skin. She saw Jenny dancing with the Duke of Stonehaven. Unlike Kate's dance card, Jenny's was always filled and even though her sister left dances blank, she never sat out, except by choice. Her beauty and poise drew men to her.

Except Wesley had chosen Kate over Jenny. Although, so had Falconridge, but she didn't delude herself into thinking he'd married her for anything other than money. Unlike Wesley who had openly adored her. He'd made her heart—

"Hello, dear girl."

Kate's breath backed up in her chest at the rasp of the familiar voice, the cherished endearment, coming from behind her. She'd known this bittersweet moment would come at some time, but she wasn't prepared for it, hadn't expected it to be so soon. It took everything within her to hold the tears of loss at bay, to force a smile on her lips as she slowly turned.

"Hello, Wesley."

He took her gloved hand and pressed a kiss to the back of her hand. "You're as lovely as ever. I heard you'd married."

Nodding, she swallowed hard. "Falconridge. Can you believe it? A marquess."

"You deserve a king."

She damned the tears that threatened to ruin this moment. "I saw that you, too, had married. Are you happy?"

"How can I be when she is not you?"

"So are you related to the king of France? His twin brother, perhaps? Locked away in the Bastille?" Jenny asked the man wearing a golden mask. Just as Kate had immediately recognized the costumed man wasn't her Falconridge because of the way he moved through the crowd, so did Jenny recognize exactly who he was by his elegant gait. Earlier in the Season, she'd spent far too much time watching his movements. He'd intrigued her from the start. "Or are you simply a man too embarrassed to show his face?"

"The latter, if truth be told."

"You're not one for always telling the truth, though, are you? I don't recall sending you an invitation, Ravensley."

"Yet another reason why I chose to come as someone being treated unfairly."

She scoffed. "You brought your misfortunes upon yourself. Does your sister know you're here?"

"No. Louisa is spending far too much time gazing at her husband to notice much else. She seems happy enough."

"I think they're well suited, but that doesn't excuse your deplorable behavior where they're concerned."

"I couldn't bear the thought of you marrying him. Now I hear you're to marry Pemburton."

"You've been so absent from Society it's a wonder you've heard anything at all."

"I have my ways. Is it true?"

Although she was angry at him for the pain he'd brought Louisa, Jenny couldn't deny she was grateful to have a moment to speak with him. From the first dance they'd shared at the beginning of the Season, she'd found herself drawn irrevocably toward him. But he was only an earl and her mother wanted her to be a duchess not a countess.

"In all likelihood he is the one I'll marry, although he has yet to ask."

All she could see were his blue eyes, but it was enough for her to read the sadness and disappointment he felt.

"Take a turn about the garden with me?" he asked.

She glanced around—

"No one's paying any attention to us," he said quietly. "We can slip out the back door over here and none will be the wiser."

"I'll be missed. I'm the hostess."

"Five minutes, Jenny. It's all I'm asking for."

Nodding, she took another look around before slipping out the side door. She was so very much aware of his nearness, but then she was always aware of him.

Instead of leading her on to the path that wound through the garden, he gently took her arm and urged her toward the side of the house, into the shadows, where the gas lamps couldn't touch them. She'd not been aware of him removing his mask, but quite suddenly she found herself wrapped in his arms, his mouth taunting and teasing hers with the memories of all the secretive liaisons they'd managed to arrange throughout the Season. He tasted heavenly, just as she remembered, and the warmth sluiced through her. He could deliver passion in ways that left her innocence intact, yet left her yearning for a few more moments with him.

He must have dropped his mask and removed

his gloves, because his bare fingers were grazing her cheek, his thumb circling beside one corner of her mouth, while his other arm continued to hold her close. Drawing back, he pressed his forehead to hers. "Ah, but I've missed you. Run away with me."

He trailed his hot mouth along her jaw, down her throat, stealing her ability to think, forcing her to concentrate on her words when she wanted nothing more than to let herself drown in the incredible sensations he was creating. "You are twice the fool if you think running away with you is even an option. You are the most impoverished lord in all of London, and my parents wouldn't sanction our union with funds."

"I don't care about the money."

"Well, you should," she said more forcefully than she'd intended. "I'll not end my life as a pauper."

"We'll find a way."

She chuckled low. "You are a fool if you believe that. You've not managed to turn your circumstances around and I haven't Kate's head for numbers. Once the passion cooled we'd be miserable."

"It'll never cool. You have no idea how desperately I want you."

And he had no idea how desperately she wanted him. It was tempting, so tempting to go somewhere completely private where intimacies could be shared with no danger of discovery.

"We shouldn't be here, we shouldn't be doing this." She pushed on his shoulders, easing him away from her. "I must return to the ball."

"I want you, Jenny, and I'll do anything, anything at all to have you."

His voice contained more determination than desperation. It excited, thrilled, and terrified her all at once. "So you've proven."

"Betraying my sister and Hawkhurst was nothing compared to the lengths I'll go to in order to have you."

"Your actions hurt me as much as it hurt them. Yes, your kiss can make me forget a good many things, but it eventually ends and when it does the memories return. I'm sorry, Alex, but I'll never marry you."

The pain of those words spoken aloud caught her off guard. She nearly stumbled as she hurried away from him, leaving him in the shadows, along with her dreams.

"I can't believe you wore a costume."

Michael gave a hard glare to Hawkhurst before turning his attention back to the dance floor. It didn't help matters that his friend was dressed in formal evening attire.

"At least we didn't have to wear masks to this thing," Michael said.

"Didn't have to wear a costume either."

"It is a costume ball. By its very nature it requires a costume."

"You've never before followed the dictates of a gilded invitation."

"I've never before been married."

"You'll do anything she asks of you."

Michael ground his teeth together. "Sadly, that's the truth of my circumstances. I'm beginning to think Louisa's brother did you a favor by ensuring that all of London knew you'd compromised his sister. If Jenny is half as stubborn at Kate—"

"Not making much progress at earning her affections?"

"I'd not thought so"—he considered the way Kate had watched him as they'd danced—"but I may have made great strides this evening."

If he'd known chain mail would have done the trick, he'd have donned it on his wedding night.

"I can't believe your patience with her."

"I have to admit—" He shook his head. No, he wasn't going to admit, not even to a trusted friend, that he found himself actually wanting to please Kate. For all his grumbling and disappointment that she had requirements that must be met, he always felt a certain sense of accomplishment whenever he caused her to smile. And when he made her laugh . . . he thought there was no sweeter sound in all the world than her laughter.

"You have to admit . . . ?" Hawkhurst prodded.

"I have to admit as much as I enjoy chatting with you, I've promised my wife another dance. So if you will excuse me, duty awaits."

"I think Louisa would warn you that as long as you view dancing with your wife a duty, she'll not come to love you."

"I suppose you don't see dancing with your wife as a duty?"

Hawkhurst, damn him, smiled broadly. "Any moment spent with her is a pleasure."

"You've effectively served to ruin my good humor."

"My apologies. I was actually hoping to offer you a bit of advice. Make her believe you'd rather have her in your arms than anyone else. To do that, you can't think of it as a duty."

Michael nodded. Being with Kate was pleasurable. He *was* foolish to view dancing with her as a duty. "Your advice is well heeded. Now, if you'll excuse me?"

"Of course."

He strode away from his friend, surprised to find he envied Hawkhurst. He'd married a woman with no funds, and yet he seemed absolutely content and madly in love. Michael had no plans ever to be madly in love. His wife was leading him around enough as it was. To love her as well would give her far too much power over him. She had enough as it was. Although, in truth, being at her mercy was not nearly as unpleasant as he'd expected it to be.

He spotted Kate standing near a set of doors leading on to the garden, talking with a man. But that wasn't what gave him pause.

It was the open, unmasked expression on her face: adoration, yearning . . . desire.

A possessiveness he didn't understand, a jealousy he'd never before experienced roared through him, almost painfully. He wanted to deny what he was witnessing, wanted to deny the desperation with which he longed to have her look at him in the same manner.

Wanted to reject the realization that no matter what he did, he would never receive such devotion from her.

Taking a deep breath, he strode toward the couple, recognizing the man as he neared: Wesley Wiggins, third son to Viscount Wiggins. A man who'd nabbed an American heiress of his own. He posed no threat to Michael, and yet, Michael couldn't help but feel that he did.

He arrived with a loudness to his heels that caused the couple to turn toward him, with Wiggins blushing almost as profusely as Kate.

"My lord," Kate said, her smile uneasy, "allow me the honor of—"

"*Mr.* Wiggins and I are acquainted." It pleased him immensely to reinforce with his address Wiggins's lack of a title.

"Oh, yes, of course. I suppose you move in the same circle, being part of the Set and all that."

"Where is your lovely wife?" Michael asked.

If at all possible, Wiggins's blush deepened. "She's not feeling well this evening. I escorted her sisters."

"I would have thought you'd have stayed by her side."

"There was little I could do to ease her discomfort."

Yet, Michael could imagine the disfavor he'd receive from his own wife if he left her while she wasn't feeling well. Perhaps it was the reason he took some comfort in pointing out Wiggins's failure. Although to his chagrin, Kate seemed unfazed by it.

"I was hoping to have the honor of dancing with your wife," Wiggins said into the silence that had suddenly surrounded them.

This dance was his, damn it. And yet, he could see in Kate's eyes . . . what? Hesitation? Uncertainty? Anticipation?

Michael wasn't certain exactly what Wiggins meant to Kate, but he sensed the man was a threat. A threat in some manner, to either Kate or Michael or perhaps their future.

He wasn't one to take threats lightly.

"Regrettably for you, I have anticipated this dance with my wife far too much to give it up now."

He extended his arm toward Kate, who looked startled. Did she truly believe he would give her to another man so easily?

She smiled at Wiggins. "It was a pleasure to see you again."

"And you, my lady."

"Do give *your wife* our best," Michael said, offering a subtle reminder that the man was well and truly spoken for.

"Thank you, my lord."

Michael escorted Kate only a few steps when he glanced at her and realized she was no longer blushing, rather she was quite pale. "Would you rather go home?" he asked.

He took comfort in the gratitude reflected in her eyes.

"Yes, actually, if you don't mind."

"I assure you I'm quite ready to dispense with my costume."

It didn't take long to have a footman locate their driver and have their coach brought round to the front. Michael helped his wife clamber inside, before joining her, taking his usual place opposite her. As they journeyed through the dimly lit streets, she seemed particularly enamored with the glow of the passing streetlamps. He couldn't help but wonder what thoughts traveled through her mind.

When he could stand the suspense no longer, he asked, "What exactly is Wesley Wiggins to you?"

"He is nothing to me."

His wife wasn't one to lie, but Michael sensed she was lying now. He had seen the heat and longing in her eyes as she'd gazed at Wiggins. And something else. Something that ran much more deeply. A flame that had once burned brilliantly and was in danger of flaring back to life. No, she wasn't lying. He'd done a rather poor job of phrasing the question.

"What *was* he to you?"

She turned her attention away from the street and met his gaze in the shadowy confines of the coach.

"My husband."

Chapter 14

Kate had expected her present husband to rant, rave, and interrogate her. Instead, following her announcement, he'd withdrawn into complete cold and calculating silence. Not a single word spoken for the remainder of the journey to their residence. Not a syllable uttered as he'd assisted her from the coach upon their arrival. She'd found his total retreat terrifying, as though he were contracting everything into a tight ball—a ball that sooner or later would have no choice except to explode.

She dearly hoped she wouldn't be in his proximity when that happened.

Now she was in her bedchamber, standing before the window, gazing out on the night, barely noticing the darkness, numbed by her encounters with both Wesley and Falconridge. Chloe had helped her change out of her costume into a rather unflattering cotton nightgown. Kate couldn't believe how much she'd anticipated the ball. And how devastated she'd been by Wesley's presence. Everything about him was so familiar, so endearing. Seeing him had effectively ruined her good humor and any plans she'd had regarding inviting Falconridge into her bed.

Surely, Jenny hadn't known he'd attend the ball. Otherwise, she'd have warned Kate. Had she even known he'd returned to London? Wesley wasn't important enough to garner much notice. He'd never inherit the title. Not as the third son. Gossipmongers paid him scant attention.

Selfishly, Kate took a bit of pleasure in the fact he'd appeared a little gaunt, not incredibly joy-filled. Was marriage to Melanie Jeffers not all he'd hoped it would be? And why had he married the little twit anyway? Because her parents hadn't threatened to cut her off?

She soundly cursed him for marrying another.

She heard the door that led to her husband's bedchamber click open. Her heart hammered against her ribs. She wasn't in the mood for his silly color-guessing game. She turned to tell him so and the words died on her tongue. From the harsh and determined look on his face, he wasn't here for any silly games.

He'd changed out of his chain mail into his silk dressing gown, but it was the fury in his eyes that sent the cold chill racing down her spine. His jaw was clenched so tightly she doubted he'd be able to speak, and as long as his hands remained fisted at his side, she wouldn't find them wrapped around her neck.

She wanted to turn away, but better to face the devil, and at that precise moment she realized she'd greatly underestimated her husband's patience. Clearly, he'd reached the end of it.

"How is it that you were married to Wesley Wiggins?" he ground out.

She swallowed hard. Where to begin? Did she even want to begin? And truly, was it any of his concern?

As though aware of all the random thoughts flittering through her mind, he pounded his fist against the bedpost. She flinched at the *thwump*, surprised it didn't rend the post in two.

"Answer me, damn you!"

She angled her chin. "I don't owe—"

"You don't want to play that game with me tonight, madam. I bargained my title for your hand in marriage, and now I'm discovering I've acquired a scandalous divorced—"

"I'm not divorced," she assured him quickly, latching on to the least damaging of her transgressions. She couldn't argue with the scandalous portion of his assessment. What she'd done had given her mother a case of the vapors.

"But you were married."

She nodded. "At seventeen. My father had the marriage annulled. When you have an abundance of money you can accomplish anything, and as you are well aware we are obscenely wealthy." She laughed bitterly. "It didn't help matters that I was underage."

"Did Wiggins exercise his husbandly rights?"

She couldn't hold his heated gaze. She looked down at his feet, his large bare feet. They were almost as frightening as his balled hands. His ankles were visible, his hair-covered calves. Did he wear anything at all beneath that dressing gown?

"Shall I interpret your silence as a yes?" he asked, with less venom, as though the words astonished him when he spoke them.

Nodding, she lifted her gaze back to his.

"Then you're not innocent as I presumed nor in need of a gentle introduction into the ways of men."

Did he truly expect her to respond in some manner to that assessment? And what did her lack of innocence have to do with anything? The fact that she did know the ways of men was the very reason she held him at bay.

"If you know the pleasures that can be shared between a man and woman, then why deny me?" He studied her intently for only a heartbeat, but it seemed enough for him to slip past her defenses and peer into realm of her heart. "Because you love him . . . still?"

She dared not risk angering him further by answering.

But apparently, he required no acknowledgment. He simply released a long deep sigh. "I saw the way you looked at him tonight, and I cannot compete with that, and so I'll not even bother to try. But neither will I be denied any longer. Close your eyes and pretend it is he who holds you. Scream out his name in ecstasy, I care not. But I will no longer be denied."

She felt the tears burning. "If you do this, I will never love you."

A deep and profound sadness touched his eyes. "You'll never love me anyway."

He stepped nearer, and with gentleness she'd not expected from him, he cupped her cheek and gathered the tears rolling along her cheek with his thumb.

"Please—" she rasped.

He touched his thumb to her lips, silencing her. "You told me tonight that sometimes pretense was enough. Pretend. Pretend it is he who holds you"—he lifted her into his strong arms—"pretend it is he who touches you." He carried her to the bed and laid her down. "Pretend, sweetheart, simply pretend."

Looking up at him, she felt her heart pounding in her chest, her throat tightening as she held a deluge of tears at bay. He asked the impossible of her.

"In the dark, all women appear the same," he said quietly. "I suspect the same holds true for men."

And with that, he turned off the gaslight, plunging them into darkness.

She heard the rasp of silk falling across skin. She felt the bed dip beneath his weight. How would she bear his touch? How would she bear his lifting the hem—

Only it wasn't her hem that had caught his attention. He'd unerringly placed his hands at her throat, his fingers lightly grazing her skin before they traveled lower and went to work unbuttoning her gown.

Did he not realize a woman's nightgown didn't have to be removed—

She felt the first brush of his lips against her neck, and all thought of advising him drifted away like fog before the morning sun. His tongue, hot, moist, trailed along her collarbone, dipping into the hollow at the base of her throat, distracting her from the task his fingers were busily seeking to accomplish.

His deep groan echoed low between them, just before his mouth left her, and she became aware of him parting the opening of her gown, exposing her skin to the air and the darkness. Feeling vulnerable, she couldn't stop the quiver that passed through her. She squeezed her eyes closed, even though the night shielded her from his gaze.

She wanted to beg him one more time for mercy, wanted to turn away from him, but her pride wouldn't allow her to cower. She would do as he'd ordered. She'd pretend he was Wesley.

Only Wesley had never folded her gown off her shoulders. He'd never slid the material down her arms, down her sides. He'd never gathered it around her waist, only to move it down farther. He'd never glided it over her thighs. He'd never pulled it free of her feet.

He'd never then cupped her ankles with palms so warm that she thought they'd melt chocolate. He'd never taken his hands on a leisurely journey along her flesh as though he were an explorer who'd discovered a hidden treasure and was measuring its worth.

And where his hands led, his mouth followed.

She gasped at the intimacy of his touch. She fought to imagine a man with blue eyes gazing at her, but she saw only green. She tried to imagine her fingers were tangled in blond hair, but she could only envision hair as black as a storm at midnight.

He kissed the inside of her thighs. He kissed just below her navel, then dipped his tongue inside. How could he aim so true, without any hint of a stumble, with no evidence of clumsiness? It was as though he was already well acquainted with the path.

She felt the brush of his chest over her stomach and then his mouth upon her breast. She very nearly came off the bed, as her fingers dug into his shoulders, to push him away, to draw him near.

She'd been married for three months, but never had she been touched such as this. Never had she known such incredible torment. Her flesh burned, she writhed for want of something that she knew not how to acquire. She barely recognized the whimpers as coming from her.

She was indeed wed to the devil, for only one familiar with sin, could be this cruel, so skilled at torture. He carried her to the brink of something she didn't understand, then left her hovering, searching, lost . . .

He returned with a growl and a fierceness that had her clinging to him as he buried his face into the curve of her neck, his mouth hot and wet against her skin, one arm strong and sure holding her close while it supported him, his other hand caressing her breast as though he'd never known anything as exquisite.

She'd never felt the full length of her naked body pressed against another's. Her feet caressed his calves, the coarse hair there kissing her soles. Beneath her hands, she could feel the play of corded muscles across his back.

How had she managed to miss the fact she'd married a man of such strength, such determination, such unbridled passion? It was as though each touch of his hands caressed her everywhere, each brush of his lips over her skin, each sweep of his tongue stroked every inch all at once. His deep-throated groans shimmered along her nerve endings.

She floated into ecstasy while writhing in hell.

Even in the darkness, she was aware of his shifting, of his rising above her. She was more than ready for him when he entered her with one long, sure stroke. The fullness of him surprised her. She'd never felt this tight, never been so aware . . .

He slid a hand beneath her hip, lifted her, and impossibly delved more deeply . . .

Nothing that had ever come before had prepared her for this moment as he rocked against her. She wanted to scream for him to stop, terrified of where he might be leading her. She wanted to yell for him to continue, terrified that he might halt before her journey was complete.

What she'd experienced before, during her first marriage, had been pleasant. Always pleasant. This was something else entirely. He'd given her a hint of his power in the forest, by the pond, but it paled in comparison with what he was delivering to her now. It was pleasure beyond comprehension, sensations almost beyond enduring.

He was rough and gentle, harsh and tender. He was all those things.

She didn't think it possible, but her body tightened more firmly around his and then she was screaming, screaming as he carried her over into a realm where she flew among the stars.

She was vaguely aware of his final thrust, the shudders rippling almost violently through him, the trembling in his arms as he held himself above her.

Her own arms, limp, fell away from him.

She was aware of his harsh breathing, heard him swallow hard. He pressed a kiss to the curve of her neck, even as he eased his body from hers. Her sensitive skin felt the brush of his as he moved off her. She heard his feet hit the floor, felt the covers being drawn over her with unexpected tenderness.

She was cognizant of movement. The door clicked, and she caught sight of the silhouette of his nude body outlined by the light pouring from his bedchamber just before he closed the door in his wake.

Leaving her alone and more lonely than she'd imagined it possible to be.

She rolled over to her side and allowed the tears to fall. What had passed between them should have been shared by two people deeply in love. It shouldn't have left her bereft. And yet it had.

Still clutching his dressing gown in his right hand, Michael crossed his bedchamber and dropped onto the sofa set before the fireplace. Leaning forward, he buried his face in his hands, hands that still carried his wife's sweet scent. The fragrance filled his nostrils, causing his body to harden painfully.

He thought he'd prepared himself for what he'd demanded of her: pretend he was another. He hadn't expected the anguish brought on by knowing she'd envisioned someone else making love to her.

He brought his head up, his chin still cupped in his palms. When had he ever made love to a woman? He bedded women. Pure, simple, and selfishly. Oh, he cared for their pleasure, always sought to please them as much as they pleased him, but what he'd experienced tonight . . .

He'd touched every inch of her with his hands and his mouth. He'd memorized every dip and curve. If he awoke blind in the morning, he could carve a perfect likeness of her.

He released a brittle chuckle. No, he couldn't do that as he had no skills at carving.

But still, he could see her so plainly. Now he knew the exquisite silkiness of everything he'd seen that night in the bathing room. He wanted to return to her now, hold her close, stroke her again, hear her cries—

He squeezed his eyes shut. Pretend they were for him.

He'd told her to pretend, not realizing he'd be desperate to do the same. Not realizing the anguish he'd feel because he wasn't the one she wanted in her bed.

Dropping his head back, he plowed his hands through his hair. At least she'd touched him. And she'd been so tight, so incredibly tight he'd almost spilled his seed as she'd enveloped him in a cocoon of wet heat. Already his body yearned to experience that sweet torment once again.

But he'd hesitated at the door, considered returning to her immediately. He'd heard her sobs. No, she'd not welcome him back tonight.

Tomorrow night, though, when she'd recovered, when she had the strength to once again pretend, he'd return to her bedchamber, to her bed. And while she pretended he was someone else, he would pretend she had no reason to imagine he was anyone other than who he was.

Chapter 15

⎯⎯∽◯◯∼⎯⎯

Stretching beneath the covers, Kate couldn't remember the last time she'd felt so well-rested, so glorious upon awakening. Her body was fairly thrumming. She released a tiny satisfied squeal. Dear Lord, but she felt marvelous.

She stretched farther, the soreness between her legs giving her pause. Her eyes flew open as memories bombarded her.

"Oh, you're awake at last."

Clutching the covers against her nakedness—she'd been too lethargic, too sated last night to find the strength to recover her nightgown and slip it back on—she jerked her head to the side, to the chair where Chloe was slowly rising.

"His lordship sent me to watch over you," her maid said. "He was a bit concerned that you were still abed. 'Tis long past noon."

The draperies were pulled back, sunlight streaming into the room so she could see Chloe's blush.

"You don't usually sleep so late," Chloe said. "Are you feeling unwell?"

"I feel fine," Kate snapped. More than fine, truth be told.

Chloe ducked her head. "I thought a dress with a high collar would do well for today."

Kate was accustomed to going nude before her servant. She threw the covers back and her gaze fell on the inside of her thigh and the bruise . . .

She furrowed her brow. No, it wasn't a bruise exactly. She remembered the lingering heat of Falconridge's mouth. Lifting her gaze to her breast, she discovered another mark he'd left behind. Scrambling out of bed, she hurried across the room to the vanity, peered in the mirror, and saw the faintest of love bites at her throat, near her collarbone.

Her husband needed to curb his enthusiasm. She started to turn, caught sight of her smile in the mirror. Had she ever worn such a self-satisfied expression?

Even when she sought to scold him for this latest offense, she didn't know if she could do it with any true anger reflected in her voice.

Did she really want him to dim his attentions when he'd succeeded in carrying her to heights she'd never before attained?

Was it possible Jenny had the right of it? That passion *was* more desirable than love?

"Where is the marquess now?" Kate asked.

"I don't know, my lady. He had the carriage brought around a few hours ago."

She wondered if he was as anxious to avoid her as she was to avoid him. What in the world did a lady say to a gentleman who'd hardly behaved as a gentleman? How could she possibly look him in the eye, knowing all the things he'd done to her, with her? She'd never had this problem with Wesley, but then his lovemaking had been much more tamed, more circumspect . . . besides, she'd loved him.

She shook her head. Not *had* loved. Still loved. It was much easier to meet the gaze of a man you loved. Because love encompassed trust. Facing Falconridge was going to be exceedingly uncomfortable. She wanted to avoid it as long as possible. Short of taking a journey back to New York, her options were limited. She needed a rousing round of shopping. Spending money always calmed her, made her better able to face challenges.

Kate turned to Chloe. "Yes, I think a dress with a high collar would do nicely for today. And have a carriage brought round for me."

She was in desperate need of a diversion.

Kate's first stop was the home her parents were leasing. She swept through the front door, a woman with a purpose. Jeremy, walking through the foyer, stopped in his tracks.

"I expected you to come by sooner than this," he drawled.

"Where's Jenny?"

"Still abed. She didn't invite him, Kate."

She knew who the *him* was. "Then it was rather rude of him to come, wasn't it?"

"It was also rude of him to marry you without our parents' consent."

Jeremy had been instrumental in convincing her not to fight her father on the annulment. He had the argumentative skills to convince a saint to sin. No doubt a talent he'd inherited from their mother.

"Did you ever like him?"

"I always liked him. I just didn't approve of his handling of you."

"Handling? You make it sound like I'm a damned horse."

Jeremy sighed. "You know what I mean. He fairly kidnapped you—"

"I went willingly."

Her brother shook his head. "I won't rehash it, except to say Falconridge didn't seem too pleased with the attention Wiggins was giving you."

"You are a master of understatement."

Jeremy took a step toward her, his brow furrowed. "He didn't take his anger out on you, did he?"

In a way he had, but it had hardly been in a manner worthy of complaining about, and she certainly wasn't going to discuss the particulars with Jeremy. "Suffice it to say my husband left no doubt regarding his displeasure over my association with Wesley. Now, if you'll excuse me, I want to visit with Jenny."

"For what it's worth, I believe Falconridge is the better man."

She released a loud scoff. "And upon what do you base that assessment?"

"He didn't do his wooing in secret as though he were ashamed of his behavior."

"He didn't woo me at all, you dolt!"

With that, she spun on her heel and darted up the stairs. She didn't want to think of all the ways Wesley had wooed her: with chocolates, and poetry, and stolen kisses. She'd never had so much attention. It had been incredibly thrilling.

She burst through Jenny's door, marched across the room, and yanked back the draperies. Jenny screeched as the sunshine poured in unmercifully. They so seldom had bright days like this that Kate took delight in tormenting Jenny so.

Jenny squinted up at her. "Kate?" She sat up. "What are you doing here?"

When Kate only glared at her, Jenny groaned. "Oh, Wesley."

"Jeremy says you didn't know he was in town."

"I didn't. And I certainly didn't invite him. I tried to warn you as soon as I saw him arrive, but I couldn't find you, and then it was too late and I got distracted—" She shook her head. "I'm sorry, Kate. Was it awful seeing him again?"

Kate sat on the edge of the bed. "Not as awful as I thought it would be. It helped that his wife wasn't at his side."

"I suspect she'll be at Stonehaven's ball. Will you attend that one?"

Kate studied her gloves. She needed new ones. "I don't know." Did she really want to see Wesley with Melanie?

"He's not nearly as handsome as your marquess."

Kate looked up. "I've told you before, I don't

judge a man on his physical attributes. They decline with time. I judge a man based on the way he makes me feel."

Jenny gave her a wicked grin. "And how does your marquess make you feel?"

Kate shot off the bed and walked to the window. She heard the bed creak, heard the light touch of Jenny's feet on the floor.

"Kate? Darling? Whatever's wrong?" Jenny said quietly from behind her.

Kate swiped at the blasted tear. Where had that come from? "He exercised his husbandly rights last night."

"Did he hurt you?"

Kate shook her head quickly, before turning to meet her sister's worried gaze. "I thought I knew . . . dear God, Jenny, I've been married. Wesley and I were intimate, but what I experienced last night . . . it was rather terrifying, but not in a horrible sort of way."

Jenny's wicked smile returned. She dropped into a nearby chair, brought her feet up to the cushion, and wrapped her arms around her legs. "Tell me everything."

"I can't. It was too personal."

"Was he passionate?"

Kate nodded. "Very."

"Was it wonderful?"

Kate bit her bottom lip, squeezed her eyes shut, and nodded.

Jenny released a tiny squeal. "Oh, you lucky girl."

Kate opened her eyes, unable to stop herself from grinning. "He was so enthusiastic he left little marks, little love bruises."

"Did you leave marks on him?"

"I don't think so. I didn't run my mouth all over his body."

Jenny's eyes widened, and Kate realized she'd said much more than she'd planned to. She rolled her eyes. "He's very amorous, very active during lovemaking. He's nothing at all like Wesley."

"You need to forget about Wesley."

"How can you say that? He was my first love."

"But he need not be your last."

"Falconridge has fairly stated that love will never be between us."

"Men often state things that aren't true. I pay them no heed."

"Now, you're an expert on men?"

"Hardly. Look at the mess I made with Ravensley."

"Did you love him?"

"Of course not, but he could stir my passions with little more than a look. I can hardly forgive him for ruining his sister's reputation and using me to do it."

"Louisa seems rather happy with Hawkhurst."

Jenny smiled softly. "I think she is. Still, Ravensley's handling of the situation was deplorable. In betraying them, he betrayed me."

"He was desperate. Mother wouldn't consent to you marrying an earl."

"Are you justifying his actions?"

"No. I just understand desperation."

"He was at the ball last night."

Kate stared at her sister as understanding dawned. "The man wearing the mask."

Jenny nodded.

"Was he the distraction?" Kate asked.

Jenny had the look of a child who'd been caught pilfering cookies. "Don't look so shocked. We only spoke for a couple of moments."

"He is to you what Wesley was to me."

"Don't be ridiculous. You loved Wesley. Ravensley is nothing more than a bit of passion."

Kate wished she could be as sure.

"You're not going to do anything silly where Wesley's concerned, are you?" Jenny asked, as though searching for a way to turn the conversation from her own questionable behavior.

"Of course not."

"What are you going to do?"

"Actually, I'm going shopping. Care to join me?"

"I'd love to, but I'm to accompany Pemburton to the park."

"Are you going to marry him?"

"Probably."

"It seems to me a woman should sound a bit more excited about the prospect of marriage."

"I'm excited about the prospect of having little love bruises."

"You're so naughty."

"Not as naughty as you."

Which brought Kate back to wondering how in the world she'd face Falconridge again.

Michael heard the bell above the bookshop door jangle, its vibrations putting his nerves on edge once again. He'd heard it numerous times since he'd arrived. A dozen or so people had come and gone while he'd lingered, looking through various books.

He didn't know why he thought he could select one his wife would take pleasure in reading, could determine which one she had yet to read.

Besides, she had sufficient money at her disposal and could no doubt purchase the entire bookshop if she wanted. While he had only a little remaining from the sale of his father's ring. He needed to use it judiciously.

What in damnation was he doing here? What did he think he was going to accomplish, except to prove that he knew little about her taste in reading, which she would no doubt consider a fault worse than not knowing her favorite color?

He simply wanted to do something that would make it a bit easier to face her later this evening, after all that had transpired between them last night. He fully intended to have her again. He would have taken her that morning, had gone into her bedchamber with the intention of waking her with a rousing session, but she'd looked so innocent, pure, so soundly asleep.

He abhorred the fact another man had gazed

on her, knew how enticingly beautiful she looked when she was all rumpled from sleep. He'd been unable to bring himself to awaken her. She'd been dead to the world. He'd brushed strands of her hair back from her face and the only part of her that had moved was her nose. A tiny little twitch, endearing in its simplicity.

So he wanted to give her something, but he didn't understand this desire to bestow a gift on her. Oh, he'd given his mistress lots of trinkets in order to keep her happy so she'd keep him happy. With Kate, he simply wanted to give her a gift. To see a softness in her eyes. To make her happy for her own sake. He had no ulterior motive, nothing he sought for himself. It was a rather strange position to be in, desperately wishing he knew precisely which book to purchase. He'd do better to simply purchase her chocolates. He couldn't go wrong there.

He took another book from the shelf and began browsing it. Apparently this story, too, involved a female in peril and a gentleman courageous enough to come to her rescue. Were these truly the type of stories women preferred? He was several pages in when he heard a familiar voice, "Falconridge?"

Slamming the book closed, he spun around to face his wife. He'd been Falconridge for so long that he was accustomed to the address, but considering what they'd shared last night, it hardly seemed intimate, personal. He nodded brusquely. "Madam."

"Do you have a penchant for romantic novels?" she asked, her furrowed brow seeming to make a mockery of her twitching mouth, as though she couldn't decide whether to be concerned or amused.

He cleared his throat. "The proprietor indicated novels in this area of the shop are favored by women."

"I see." She took a step nearer, clearly deciding to be amused. "Why would you prefer to read a novel favored by women?"

"Not me, madam." He shoved the book back into its place on the shelf and busied himself scanning other titles. "I was searching, trying to determine . . . damnation," he muttered beneath his breath. It had been a silly plan.

She reached past him, bringing her sweet scent nearer, and took the book he'd just returned to its proper place. "Does it appear to be any good?" she asked.

"It's about a governess and a widower. Not a very pleasant fellow actually."

"Handsome, though, I suspect. The hero is always handsome."

"What are you doing here?" he asked.

"I recognized your carriage and driver parked on the street and since I was in need of a book, I thought"—she laughed lightly. "I don't know what I thought. Do you come here often?"

"I've never been here before."

"Why today?"

"If you must know, I sought to purchase you a

gift; however, I know nothing about your reading preferences and, therefore, it was a futile effort. And it wouldn't really be my purchase would it since you'd be the one paying the charges?" He was weary of discussing his stupid attempt to be the type of husband she wanted. "How are you feeling this afternoon?"

She nodded, looked away. "Quite well."

"What are your plans?"

"I haven't any really. I just . . ."

"Would you care to join me in the carriage? Perhaps take a ride through the park?"

She held up the book, smiled. "After I make a purchase."

While Kate made her purchase, Falconridge went out to inform her driver she'd have no further need of the coach. She didn't know why she was anticipating sharing a carriage ride with him. Perhaps because he'd seemed charmingly disconcerted by her presence, disgruntled by the fact she'd ruined what obviously he'd planned to be a surprise. Or perhaps it was that seeing him again wasn't nearly as embarrassing as she'd expected it to be, was actually quite thrilling.

She could tell by the way his gaze heated whenever he looked at her that he was thinking about what had transpired between them last night. She wondered if she was as easy to read.

"Here you are, my lady," the clerk behind the counter said, handing her the book wrapped in brown paper for safekeeping. "I hope you'll enjoy the story."

"I know I shall. I've already read it."

She walked out of the shop, to find her husband waiting by the carriage. He assisted her onto the seat, and she very deliberately scooted all the way across. He stayed as he was, studying her.

"I don't think I could be any more clearer if I sent you a gilded invitation," she finally snapped.

Grinning, he gave a slight nod. "I suppose not."

The carriage rocked as he climbed in and took his place beside her. She could smell his sharp, citruslike fragrance, remembered the scent of it heated with passion.

"Take us home through the parks," Falconridge instructed the driver. "Leisurely."

They journeyed in silence for several minutes, before she finally said, "I'm not overly fond of the English tradition of calling aristocratic men by their titles. Falconridge sounds so harsh. I barely remember the ceremony." She shifted her gaze to him. "I seem to recall your name was Michael."

He nodded slowly.

"I believe I shall call you Michael, then."

"If it pleases you."

"It does."

"Did I please you last night?"

She gasped. "A gentleman wouldn't ask such a thing." She expected him to say a lady wouldn't scream out in ecstasy.

"No, he wouldn't," he said quietly. "I'd not expected you to welcome my company today. It's a pleasant surprise that you have."

"I suppose you intend to continue with what you began last night."

"Indeed."

She arched a brow. "What? You're not going to say your usual, if it pleases you?"

"I think it did please you. More importantly, you pleased me." He trailed his gloved finger along her cheek, tucked a stray strand of hair behind her ear. "Why didn't you tell me you'd been married?"

"I know gentlemen prefer their women pure."

"I've never fancied virgins."

She could hardly countenance they were discussing such intimate details in broad daylight.

"You can't deny you were angry."

"Would it not bother you to discover I'd been married?"

She shifted slightly in the seat to better see his face. "Were you?"

"No."

"Was there ever a woman you wished to marry, other than me, I mean?"

"No."

"You're not comfortable with the direction of our conversation."

"No. I do not see the need to meddle in our pasts."

"You seemed quite willing to meddle in mine last night."

"That was different."

"How so?"

"I didn't have to answer any questions."

His eyes held a gleam that drew her, just as they had when they'd traveled from London to his estate. She found herself chuckling as their driver turned into the park. And more than ready to shift the conversation to something a little less likely to cause either of them to feel uncomfortable.

"The flowers in English gardens are always so lovely," she said.

"I suppose you have a favorite, and I shall have to guess it in order to prove—"

"Forget-me-nots." She looked down at the book in her lap, wondering why it was so difficult for them to get to know each other. "I like forget-me-nots."

"Is that because blue is your favorite color?"

She peered over at him coyly. "There are other blue flowers. Besides, I thought you guessed blue already."

He grinned. "I suspect I did. If it's not your favorite color, then why that particular flower?"

"I think because of what it symbolizes. That one is always remembered."

He looked away, but she thought she caught a glimpse of sadness in his eyes before he did.

"Yes," he said quietly. "There is no joy in being forgotten."

"I can't imagine anyone forgetting you."

He shifted his attention back to her. "I shall do all in my power to see that you don't forget me."

She watched as the heat in his eyes intensified until she was the one who turned away. She
thought forgetting him would be an impossibility.

She straightened at the sight of a gentleman
astride a horse. "Is that Pemburton?"

"I believe so. Why?"

"Jenny told me she couldn't accompany me because she was going to the park with him. How
strange."

"Perhaps she meant someone else, or perhaps
their outing will be later."

"Perhaps."

Although she had a rather bad feeling about
things.

Oh, Jenny, please don't do anything silly.

"Are you all right?" Falconridge asked.

She nodded, smiled. "I'm fine."

She could only hope the same remained true of
her sister.

Kate didn't want to be fascinated by her husband, and yet she couldn't deny that she was.
They'd not spoken a great deal as they journeyed
through various parks, but he'd spoken a little
about his schooling, she'd told him of hers. She'd
even confessed how much she'd envied Jeremy
because he'd had the opportunity to attend a uni-
versity.

"Why would a man have need of an educated
wife?" Michael had dared to ask her.

She'd given him an earful there. Perhaps she'd
show him. She'd join a suffrage organization. Surely

her newly acquired title carried some weight behind it, and with her financial status secured, she could very well make a difference.

But as she stood in her bedchamber, gazing out the window, women's rights were the last thing on her mind.

Their pleasant afternoon had led to a pleasant enough dinner. An hour of quiet reading afterward, and then they'd retired to their respective bedchambers, he with the promise of coming to say good night.

He'd then proceeded to ruin a perfectly lovely evening by glancing over his shoulder at her with a knowing grin and saying, "I suppose a more accurate statement would be that I'll be in to *show* you good night."

Now her stomach was all aflutter. She moved to the bed, then crossed back to the window. She didn't want him to think she was anticipating his visit.

But dear Lord, help her. She was. Her nipples puckered with the mere thought of him walking into her bedchamber. She strolled to the chaise, sat, got up, and walked back to the window. How was it that it took him longer to prepare for bed than it did her?

Tonight she'd not bothered to braid her hair. She'd very nearly dispensed with buttoning her gown.

She walked back to the bed, fluffed a pillow, and froze when the door finally opened. She considered dashing back to the window, but instead she lifted her chin and met his gaze as he strode into the room, wearing the now ever-so-familiar dressing gown.

He fairly prowled around the corner of the bed, like some great cat. She faced him as he got nearer, crowding her as he reached past her—

"You don't have to extinguish the light," she said, surprised by the breathlessness of her voice.

He gave her a questioning look. She angled her chin defiantly. "I can close my eyes."

He seemed to ponder her strange prelude to their lovemaking, but she refused to acknowledge she wanted the light, wanted an opportunity to see him, even if it was through eyes that gave the appearance of being closed. She wanted to see all she'd touched last night.

She made a move to climb into bed, but he gently took her arm.

"Not yet."

She watched as his gaze moved slowly from her eyes to her mouth and lingered there. Licking her lips, she was acutely aware of his eyes darkening, his nostrils flaring. He was going to kiss her. She was certain of it. When he lowered his head, she closed her eyes, angled her chin up so their mouths could meet—

Only he kissed the underside of her jaw, provocatively, his tongue teasing as much as his lips. She felt the sensations stretch all the way down to her toes. He blazed a trail all along her throat. No hurry, no rush, as though they had all night.

She didn't remember reaching out, but suddenly she felt silk beneath her fingers and she didn't want silk. She wanted the velvety smoothness of flesh. She slipped her hands beneath the opening, felt the heat of his skin. His groans and moans were the most beautiful symphony she'd ever heard. How was she to have guessed that she could play him as easily as she could a piano?

She peered through lowered lashes and watched the intensity with which he studied her as he worked loose the buttons on her gown. Appreciation lit his eyes, even as they smoldered. Against her palms, grazing over his throat, she felt him swallow.

She'd never known this much power before. The way he looked at her made her feel beyond beautiful. Made her feel that even if she were a pauper, still would he appreciate the gift he was skillfully unwrapping.

The gown slid to the floor, pooled at her feet. He raised his eyes to her, and she quickly shut hers more tightly. What did hers reveal to him?

She stepped out of her gown, moved to the bed, and again he took her arm and said in a voice hoarse with desire, "Not yet."

Not yet? Did he not realize that she could barely stand? That she was in danger of becoming a pool at his feet in the same manner that her nightgown had? She thought she should feel self-conscious standing before him completely nude, but his gaze held nothing lascivious. Rather he looked as though he were appreciating a fine work of art.

Then his eyes met hers and she realized hers

were as wide open as his. Her hands had moved lower until they were at his waist, butting up against the sash that held his dressing gown in place.

Holding her gaze, he slid his hand beneath hers and easily loosened the sash. With a sleek roll of his shoulders, he dispensed with the dressing gown entirely and she saw what she'd only felt last night. He was truly magnificent. Firm and fit and quite . . . proud.

Gliding her hands back up his chest, she slid her eyes closed. Expected him to guide her to the bed. Instead, his mouth and hands were trailing over her as she stood before him, quivering with need, shivering with desire. He kissed and stroked, tasted and touched, his mouth moving lower, across the swells of her breast, lower still. She heard his knees pop as he crouched before her. Opening her eyes, she looked down on his dark head, remembered it so often drenched with rain.

She'd told him she couldn't give herself to someone for whom she held no affection. She couldn't say she loved him, but running her fingers through his hair, she could admit that she had come to care for him. Somehow, against the odds, in a very short time, she'd grown quite fond of him with his pitiful attempts to please her that weren't pitiful at all.

He skimmed his mouth along the hollow of her hip. And then he was kissing her more intimately than she'd ever been kissed and frenzied passion spiraled through her. She imagined his mouth on hers, drinking just as deeply. She dug her fingers into his shoulders, wanted to bring his mouth to hers. But he took his time, working his way back up, turning her as he did so, gently pushing her back on to the bed, until she was sitting on the edge and he was journeying up her body, laying her down as he went.

Standing between her thighs, he plunged inside her and began to ride her with a fierce determination as though his body was as close to exploding as hers. She was clutching him, holding on, her legs wrapped around his waist as passion rose between them. She didn't know if she'd ever seen anything as beautiful as the movement of his body, joined with hers. And when the cataclysm came, it bowed her body beneath his. He threw his head back, lost in his own pleasure. She gloried in the sight of it, found it as satisfying as experiencing her own release.

On strong, yet trembling arms he held himself above her. He lowered himself slightly, kissed her throat, and eased out of her. He studied her for a moment as though he wasn't quite certain what to do, as though what he'd just experienced had stunned him. He reached down, then draped her nightgown over her, while clutching his dressing gown in his other hand.

"Good night," he rasped, before stumbling back, straightening, and striding from her bedchamber.

She brought her legs up, rolled on to her side,

and pressed her nightgown against her chest as though it were the rag doll she'd slept with when she was a child. How could he give her so much, yet leave her with so little?

Michael stared at the empty bed in his bedchamber. It held no appeal.

He'd wanted to crawl beneath the covers completely and fully with Kate. He'd wanted to hold her close, fall asleep with the sound of her breathing filling his ears.

He'd never wanted that from a woman.

Ride her until the end of the journey—and then travel on alone. It had always been his way. But with her, he wanted so much more.

When her eyes were open, was she seeing him or another?

He'd thought to acquire wealth so easily, and now he thought he might willingly give it all up to have her want *him*—just once.

Chapter 16

Stonehaven's ball was perhaps the most well attended of the Season.

Earlier Kate had danced once with her husband. She was anticipating doing so again. She couldn't deny she cherished the way he looked at her, as though he were coming to appreciate her as much as she was him. Oh, he still had his moods and he wasn't very forthcoming with revealing information about himself, but she had to admit that the intimacy they shared in the bed seemed to be flowing over into their lives. That he would stand behind her when she was at the desk looking over the accounts. He would lean near and point out a particular purchase. Sometimes his cheek would almost touch hers, and she wondered if he took delight in tormenting her with his nearness.

Sometimes she would be fairly melting by the time they retired for the night.

"Are you blushing?" Jenny asked.

Kate waved her ivory fan. "It's so warm in here."

"I'm thinking of stepping out for some air. Did you want to join me?"

"That sounds lovely."

Jenny slipped her arm through Kate's. "The Season is near to ending, and I'll miss it terribly."

"I'm sure you'll be invited to all sorts of country parties."

"Perhaps I'll come spend some time with you at your estate."

Kate welcomed the feel of the softly blowing breeze against her skin, as they stepped on to the veranda. "I'd like that, but you must give us a few months to get everything back in order."

"Oh, Kate, I don't care about all that. I'd be there to visit with you, not to check out the particulars of your house management skills." Jenny stopped in her tracks on the pebbled path and looked back over her shoulder. "Oh, dear, I forgot something. Go on without me. I'll catch up."

Before Kate could inquire as to what her sister could have forgotten, Jenny was hurrying back toward the terrace. Kate thought about returning to the ballroom, but it was a lovely fog-free night and other guests were walking about. Why not her?

Although if she'd realized Jenny was going to abandon her, she'd have asked Michael to join her. She'd begun to enjoy his company even when he wasn't talking. There was a comfortableness in having him near. The one thing she couldn't determine was why he never kissed her. And why he never lingered in her bed. He *showed* her good night and then he left. And she so wanted him to stay—but not because she asked him to. She wanted him to stay because it was what he wanted.

"Hello, dear girl."

The voice coming out of the shadows almost had Kate hopping out of her shoes. She spun around and could see Wesley crooking a finger at her, beckoning her to join him behind the trellis of roses. She cast a furtive glance around her, pausing momentarily at the spot where Jenny had left her. Had this rendezvous been pre-arranged by her sister? She had a sneaking suspicion that it had been.

"I only want a word, Kate," Wesley whispered.

She'd seen him arrive with his wife, had even taken a moment to speak to both of them, although she couldn't imagine what it was about Melanie that had caused Wesley to marry her. Her money, of course. The girl, bless her heart, had the largest set of teeth imaginable. Kate wondered if in the dark, Wesley imagined she was Kate.

"Please, Kate," he urged.

Reluctantly, she joined him. "This is entirely inapp—"

Then he was kissing her, kissing her as though they were still married, kissing her as though it was his right, kissing her as though he still loved her, as though his very happiness depended on it.

Kissed her with an intimacy she never received from her husband. Michael made love to her, but he never kissed her mouth. He kissed her neck, her breasts, her thighs. He'd even kissed her toes, every one of them. He never pressed his lips to hers, never swept his tongue through her mouth.

Pulling back, Wesley cradled her face between his hands. "I miss you desperately."

Breathless, she stared at him. "Need I remind you that you're married?"

"Which only serves to add to my misery. Melanie, bless her, is not you."

"But you knew that when you married her."

"Yet, what choice did I have? What choice did either of us have? Your mother saw to that. I shall never forgive her for tearing us apart."

"Mother is not entirely to blame. As long as you were unmarried there was a chance I could convince them that we were meant for each other. You didn't wait."

"I admit I became impatient. She wouldn't even let me see you. She returned every letter."

"You wrote me?"

"Of course, I did. I thought I could be happy with Melanie. But she hasn't your fire. I want you back in my life, Kate, even if it's only a moment here or a moment there. You are an addiction that I simply—"

"Remove your hands from my wife, sir, if you wish for them to remain unbroken."

Whether or not Wesley actually did as he was commanded was a moot issue, because Kate spun around to face her husband, effectively removing Wesley's hands from her person for him. She knew the sound of Michael's voice when he was angry, and this was beyond seething. What she felt undulating off him now was raw fury.

"Michael—"

"It would be best if you not speak at this precise moment, madam."

Wesley chortled, actually chortled. "You have no hold over her."

"She is my wife."

"Only because her father outbid all the others."

Kate snapped her head around to look at Wesley. "What?"

"Did he not tell you? He put himself up for auction—to the highest bidding American father."

She turned back to Michael. "I don't understand. My father said you asked for my hand—"

"Only after he was assured your father would provide a settlement higher than any other."

She wanted Wesley to shut his mouth, wanted Michael to deny the charges. To say something, anything. To laugh out loud at the ludicrousness of Wesley's words. To punch Wesley in the face.

"Is what he said true?"

Even in the dimly lit gardens, she could see the struggle being fought, the struggle to deny, the one to admit. That he had to struggle at all was answer enough. She felt the tears begin to burn her eyes. "You had men bid on you?"

"He did."

She spun around. Wesley jerked back. She could

only imagine what emotions might have been visible on her face. "How do you know so damned much?"

"Because Melanie's father was one of the men he invited to the private—and secretive—auction." Wesley fairly spat each word.

"My father wouldn't be so desperate for me to marry . . . he wouldn't debase himself . . ." She jerked her attention back to Falconridge. "I knew money was involved, but not to the extent that it was all I am to you. Money. That's all I've ever been."

"Kate—"

"Damn you to hell."

She lifted her skirts and hurried from the garden, avoiding the house, seeking out the gate. She emerged at the circular drive where so many carriages were waiting for their owners. Swiping at her tears, she searched frantically for Falconridge's coach. She had to escape, had to get away . . .

When at last she found it, the footman opened the door for her. "Take me to my father's," she instructed as she clambered inside.

"What of his lordship?"

"He's not coming."

Even though her parents' house was not that far, the journey seemed to take most of her life to complete. Images tumbled through her mind: her wedding day, Falconridge's startled expression when she'd mentioned his asking for her hand, laughing with him, his hands and mouth—

The coach came to a stop and she flung the door open before the footman could get to it. If she hadn't feared she'd trip and break her neck, she would have hopped out. Instead she waited impatiently for his assistance.

She raced up the steps and pounded on the door. As soon as it opened, she barreled past the butler.

"My lady—"

"Where's my father? The library?"

"Yes, my lady. I'll announce you—"

"Oh, please. I don't need announcing."

As a matter of fact, she suspected her presence and agitation would be announcement enough.

Her father was exactly as she'd known he would be: sitting behind his desk, peering at his ledgers through a cloud of smelly cigar smoke. He looked up, his eyes widening as though he'd expected someone else, and then they narrowed, his brow furrowing as he slowly came to his feet.

"Kate, what's wrong? What are you doing here this time of night?"

"You *bid* on him?"

Her father's shoulders slumped forward. She'd never seen him take that sort of defeated posture, but almost immediately he straightened.

"Damn, Falconridge, I thought he was a man of his word."

"A man of his word?"

"The auction was to be kept secret. I didn't think you'd ever hear of it—"

"He didn't tell me. Wesley did."

Her father's eyes narrowed further as he snatched up his cigar, took a deep puff on it, a habit he indulged when he was involved in difficult ciphering. "Jeffers," he finally mumbled. "I'll sue him for breach of contract."

Kate stepped nearer to the desk, braced her hands on it, and leaned toward him. "I can't believe you would think a man who would auction himself off like a . . . a fancy heirloom was worthy of marrying your daughter."

Her father reached out and lifted the lid on the carved wooden box that held his precious cigars. "Want one?"

It was their secret, her guilty pleasure. She'd spent many an hour going over the books with her father, puffing on a cigar as though she'd been born a son rather than a daughter. She shook her head. She wasn't in the mood tonight to share in their little ritual.

He walked over to the liquor cabinet and splashed whiskey into two glasses. He brought them over and held one out to her. "You'll want this. Sit down, Kate."

"Papa—"

"Take the whiskey and sit down, sweetheart."

She did as he bid her, watching as he took the chair beside hers, close enough that he could take her hand if need be. When had he grown so old?

"A father isn't supposed to have a favorite among his children," he began, "but the Lord knows, you know, your mother knows—hell, Jenny and Jeremy know—you've always been mine."

"If you loved me so much why didn't you let me stay married to the man I loved? It makes no sense. You said he was a fortune hunter. Well, what do you call a man who puts himself up for auction to the highest bidder?"

"Honest. You gotta give him that, Kate. The man was honest about what he was doing, what he wanted, and what he was offering."

"I don't have to give him anything," she grumbled, before sipping on the whiskey, allowing the familiar flavor to roll over her tongue and down her throat. "He doesn't love me and I wanted love. Wesley at least loved me."

"I could argue that. Hell, I have argued that. But not tonight. That's not why you're here tonight."

"No, it's not. I want to know why you could bid on a man—"

"Your mother wanted you to marry an aristocrat, a man with a title. There was one for sale and so I bought it."

"Because you didn't think I could acquire one on my own?"

"Because I was running out of time, darling, and you weren't *trying* to acquire one on your own."

Kate's stomach lurched at the implications. "Jenny thinks Mother's ill, that that's the reason you keep taking her to the seaside."

He tossed back his glass of whiskey before nodding.

"How ill?"

"Ill enough. She didn't want you girls to know."

"Does Jeremy know? Is that the reason he's

spending time in London with us instead of gallivanting around the world?"

He nodded, wrapped both hands around the empty glass, and leaned forward, elbows on his thighs. "I didn't love your mother when I married her, Kate. I married her because I saw in her a strong-willed woman who wouldn't settle for failure, a woman with ambitions that outshined mine. And I knew together we'd be unstoppable, that we could reach heights of success that neither of us had grown up knowing. When those New York knickerbockers snubbed your mother, when they didn't send her an invitation to their balls . . . we have more money than any of them, Katie, and it wasn't enough. We built the finest house and wore the nicest clothes, but it wasn't enough. When your mama looked in the mirror she saw a young lady who got married in her best dress, and it was frayed around the edges. And the man she married, he wasn't dressed much better."

He wore a sad smile as he studied the empty glass in his hands. Kate took it from him and replaced it with hers. Nodding he gulped the whiskey.

"I don't know when I fell in love with her, Katie. One day she was scolding me about something, she was always scolding me to reach farther than what I could touch, but this one day, I just looked at her and thought, I love this woman. With everything in me. I am where I am today, because your mother believed in me, even when I didn't believe in myself." Tears welled in his eyes. "I will do anything and everything to see that she dies happy."

"But if you'd only told me—"

"It makes it too real, sweetheart. If no one knows, then I can pretend it's not true."

"What does she have?"

"It's a cancer and I'm not going to discuss the particulars."

"How long?"

"A year. Maybe more. You know your mother. She believes in doing things her way. I suspect she'll give Death a run for his money."

Kate felt as though she no longer had any stability in her world. It had been a long time since she'd wanted to feel her mother's arms around her. She'd always been closer to her father.

"You should tell Jenny, Papa."

He nodded. "I know."

For several moments they simply sat in quiet reflection.

"Is your marquess so awful?" he finally asked.

She shook her head.

"Maybe one day you'll look at him and think, I love this man and maybe you'll think of me with a little more kindness." Reaching across her lap, he squeezed her hand. "Don't let your mother know that you know . . . about any of this."

"I won't." She stood up. "I understand why you did what you did. Perhaps a part of me even admires you for it. But I can't forgive you for it."

And with that, she turned and walked out of the room.

* * *

Michael made it as far as the steps in the foyer.

In Stonehaven's garden, he'd made a move to go after Kate, but Wiggins had grabbed his arm.

"Let her go," he'd ordered.

Michael wasn't about to listen to anything the man had to say. He'd made that clear by delivering a hard punch to the man's face. He thought he might have broken his hand in the process. He'd finally made his way out to the street, only to discover their coach gone.

He'd walked until he found a hansom cab for hire. And had returned home to discover his wife hadn't.

So he tugged off his gloves, loosened his neckcloth, dropped down to the third step of the stairs that swept up to the next landing, and considered his options.

She'd no doubt returned to her parents' home, and the very real possibility existed that she would never return to this one. The disappointment and revulsion at learning her husband had sold himself was far too clear. He'd thought looking at his own reflection in the mirror had been hard enough, but gazing into her eyes—

With a deep sigh, he dropped his head into his hands, pressed his fingers against his skull.

He'd kept his part of the bargain. The money was his, hard-earned. He wouldn't allow it to be taken away. They could turn it all over to him and take back their daughter who believed love was so damned important . . .

He was weary of playing her games. Favorite colors and flowers and books . . .

He'd had enough. She could rot in hell for all he cared. He didn't need her. He needed—wanted—her money. That was the extent of his longing. She could go back to Wesley Wiggins—

The anguished cry echoed around him. He couldn't bear the thought of her with another man. Couldn't bear the thought of her gracing him with smiles, of laughing with him, of peering over at him impishly on the verge of delivering some tart comment designed to put him in his place.

He didn't want her with a man who knew her favorite color.

He wanted her.

He wanted her smiles, her laughter. He wanted the way she took charge, her no-nonsense approach to life. He wanted the contentment he felt when he danced with her, the joy he experienced when he gazed at her first thing in the morning. He wanted her cries and whimpers of passion at night, even if they were stirred to life by the memories of another man.

He cursed at the bittersweet moments that plagued him. If he truly cared for her as he'd begun to suspect he did, he should be willing to give her up, to place her happiness above his.

Instead, he sat on the cold, hard steps trying to determine how he could convince her that he was worthy of her affection.

Chapter 17

———∞———

Michael stood within the Rose entryway waiting to be announced. He was damned tempted to rush up the stairs and pound on the door of every bedchamber until he found his wife. He'd sat on the hard steps of his own stairs until dawn—waiting for her return. When the sunlight had begun filtering in through the windows, it had brought a darkness to his soul, the likes of which he'd never known.

He'd been hit with the realization that he didn't want to lose Kate. And not because of the funds that she'd brought with her, but because of the smiles and laughter she brought with her and even her damned notion that he should earn her affection.

But it appeared he was in danger of losing her, because he'd yet to determine how to gain her affection.

So he'd begun considering his options. He'd purchase her a dozen bouquets of forget-me-nots. Two dozen boxes of chocolates. A hundred, no a thousand books. And as he thought of each item, he dismissed it.

He didn't have the power to earn her love, but perhaps he could earn her understanding.

He heard light footsteps coming down the hallway. The butler bowed slightly. "My lord, if you'll follow me, Mr. Rose will see you."

Michael followed the man to the library where he spotted James Rose pouring amber liquid into two glasses. Rose glanced over at him. "Falconridge."

"Rose."

Rose turned from the table and handed him a glass. "I know it's a bit early in the day but I figure we can both use a good stiff drink. And don't worry about a thing. Kate was here last night and told me everything. We're going to sue Jeffers for telling that no-account son-in-law of his about our arrangement." He tossed back his drink in one swallow. "The money will go to you, of course, as I have no need of it, but I have the best lawyers already on retainer—"

"I don't care about any of that. I'm here for Kate."

Rose looked as though Michael had tossed the expensive whiskey in his face. "What do you mean you're here for Kate? She returned to your residence last night."

"No, she didn't."

"Of course she did. There was no where else for her to go. You just didn't see her arrive."

"As I was sitting on the stairs of my foyer until dawn, there is no way I could have possibly not seen her arrive. Are you certain she isn't here?"

Rose nodded. "Absolutely positive. She was understandably upset with me. She rushed out. I followed, saw her get safely into the coach. I just assumed—" He dropped down into a chair, hung his head. "I think she's feeling betrayed. Not the first time. I explained to her that I wouldn't have even bothered to attend your auction if she'd been trying to find a husband, but she was content to stay in her room and read. I needed her married."

Michael set his still-full glass on the desk. He needed his wits about him, and he wasn't particularly interested in what had brought them to this moment. It was done and he no longer had control over it. He'd grown accustomed to not having control. He did the best he could. "Do you know where she might have gone?"

Rose lifted his head, met Michael's gaze. "No. She hasn't any friends here." He sprung to his feet. "Damnation! I gave her control over the money. She could have bought a ticket to anywhere in the world. We may never find her."

"I'll find her." He turned to leave.

"I should have given control to you."

Michael turned back to him. "No, you shouldn't have. Kate has a keen sense of money—just as you told me. I wish I'd been in a position . . ." He looked down at the floor. No frayed, worn rugs there. He lifted his gaze. "The yearly stipend you promised. It won't be necessary."

Rose took on the look of a man who'd placed a wager at the racetrack and just watched the horse cross the finish line well ahead of the others. "I never thought it would be."

Michael wished none of it had been necessary. "I wish I *had* asked for her hand. She deserved that, at least."

"Let me grab my coat and I'll help you look for her."

"That won't be necessary." For the first time since he'd gone into the garden last night, he actually smiled. He might not know her favorite color, but he did know this. "As impossible as it seems, I believe I know where she is."

"It's so nice of you to pay us a call, my lord, even though the hour is unconscionably early for a social visit," the Duchess of Hawkhurst said, as she poured tea into a china cup. "That seems to be an unfortunate habit you have—not calling at the appropriate hour."

Michael had arrived only to be kept waiting while he was announced to Her Grace, who apparently had decided she didn't need to greet him until the tea had been properly steeped and was ready for pouring.

"I want to see her."

She peered up at him. "And who would that be, my lord?"

"My wife," he ground out.

Hawk, standing against the fireplace as though his presence were needed to support the wall, cleared his throat, and Michael reined in his impatience.

"She is here, isn't she?"

"Do you take sugar with your tea?"

"I'm not here for tea, Your Grace. I'm here for my wife."

"And why would you think she's here?"

"For pity's sake, Louisa, stop torturing the man," Hawk said. "She's here, still abed, after arriving in the middle of the night."

Michael didn't know if he'd ever felt such relief, not only because Kate was safe but because he'd managed to deduce where she would go if she had no where else to go. "Will you let her know I'm here?"

"I promised her that I'd provide her with a refuge as long as she needed it," the duchess said.

"A refuge? I'm not going to beat her."

"What are you going to do?"

Devil take all women!

"Forgive my impertinence, Your Grace, but I don't feel I need to explain myself to you, but I will explain things to my wife."

"She's feeling quite vulnerable right now."

"I only wish to speak with her. If she doesn't want to leave with me"—he could barely stand the thought of her remaining here—"then she need not, and I'll personally pack up her clothes and bring them to her. Ask her. I've been as accommodating as I could be. That will not change, but it is imperative that I speak with her."

The duchess glanced at her husband. Hawk nodded. She sighed as though she'd lost some great battle. "Very well. I'll let her know you're here, but I'll not force her to see you. She's been forced to do things she didn't want to do far too often. I'll not be party to making her life any more miserable than it already is."

She rose to her feet and swept from the room with more righteous indignation than Michael had ever witnessed. Once she was out of sight, Hawk murmured, "I tried to warn you that secrets—"

"Yes, yes, yes. You're ever so wise and knowing. How fortunate for me that I have such a clever friend."

"More clever than you for certain, because I know the way to a lady's heart doesn't involve bringing her to tears. She was quite distraught when she arrived. Louisa was with her for a good part of the night."

Hawk's words effectively doused Michael's irritation with him. "I'd never planned to deceive her about how she came to be my wife, but once I realized her parents had told a different tale . . . what was I to do? Reveal them as liars?"

"It might have been better than perpetuating the lie."

Michael waved that off. "It no longer matters. It's only important that she come to understand why."

"Do you think seeing her now is the right move?" Hawk asked quietly.

"What would you do in my place if it were Louisa who wanted nothing to do with you?"

Hawk arched a brow in surprise. "You've come to care for the girl."

Care hardly seemed a strong enough word to describe what he felt for Kate. In a short period of time, she'd come to mean everything to him. He couldn't imagine his life without her.

"She wanted to be desired for more than money. Yet we can't survive without the funds she brought into the marriage. How do I convince her that she is more important?"

"Simply tell her."

Michael shook his head. "If I've learned anything at all about Kate these past few weeks, it's that she must be shown."

And in the showing, he knew he could very well lose her forever.

"Kate?"

Kate heard the soft voice, but she wanted to stay buried beneath the covers where not even a whisper of sunlight could touch her. Oh, her head hurt and her eyes felt gritty and swollen from all the tears she'd shed once she'd arrived here.

"Kate, you need to wake up."

She eased the blanket down only enough to look out from the cocoon of her haven and see the Duchess of Hawkhurst standing over her. "To wake up would indicate that I'd slept. And I haven't."

Louisa sat on the edge of the bed, moved the covers down farther, and tenderly brushed the loose hair back from Kate's face. "Falconridge is here. He wants to see you."

"You sent word to him—"

"No. He simply arrived and asked to see his wife as though he knew you were here. But neither Hawk nor I sent word."

"Then how did he know?" she asked, baffled.

"I don't know, but he looks as though he's had as rough a night as you. I'll help you get dressed."

Kate shook her head. "I need more time to sort things out. Tell him I'll return home when I'm ready."

"I'm not certain he's in a mood to accept that as an answer."

"That's just too bad. He sold himself, Louisa. And my father purchased him, not only placing a value on him, but a value on me. I can't be part of this. I won't be part of it. He doesn't own me. I won't do as he bids."

"He must have been very desperate—"

"Or incredibly lazy. I've heard the snide comments about what American heiresses will bid for a nobleman, but I didn't think anyone would actually take them to heart." She sighed. "Tell him I'm not at home. Tell him to go to the devil."

Louisa released a deep breath of obvious exasperation. "I shall try, but I think you should prepare yourself for my not meeting with success. He seems quite determined to have his way."

"Yes, well, I can be just as stubborn, and well he knows it." Or at least she thought he did. But he knew so little about her. How *had* he managed to deduce that she was here?

"Did he go to my parents' house first?" Kate heard herself murmur.

"I'm not sure," Louisa said. "Perhaps you should go down and ask him."

"No, I don't want to see him. Simply tell him that it would please me if he left. He always does what would please me."

"A woman can't ask for much more in a husband than that."

"A woman can ask for love," Kate said quietly.

"He must hold some affection for you or he wouldn't come looking for you."

"I have complete control over our purse strings, Louisa. Without me, he has no access to funds. And he needs a good deal of funds to renovate his residences. Just tell him what I said. He'll leave." Lying down, she pulled the covers back over her head. There was comfort to be found in the cozy darkness.

It was several minutes before she heard the door open again. "Did he leave?"

"No, he did not," a familiar deep voice answered back.

She jerked the blankets down and glared at her husband who was slowly closing the door behind him and watching her intently as though wondering if she might pick up an object on the bedside table and throw it at him. If they were her things, she very well might have. Even Louisa had betrayed her. Was there no one she could trust?

"Don't be angry at your hostess. She believes I left. Her mistake was in taking me at my word and not escorting me to the door."

"So you lie as easily to her as you do to me."

"I never lied to you, Kate. I may have danced around the truth a bit, but only because I realized your parents didn't want you to know the particulars of our arrangement."

"You said you approached my father—"

"And I did. With an invitation to the auction."

"Who all did you invite?"

"Your father. Jeffers, Blair, Haddock, and Keane."

She pushed herself up and sat back against the pillows, settling the blanket at her waist. "Rather austere company. The wealthiest of the wealthy. At least I can't fault you for not aiming high."

He walked over to the window and gazed out, squinting against the brightness of the morning. "In my youth I would stay in this room when I visited Hawkhurst."

It seemed a strange change in topic, and yet at the same time, it was revealing something that she couldn't quite comprehend. "But your own residence isn't that far away."

"Still, it was more pleasant here. Hawk's mother had a tendency toward kindness."

"And your own mother didn't?"

"My mother was hardly ever home. I think she and my father saw me as a necessary nuisance. The required heir and nothing more except a bother. A nanny and a governess saw to my care. They were neither kind nor particularly pleasant."

"I had a governess. She wasn't so awful."

He peered over his shoulder at her. "Did she lock you in a closet if you didn't eat your peas?"

She slowly shook her head. "Did yours?"

"To this day I refuse to eat peas willingly."

"But you were the young lord, the heir—"

"I suspect that was the reason she took such delight in tormenting me. She was quite clever. She had me convinced I'd be a grave disappointment to my parents if they ever learned I had to be punished for behaving poorly, so I suffered through her cruelties in silence."

"Is her punishment the reason you don't suffer confinement well?"

"Probably."

"Is all of this the reason you hate your mother, that you don't go see her—"

"I don't hate her. I've always loved her, even though she had no time for me. And I go see her quite often."

"But you've never taken me to meet her."

"I had my reasons."

He crossed the room, stood at the foot of her bed, and wrapped his hand around the bedpost. She could see him more clearly now. He looked as though his night had been as horrendous as hers. His eyes were red-rimmed, but she couldn't imagine him weeping. No doubt he'd imbibed and become lost in his favorite liquor or perhaps it was simply lack of sleep that made him appear so war-weary. His hair was untamed, as though he'd run his fingers through it a thousand times. Other than that his clothing was impeccable, his grooming perfection.

She felt her defenses crumbling and forced herself to shore them up. How could she resist him when he looked at her as though he'd like nothing more than to gobble her up? She shifted her gaze to his hand, holding the bedpost until his knuckles turned white, as though he needed that solid anchor to keep his distance.

"Your hand looks swollen."

"I rammed it against something last night."

"In anger?"

He nodded.

"Does it hurt?"

"I suspect the discomfort pales when compared with the pain I've brought you."

"I promised myself I wouldn't ask, but I have to know. After my father outbid the others, did you tell him that it was me you wanted to marry?"

She could see him struggling to hold her gaze. "No."

"You wanted to marry Jenny."

"I thought she stood less chance of being disappointed."

"Because you can't love me?"

"I don't know how to love you, Kate. Love is not something with which I'm intimately familiar. I can tell you that I never meant to hurt you."

"And how did you plan to accomplish that when your selection of a wife was based on the highest bidding father? You couldn't even be bothered to court a lady. You wanted the fastest, easiest—"

"What I did was not easy." It sounded as though he'd shoved each word out from the depth of his soul. "It cost me everything that I valued, my pride, my dignity as a man. And now it's going to cost me you. I need you to understand why I did it."

"Your reasons are obvious. The condition of your estate, your London residence—"

"I could live with the deteriorating conditions of my life. There's more, but I have to show you. Give me an hour of your time and if at the end of it, you want to be rid of me, then we shall find a way to make it happen."

Even now, as much as she hurt, she didn't want to be rid of him. She wasn't certain what she did want. But she did know what she didn't want.

"I don't have proper clothes here. All I have is the gown I wore to the ball last night and it's hardly suitable attire—"

"Our residence is not that far away. We'll stop there first."

"Where are we going after that?"

"To visit hell."

Chapter 18

Kate had tried to get more information from her husband on the pretext that she needed to know exactly where they were going so she could dress appropriately. But he'd refused to offer even a hint, and she knew him well enough to know that he could be as stubborn as she. They were alike in that way.

So she'd decided on a simple gray dress with red velvet trim, an elegant matching cape, and a tidy hat that sat perfectly atop her upswept hair. She'd even spent a few minutes with slices of cucumber over her eyes to reduce the swelling. She fully intended to arrive at hell looking her best.

If he'd sought to intimidate her with his succinct response, he'd learn she wasn't easily intimidated. Although she suspected he was well aware of that. They'd not spoken on the way to their residence, and he seemed determined to be equally noncommunicative as they made their way to wherever it was he wanted them to go.

"How did you know I was at Louisa's?" she finally asked, because the oppressive silence was beginning to grate on her nerves.

Sitting beside her, he merely angled his head slightly to meet her gaze. "I simply knew."

"Did you go to my parents' first?"

He nodded. "I spoke with your father this morning. He was quite concerned. I sent word to let him know you were all right."

"I'm still angry at him."

"Still angry at us both, I suspect."

"Both of your actions degrade me."

"I beg to differ. They degrade us, but you're innocent . . . above all this."

It seemed to be a time for honesty between them.

"I didn't arrange to meet Wesley in the garden last night. Jenny and I were going for a stroll. She forgot something and left me . . . and Wesley was there. I was so surprised by his appearance that I didn't leave immediately, and I should have."

"Thank you for that."

"You know, one of the reasons that I wanted to marry a man who loved me was because when you love someone it's much easier to forgive their faults, and I have a good many faults."

"Will you think more of me if I list them rather than your favorite color?"

His eyes held the familiar glint of teasing.

"Are you saying that you've noticed them?" she asked tartly.

"I'm saying they're easier to deduce than your

favorite color, but then I have faults of my own and far more than you."

"You're very secretive."

"I'm not accustomed to sharing."

They began to move into an area of London sparse with buildings and people. Just as quickly her curiosity intensified. What if he had a child . . . someone he visited in secret?

"Are we going to see someone or some*thing*?" she asked.

"A bit of both. It's just up here." He indicated a building in the distance that became visible whenever there was a break in the trees. A wrought iron fence apparently circled the property.

"Is it one of your residences?"

"No. It's the Glennwood Lunatic Asylum."

Her heart skipped a beat, and she twisted around to face her husband completely. She'd read far too many novels where the innocent lass was locked away . . .

"Why are we coming here?"

He was studying her, a speculative, yet grim expression marring his handsome features. "Good Lord. You're afraid I'm going to lock you away." Reaching out, he tucked stray strands of hair behind her ear. "Perhaps *I* should have insisted you deduce my favorite color."

"What has your favorite color to do with anything?"

"Perhaps if you knew it, you'd know me well enough not to have such silly notions."

She was a bit disconcerted he could read her so easily. When had he begun to have such an understanding of her thoughts . . . her needs . . . her fears?

"If you were going to lock me away, you would have done it the first night," she said with conviction. "And your favorite color is black."

"Wrong on both accounts. It's not as easy to deduce someone's favorite color as you might think."

She realized that their discussion had taken a silly turn, and that perhaps he was perpetuating it because he wasn't at all comfortable with where they were going and what he was about to share. As the driver turned the carriage on to the dirt path and through the gates where "Glennwood Asylum" was carved in stone on either side of the gates, Michael's eyes grew incredibly sad. Reaching out, she wrapped her hand around his and squeezed comfortingly. "Why are we here, Michael?"

"I want to introduce you to someone."

"Who?"

"My mother."

"But you said she was ill . . . with a cancer."

"No. I said she wasn't well. Your mother voiced her concern that it was cancer. I never acknowledged it, although I suppose cancer is as good a way as any to describe her condition. It's as though something is eating away her memories."

"I don't understand."

"I'm not sure anyone does."

The driver brought the carriage to a halt in front of the looming building. Kate wasn't certain when she'd stopped squeezing Michael's hand and he'd begun to squeeze hers.

"Kate, I need you to understand why I . . . stepped on the bidding block, as it were."

"Not for new wallpaper or draperies."

"No." He gave her a wry smile. "Besides, you wanted to meet my mother."

She swallowed hard. "Is it contagious?"

"I don't believe so. At least I've not displayed any symptoms. I don't think. Although I suppose I wouldn't remember if I did."

"What are you talking about?"

"My mother's affliction. She doesn't remember things."

Kate shook her head in disbelief. "That's not a reason to be placed in an asylum. Sometimes I can't remember where I set down my book or my purse—"

He cradled her face and there was such a depth of sorrow in his eyes that she almost wept.

"Kate, my mother doesn't remember me."

Before she could respond, he moved away, opened the carriage door, stepped out, and turned back to her, his hand extended. "I need you to come with me so you'll understand."

Only she was afraid, afraid to know the truth.

And yet, how could she not stand beside him. He was her husband. And more, he'd become someone she'd begun to care about. "Don't be afraid, Kate."

Only she was. "I've never known anyone who belongs in a place like this."

"I'm not sure anyone belongs in a place like this." He took her hand. "Come meet my mother."

Taking a deep breath, she alighted from the carriage. "How could she not remember you?" she asked as they walked toward the door.

"To her, I'm as inconsequential as the book you mentioned misplacing earlier."

"You can't possibly believe you mean that little to her."

"Some days I no longer know what to believe."

Forcing herself to walk through the door he opened for her, she stepped into a cavernous entryway. Stairs swept up either side, and she thought she could hear the distant tormented cries of lost souls.

A young man sitting at desk came to his feet. "Lord Falconridge." He smiled. "Your mother is having a good day. She's in the garden."

Michael looked as though he'd smashed into a brick wall. "A good day? Do you mean she's getting better?"

Kate heard the hope in his voice, saw it reflected in his eyes, leaving her with no doubt as to the extent of his affection for his mother. And yet he claimed not to know how to love?

"I'm not certain I'd go that far," the young man behind the desk said. "You'd have to ask Dr. Kent." He called out to another man passing through the entry. "Charles, will you take Lord Falconridge to see his mother?" Then he turned back to Michael.

"I'll let Dr. Kent know you're here."

Charles, who looked to Kate like a man she'd never want to meet in a darkened street, lumbered through the foyer to a set of double doors at the back.

"Was this someone's residence?" Kate asked, anything to distract her from the upcoming meeting. She didn't want to be nervous, and yet she was.

"I'd heard once that it was," Michael said. "But I don't remember who it belonged to."

They stepped outside. Michael reached out and touched Charles's arm. "I see her. Thank you."

"Good day, m'lord." Charles went back inside, leaving Michael and Kate.

"It's a lovely garden," Kate said for want of anything better to say.

"Let me speak with her first, prepare her for the introduction," Michael said quietly. "Wait here until I return for you."

"Let her know that I'm looking forward to meeting her."

"She doesn't always understand"—he shook his head—"I'll let her know."

Kate watched as Michael strode to a table beneath the shade of a towering tree, where a woman sat in a very simple dress, her wispy silver hair flowing over her shoulders. He bent slightly, before speaking, and while Kate couldn't hear the words, she could see his mouth moving.

Suddenly the woman lunged, and Kate watched in horror as she ferociously attacked Michael.

* * *

"You're a liar! I have no son! You're a liar!"

Standing in the garden, Michael could still hear his mother's shrill shrieks, her accusations echoing around him. She'd hardly seemed aware of her surroundings until he'd spoken, and then she'd come at him with a viciousness that had astounded him.

Out of the corner of his eye, he'd seen Kate rushing—what? to his rescue?—and he'd slapped his mother. Slapped the woman who'd given birth to him, to try to calm her down and all he'd managed was to worsen the situation.

It had taken two attendants to pull her away from him, to drag her—screaming and sobbing—back to her room. While Kate had stared at him, obviously horrified, by what she'd witnessed.

"What happened?" she finally asked.

He shook his head. "I don't know. I told her I wanted to introduce her to my wife."

"My lord!" Dr. Kent hurried over, his long legs eating up the distance between them. "I heard there was an incident. I'm frightfully sorry. I should have been here—"

"It doesn't matter. They won't hurt her—"

"We've had to restrain her."

Michael squeezed his eyes shut. He'd seen the awful jacket they used. He looked over at his wife. "Lady Falconridge, allow me to introduce Dr. Kent. He runs the facility."

He bowed toward Kate. "My lady, 'tis an honor to have you here."

"An honor? For God's sake, it's—" Michael began.

Kate placed her hand on his arm. "It's all right, Michael." She looked at Dr. Kent. "Do you know what ails the dowager marchioness?"

"A severe form of dementia, the likes of which I've never seen. She doesn't respond to our treatments. As I'm sure his lordship has told you, she's incurable. Our policy is to only house those we can cure."

"Thank you, doctor," Michael said. "We'll take our leave now."

"What about your mother?"

"I shall let you know when arrangements are made."

As Kate placed her hand on his arm, she asked, "May we walk to the front by going around through the garden, instead of through the facility?"

"If you prefer."

"I definitely prefer." She opened her purse and removed a linen handkerchief, pressed it to her mouth to dampen a corner, then tenderly touched it to his cheek. "She scratched you—"

He stepped away from her.

"Michael, it's bleeding."

He thought if she were kind to him, he might crumble. Right there, in the midst of the garden, within the walls of the asylum. Instead, he reached into his jacket, removed his own handkerchief, and pressed it against his cheek, still feeling the sting from his mother's sharp nails scraping along his face, no doubt leaving bloody furrows.

"How long has she been here?" Kate asked softly, as though she realized he could easily shatter.

He didn't want to talk. All he wanted was to return home and bury himself deeply within her.

"Five years."

God, it had been a mistake to bring her here, to try to show her, to explain—

"I'll meet you at the carriage," he said.

Stunned, Kate watched as her husband began striding toward the copse of trees. "Michael!"

Lifting her skirts, she hurried after him, not catching up until he'd reached the trees. Their leaves rustling in the breeze sounded obscene. Nothing here brought comfort.

"Michael—"

"Go to the carriage, Kate."

How could he demand that of her when she could see how badly he suffered, how much he hurt? It was one thing to be told that his mother didn't remember him, but to hear the words flowing from her own lips.

"Why did she say she has no son?"

He spun to face her and the anguish she saw in his eyes nearly felled her.

"I told you! Because she doesn't remember me!"

He dropped to his haunches, dug his elbows into his thighs, and pressed the heels of his hands to his forehead.

"Why did she attack you?"

"She's in a damned lunatic asylum! You can't actually believe that I can explain her behavior."

"Why didn't you tell me about her sooner—"

"Allow me to repeat: My mother is in a damned lunatic asylum!"

He lowered his hands and dropped his head back, his gaze on the clear sky.

"You're bleeding again."

"What does it matter? What does any of this matter?"

Her heart ached for him as it had never ached before. Everything in her life seemed so trivial in light of his torment. She'd never felt so helpless, so unprepared for anything as devastating as what he endured.

"We can find a better doctor," she said. "We have enough money that we can make her well again."

He searched her face and she could see the wonder in his eyes. "So innocent, so naïve."

"We can at least try—"

"Do you think I haven't?"

"Oh my God." She knelt in front of him, studied his face, felt the tears stinging her eyes as understanding dawned. "She's the reason you . . . you auctioned yourself."

"Private asylums have an expectation of curing people. I don't want her in a public asylum. Now that I have funds, they've agreed to keep her here a while longer, but I need to make other arrangements for her. I want to bring her home. I want to build her a haven near Raybourne, hire a staff to care for her." He squeezed his eyes shut. "She's a marchioness. She deserves better than this."

Kate saw a boy who wasn't raised in the shadow of his mother's love, who as a man distanced himself from that very emotion—even now. Not acknowledging that it was love that drove his actions. It could only be love for his mother, not respect for her position as a peer that had caused him to sacrifice his pride.

"I think . . ." She swallowed. "I think we should visit the bank on our way home. We need to alert them that your signature will work as easily as mine for releasing funds."

"That's not the reason I brought you here."

"I know. You wanted me to understand why you did what you did." Oh, God, she wanted to weep for what he'd suffered, for the burden she'd inadvertently added to his life. "But I think it was rather silly of my father to trust you with his daughter and not his money."

He studied her as though he wanted to say more and she wondered if a time would come when he'd ever feel comfortable revealing his innermost thoughts to her. She supposed what he'd revealed today was a start.

Unfolding his body, he reached down, slipped his hand beneath her elbow, and helped her rise. It seemed appropriate that they not speak as they walked to the carriage, because it was as though they were leaving a place of mourning.

Chapter 19

～○○～

Several hours later, Kate's generosity in giving Michael access to all their funds still overwhelmed him as he stood in his office, looking at the floor plans he'd drawn more than six months ago. At Glennwood, he'd been unable to find words to adequately thank her. Every thought that came into his head seemed trivial, insignificant, trite. All the things he'd dreamed of accomplishing when he'd sought out a wealthy heiress seemed within easy reach.

All because he'd dared to share with her the truth about his mother.

Kate had been understanding, sympathetic, and comforting. They'd journeyed home with her hand wrapped around his, as though she were silently communicating that no matter what happened, what troubles they faced, she'd always be there for him. For the first time in his life, he truly didn't feel alone.

The realization terrified him. He was afraid to trust this feeling of . . . sharing. And yet, he feared more that it might slip away.

He'd watched Kate during dinner. It was strange that the magnitude of what he'd done—taking her as his wife—was only just beginning to sink in. She'd be at his dinner table every night for the remainder of his life. She'd be in the bedchamber next to his. He'd told her father that she'd deserved to be asked for her hand. How did he compensate for such a glaring injustice? Staring at his drawing, he wondered how he could give her now what he should have given her before?

He'd taken her hand in marriage, been given her father's funds, and all she'd asked for in return was that he earn her love by deciphering her favorite color. What a botched job he was doing of that.

Following dinner, she'd gone to the library to read while he'd come to his office to look over the dreams that would now become reality—because of her generosity. He'd brought the plans with him, so he could discuss them with the builders. At Raybourne, Michael hadn't told Kate why building the house was important to him. Now he no longer needed to tell her anything.

Strange, how suddenly he desperately wanted to. How desperately he wanted to tell her everything, share his sins, his transgressions . . . he didn't want her looking at him as though he were noble. He wanted her to see him for what he truly was. He needed her to hate him as much as he hated himself—

It was so much easier to deal with hate than love.

And God help him, he was coming to love her.

* * *

Kate sat in the library, the book open in her lap, the pages unread. She didn't know why she'd thought things between her and Michael would change after his revelations this afternoon and her willingness to remove all restrictions from his spending. What truly bothered her was that she was becoming as morose as he.

Following dinner, he'd excused himself to adjourn to his study, no doubt because he preferred brooding in solitude. It hurt to see him so, and she wondered when she'd begun to care for him so much that seeing his misery was a personal attack against her own happiness.

She thought about seeking him out, insisting that he spend the evening with her, but she was weary of his doing everything simply because it was what she wanted. She wanted him to want to be with her. She wanted—

She glanced up as the door to the library opened, and he walked in holding a scroll. It was embarrassing, the joy that shot through her at the sight of him. Did he ever experience such gladness upon seeing her?

"I wanted to share something with you," he said quietly.

Closing her book, she couldn't have been more pleased if he'd told her he'd planned to present her with the Crown jewels. She rose elegantly, trying not to appear too giddy.

He began clearing the desk, then spread the scroll out, anchoring one side with the lamp and the other side with a book.

"I recognize it. The house you want to build near the pond," she said.

"Yes, I'm building it for my mother. I thought you might be interested in the details."

"I'm very interested." And she wished they weren't quite so formal with each other, as she moved around to stand beside him, so she could have the same view as he did.

"I want to move my mother out of Glennwood. I want to give her a place where she can feel safe and secure."

"Why so small? We can well afford something much grander than this."

"My mother gets easily lost. It was one of the . . . it was the reason I began to suspect something was wrong."

When several heartbeats of silence followed, she looked up at him. He was looking at the parchment, but she didn't think he was seeing the lines and numbers. She thought he was trapped in his memories. "What happened?" she asked softly.

"It was at the country manor. As you've seen, it's quite large. A hundred and thirty-seven rooms. Hallways, alcoves. She got lost. Not just lost, but terrified. She was shrieking. She couldn't find her way back to her bedchamber. It was past midnight. I'm not even sure why she left her bedchamber to begin with." He leaned over the drawing, tracing a finger over the lines that he'd drawn. "I want to give her a small house. A front room, the parlor if you will. To the side will be the dining room. A large opening between the two. The back of the parlor will lead into her bedroom." He cleared his throat. "I want her bedroom to look familiar. My mother slept in your bedchamber before you did. I would like to move the furniture into her new home."

He shifted his gaze to her as though he expected her to object.

"I think that's a lovely idea." Then because she longed to see him smile, she said, "Until I purchase new furniture for the room, I think you and I shall play hide and seek every night." He stared at her; she explained, "I'll sleep in a different bedchamber and you'll have to seek me out. We could make it a game."

"Do you think this humorous?"

"Your mother's situation, no. But I'd like to see you smile."

He scoffed. "Smile."

He said it as though he could barely remember what the word meant.

She touched a small area on the drawing. "What's this?"

"That's where the nurse will sleep. I want to hire three nurses, each to look after her for eight hours, so she is never alone. They'll stay in the main manor except when watching her. And of course, a lady's maid, a housekeeper, a cook, although they can stay in the main residence. My mother can be trying at times."

"You've given a lot of thought to this."

His attention was back on the drawing. "Yes."

She studied his profile, his proud, arrogant profile, with the three scratches along his cheek that she selfishly hoped wouldn't scar and mar his features. "I don't know if I've ever heard of anything so noble—"

"Noble?" He released harsh laughter. "You have no idea the things I've done, the things I approved them doing to her." He walked to the corner table, poured whiskey into a glass, and downed it. "I let them dunk her in freezing water because they said the shock of it would bring her back to her senses."

He poured and downed another glass.

"When she was hysterical, I let them restrain her in this jacket that prevented her from moving her arms."

He poured and downed another glass.

"You were desperate for her to be well."

He spun around and glared at her. "I was desperate to end my own aguish." He took a step toward her. "I want to forget her as easily as she has forgotten me." He grabbed her arms and shook her. "Do you not understand? I hate what she has made me become, what she has forced me to do." He shook her again. "I just want to forget."

If tears accompanied his last rasped declaration, she couldn't say because he drew her close, buried his face in the curve of her neck. "Help me forget, Kate. Help me forget."

He held her close, this man who'd insisted he'd no longer be denied, held her close and waited, as though having hurt her with the revelations of the past two days and nights, he feared she'd not welcome him into her arms, into her bed. She ran her hands up into his hair, allowed the rebellious strands to wrap around her fingers.

"Yes," was all she whispered, and all he needed.

Bending down, Michael lifted Kate into his arms and carried her from the room. He wondered if she had an inkling how desperately he wanted to become lost in her fragrance, her warmth, the silkiness of her body. Or did he guard his desires as carefully as she guarded her favorite color? Did he want her to know? Did he want to be that vulnerable? If he lowered his defenses, would she hurt him as his mother had?

Would she say hateful things and accuse him of wrongdoings for which he was innocent? Would she grow to despise him for actions taken or would she come to care for him regardless of his faults?

As he carried her up the sweeping stairs, taking two steps at a time in his eagerness to be with her, it was terrifying to contemplate how dependent he'd become on having her near. Last night the house had seemed so quiet and empty. How could one woman have such a presence that her absence could be so keenly felt? And what would he do if she ever left him and didn't return?

On the one hand, he resented that she was managing to claim so much power over him. On the other, it awed him that he had the ability to care this much. He'd built a wall around his heart to protect it, and she was slowly brick by brick, smile by smile, laugh by laugh, kindness by kindness, tearing it down. Tomorrow he'd refortify it.

Tonight he simply wanted the haven she could provide.

He swept into her bedchamber with a single-minded purpose: divest them of their clothing as quickly as possible. But her hands, touching him, stroking him, as though she were as eager for him as he was for her, kept getting in the way. "Make yourself useful and start unbuttoning my clothes," he said, as he went to work on hers.

"Always the romantic, my husband," she murmured, kissing his neck, sending a shiver through him, as she began working on the buttons of his shirt.

Leaning back slightly, he saw that her eyes were closed. For a moment, he'd dared to think that she was here in the room with *him*. But she'd already begun to drift away into the realm where she was with another. If he hadn't needed to escape his own anguish so desperately, he might have stopped but he couldn't deny Kate her own escape.

So when all their clothes had been removed, he laid her on the bed and concentrated on his need. His need to lie beside her and glide his hand over the swell of her hip. His need to nestle his face in the curve of her neck where the haunting fragrance of her perfume still lingered. His need to lower his head and feel the hard bud of her nipple between his lips. His need to ease down farther and taste the saltiness of her desire. His need to feel her hips buck against him, to hear her whimpers and cries echoing around him, to feel her fingers becoming entangled in his hair, to experience the weight of her legs wrapping around him, holding him impossibly tightly.

She was kindling to his fire, and he stroked the flames with his tongue until she was writhing against him, lost in her own world, in a place where another man touched her, sparked her passions. Did it make her unfaithful?

It didn't matter. As her body tightened and shuddered, as her gasps surrounded them, as she dug her fingers into his shoulders, it didn't matter. She was so incredibly wet and ready for him, the tremors still cascading through her body as he glided effortlessly into the hot haven where she welcomed him with a tight, firm pulsing.

He rose above her, gazed into her languid eyes . . . they'd turned blue with passion, a blue such as he'd never seen. And then her eyes slid closed, and the moment that was theirs disappeared.

He ignored the pain that ripped through him—he'd given her license to dream of another—he couldn't hold it against her for finding her comfort in memories while he found his in her. He rode her like a man obsessed, each stroke building the pleasure, each stroke carrying him farther away from everything he wanted to forget: his mother leaving his boyhood care to cold women, his mother not loving him enough to remember who he was, his wife loving another.

When Kate's arms came around him, holding him close, he lowered himself, and buried his face in the crook her shoulder, each powerful thrust increasing his pleasure and bringing her back to the peak if her cries were any indication.

She called out to the heavens, arching against him, while his own release came swift and hard, nearly blinding him with its intensity. He held her close, struggling to catch his breath, kissing away the dew that had gathered at her temple. His mind was an empty oblivion where nothing existed except the remnants of pleasure, the silkiness of her flesh against his. He wanted to remain here all night.

Instead he pressed one last kiss to the slope of her throat, before easing away from her. His knees nearly buckled beneath him as he stood, caring little about retrieving his clothes. He'd send his manservant in to fetch them in the morning. For now, he merely wanted to fall into his bed while the memories of being with Kate were still powerful enough to carry him into blissful slumber.

Kate stared at the canopy, allowing the tears to well and slide unimpeded toward her pillow. After all they'd shared today, after what they'd just shared in her bed, how could he leave so easily?

Help him forget, he'd asked of her with a desperation that had torn at her heart. How could he give so much to her here—take so much—and not stay with her for a while longer?

Chapter 20

Kate spent the following morning with her mother. It was terribly difficult not giving any indication that she knew of her mother's illness. But now that she did know of it, she felt guilty for not noticing sooner her mother's sallow complexion, how her eyes no longer sparkled. She'd always thought of her mother as a locomotive, unstoppable. It was disconcerting to realize she was only human after all.

But her spirit was formidable, and Kate had little doubt that her mother wouldn't draw her last breath until she'd seen each of children married—to a person of her choosing.

She carried that thought with her after she returned home and wandered through the house, searching for Michael. She found him in the study, drawing lines on a large sheet of paper. "What are you doing?"

He glanced up. "It was an idea I had for one of the rooms at Raybourne. I thought to convert it into a library."

"You already have three libraries."

"But this one would be warmer, cozier. Would reflect the softness of a woman. It would be more welcoming than austere. I thought to call it Kate's Library."

Kate's sob echoed through the entry hallway as tears filled her eyes and spilled over on to her cheeks. His thoughtfulness was simply too much.

"Kate, it's nothing to weep over. It was only an idea. We don't have to do it."

She shook her head frantically, the emotions of the past few days building. "My mother's dying," she rasped. "That's the reason my father attended your stupid auction, that he was so willing to outbid the other fathers."

"Oh, sweetheart, I'm so sorry." He came out from around the desk, lifted her into his arms, and cradled her against his chest. She wound an arm around his neck and buried her face in the nook of his shoulder. He smelled so good, as comforting as the library he was designing for her.

Michael carried her up the stairs to her bedchamber, while her tears dampened his shirt and the weight of her grief tore at his heart.

He laid her on the bed, knelt beside her, and brushed her hair back from her face.

"I've never liked my mother," she said in a voice that spoke of sadness and profound loss. "She's always been so hard, so demanding." She released a brittle laugh. "Everything has to be done her way." She lifted her gaze to his. "But I don't want her to die."

"No one thinks you do," he said quietly.

"My father told me that he didn't love her when he married her, but now he'll do anything to see that she's happy."

"Which worked to my advantage."

"I can't imagine my life without her."

"She's not in the grave yet, Kate."

"Perhaps she can spend some time with us at Raybourne."

"If that would please you."

She'd spent so much of the past few years avoiding her mother that it seemed odd now to want to have her so close. But she had no regrets where her mother was concerned. Still, she felt she needed to warn him. "She can be quite meddlesome."

"I shan't be bothered by that."

"Even if you were bothered, I don't think you'd tell me."

"Any member of your family is always welcome in our homes."

Sighing, she sat up. "We also need to begin making all the arrangements so your mother can come to Raybourne."

He nodded. "I'd planned to speak with the builder this afternoon. Shall we have a luncheon in the garden first?"

Reaching out, she brushed his hair back off his brow. "I'd like that very much."

Following lunch, Kate and Michael mapped out a strategy. He would secure the builder, while she began interviewing and hiring the additional staff for the estate. Together they would interview nurses when the time came because Michael was far more familiar with what was required in that regard, but he respected Kate's opinion on the matter.

That he wanted her to help him meant more to her than she could express.

She was in the library writing out the list of staff positions that she wanted to fill when the butler entered the room, silver slaver in hand.

"A gentleman has come to call, my lady."

Neither her father nor her brother would stand on ceremony if they'd come to visit her. She had an uncomfortable feeling regarding her caller. She looked at his name embossed on the card, both surprised and not surprised that his name didn't cause its usual thrill. They were both married now and any sort of excitement over his arrival was inappropriate. But more than that, she was more irritated by his arrival than anything.

And she didn't want to contemplate Michael's reaction should he discover she'd entertained Wesley in his London home.

"I'll meet with him in the garden." She was being polite to see him, but making sure they weren't in a situation that would arouse speculation. Surely no one could fault her for the discretion.

She patted her hair, self-consciously ran her fingers over the high collar of her dress. Beneath the cloth was once again, evidence of Michael's enthusiastic lovemaking. She wondered briefly what Wesley would think if he saw the marks. Considering he'd never left one behind, she doubted he'd know what they were.

When she got outside, he was standing at the edge of the terrace. He turned as her footsteps echoed around them. She came to an immediate stop at the sight of his bruised and swollen cheek. "What happened?"

"Your husband happened."

She remembered Michael's swollen hand, his comment that he'd rammed it against something. She didn't know why she took perverse pleasure in the fact it had been Wesley's face. "For all his brooding he never struck me as the type of man who would hit another."

"Yes, well, he is. Extremely barbaric."

"I don't suppose I need to point out he would be none too pleased to see you here," she said.

"All that matters to me is that you're pleased."

"Quite honestly, I don't know if I am. My husband—"

"Isn't about. I waited until I saw him leave."

She didn't like the fact he was spying. "What do you want?"

"I want you, of course."

"Yes, well, it's a bit late for that."

"Let's walk, shall we?" He glanced around. "Servants may be discreet, but they still have ears."

"As long as we remain visible. I'm not going to slip behind any trellises."

"I just want to talk."

Nodding, she stepped on to the cobbled path that wound through the gardens.

"I wanted to make certain you were all right after my revelation the other night."

"I'm fine."

"After he took his fury out on me, I wanted to reassure myself that you remained unharmed."

"You waited two days to reassure yourself," she felt the need to point out.

"Because I couldn't catch you alone before now. I'm grateful to see that you're unharmed. I have something for you."

They were well beyond the house now. He removed a slip of paper from inside his jacket.

"I penned you a poem."

She thought of all the poems he'd written her. She'd kept them all, housed them safely in a box she kept at the back of her wardrobe.

"I'm not sure you should have done that," she told him. "You're married."

"It doesn't stop my longing for you."

She shook her head. "Wesley—"

"Please take it."

She did as he requested, clutching it in her hand. "I can't promise to read it."

"It is enough that you have it. Are you going to remain married to him?"

"I beg your pardon?"

"I would divorce Melanie in a heartbeat if you were available again. Or better yet, we could both get an annulment. Neither of us has been married that long. It's a much quicker resolution than a divorce."

She laughed mirthlessly. "I can't believe you're suggesting this."

"I never stopped loving you."

Her heart lurched with his admission and she shook her head. "Falconridge is my husband. He needs—"

"But he doesn't love you. He married you strictly for your money."

"I don't need you to remind me what he did." She almost told him that Michael had his reasons, but she'd not justify them to Wesley. Michael was a very private person.

"Even if you won't leave him, there's no reason we can't see each other," Wesley said.

"Why is it that it continually escapes your notice that we're married?"

"They are both marriages of convenience. No one expects faithfulness from one's spouse under those circumstances."

"I do." She held up the crumpled paper. "Thank you for the poem. I'll have the footman show you out."

"Kate." He reached for her and she stepped back.

"You broke my heart the day you married her. You can't come to me now with poetry and promises and expect me to be glad to receive either."

She spun on her heel and rushed to the house, desperate to escape her doubts as much as she wanted to escape him.

* * *

Much later that night, Kate lay breathless and trembling beneath her husband, while another shudder racked his body. She was fairly certain they'd peaked at the same time, her cry and his groan sounding in perfect harmony. She swept her hands up over his dew-slickened back, eliciting a soft moan from him, before he tenderly moved away from her.

The customary bereavement at his leaving swamped her. She'd left candles burning tonight to add to the ambiance of his nightly visit. She watched as his silhouette moved around the bed, headed for the door—

"Michael, will you stay and hold me for a few minutes longer?" she asked, quickly. *Stay and make me forget about Wesley's visit and the lovely poem expressing his love for me that I'd been too weak to resist reading.*

"If it pleases you," he said quietly, slipping back beneath the covers. "I'll hold you as long as you like."

She nestled against his side and placed her head in the nook of his shoulder. One of his arms came around her back, holding her close, while his other hand began to trail idly up and down her arm.

She despised that she'd had to ask him to stay, that he never stayed of his own accord. That he didn't care for her enough to want to relish the moments afterward.

She rose up on her elbow. "Go on. You can go now."

In the flickering shadows cast by the flames of the candles, she could see his brow furrowing.

"Kate, what's wrong?"

She shook her head. "I want you to be here because you want to be here."

"I do want to be here."

"No, you don't. You always leave as quickly as possible—"

"I assumed that would be your preference."

"Oh." She studied him, wishing tonight they'd left the lights on. "What's your preference?"

Cradling her cheek with his palm, threading his fingers through her hair, he drew her back to his chest. "To hold you for a bit longer."

Snuggling more closely to him, she relished the almost inaudible moan that escaped from him and the slight rumble of his chest that caressed her cheek. There was such an earthy fragrance to him after they made love. Burying her face in the crook of his shoulder was much more pleasant than burying her face in the pillow upon which he'd lain before leaving her.

With her finger she circled his nipple, took pleasure in his low groan.

"Why don't you ever kiss me?"

It was subtle, but she felt him stiffen beneath her, as though every muscle dreaded his revealing the answer.

"I thought it would be easier for you to pretend if I didn't," he finally said.

She angled her head so she could see his profile more clearly. "I don't understand."

Very tenderly, he moved her hair aside, hooked it behind her ear.

"I know when I come to your bed, you pretend I'm someone else. My touch, my scent, my groans, the feel of my body . . . I can't change them or prevent you from being aware of them. But my taste . . . I thought not kissing you would make it easier for you to pretend."

A tightness nearly crushed her chest. He'd told her that first night to pretend he was Wesley. Did he honestly think when he carried her to such wondrous heights that she could think of anything at all?

She was surprised by the disappointment that assailed her because he might think she could do it, because he had great success himself at thinking of someone else.

"Who do you pretend I am?"

Once again, he began stroking her arm. "I'm married to the loveliest woman in all of London. Why would I have a need to pretend I'm with anyone other than you?"

Tears stung her eyes. It wasn't poetry but it was so damned close and so heartfelt. A small sob escaped.

He rolled her over, the concern in his eyes only making her cry harder. "Kate? What's wrong?"

She couldn't explain. That tonight he touched her heart. She cupped his chin and stroked her thumb over his lips. "Will you kiss me?"

"If it pleases you."

She nodded. "It would."

She watched as his Adam's apple slid up and down as he swallowed. She didn't think he'd looked this nervous when he'd stood in front of the church exchanging vows with her. "I won't bite."

He released a low laugh. She pressed her fingers to his chest. "You don't do that often enough."

"I do it more frequently since you've come into my life."

Then he lowered his mouth to hers and she wasn't thinking about laughter. She was thinking only about the wonder of his kiss, the way his tongue slowly outlined her lips, his hand cupping her cheek, and his thumb stroking near the corner of her mouth until it became part of the kiss. It was strange—considering all the liberties his tongue, lips, palms, and fingers had taken with her body all these many nights—that she should find his kiss just as erotic, just as persuasive, just as capable of delivering passion as anything else he did with her.

As she sighed, he slipped his tongue between her parted lips, eagerly exploring her mouth with bold sweeps that dared to leave no portion untouched. Her own tongue responded in kind, darting and teasing, coming to know the shape, texture, and taste of his mouth. The wine at dinner and the chocolate cake he'd had for dessert. And it occurred to her that their dessert was always some form of chocolate: cake, pudding, raspberries with a chocolate glaze. And she found herself laughing at the sweetness of it.

He pulled back and grumbled, "Just what a man wants to hear when he's attempting to seduce a woman. Laughter."

Before he could escape, she wrapped her arm around his shoulder, pressed her hand to the back of his head. "I just realized our dessert at dinner always includes chocolate in some manner. That's your doing, isn't it, because you know how much I adore chocolate?"

He grinned, a beautiful self-satisfied smile. And she had her answer. "What else have you done that I haven't noticed?"

He kissed the corner of her mouth. "The gardener is adding forget-me-knots, but they won't be in bloom until next year."

Smiling, she twisted her head until she could meet his mouth squarely, kissing him as deeply as he had her only a short time before. "What else?"

"You want all the surprises ruined?"

"You have a surprise planned?"

He looked entirely too smug.

"A poem. You've written me a poem."

"Can't stand poetry. It's silly drivel."

"But I love poetry."

He grimaced.

"What then?"

He shook his head.

She ran her fingers up the sides of his chest, and he jerked. "You're ticklish."

She began tickling him until he grabbed her wrists and held her arms up over her head with one hand.

"You don't want to play that game with me, madam."

"What's my other surprise? Tell me, please."

"You might not like it."

"Better to tell me now, then, don't you think?"

He had her pinned down, his leg draped over her hip. He studied her. "A puppy."

He said it so quickly, she almost didn't catch it.

"To keep you company when I'm not available. So you're not quite so lonely. Since you don't suffer loneliness well." He looked completely disgruntled as though he wished he'd kept it to himself, when all she wanted to do was hug him fiercely but he held her hands. "It's Lord Bertram's litter."

She couldn't help herself. "Lord Bertram gave birth to puppies?"

"No, his cocker spaniel did."

She laughed. "Oh, Michael, can you never deduce when I'm joking? If you won't laugh then kiss me."

"Given the choice between laughing or kissing you, I'll always choose kissing you."

His mouth blanketed hers, and he kissed her deeply, hungrily, as though he were a man who'd been denied all manner of sustenance only to suddenly find himself presented with an unlimited feast. She couldn't believe the thoroughness of his attentions.

They'd already made love once but his kiss caused desire to swirl through her. Or perhaps it was simply the words he'd uttered before. Her non-poetical husband was very poetical, in a simplistic, honest sort of way. Not flowery or verbose and certainly not prone to rhyming, but he spoke poetry just the same.

And more, as his tongue waltzed with hers, in an ancient rhythm of thrusting and sparring, it became obvious that he thoroughly enjoyed kissing. How was it that he'd denied himself so simple a pleasure these many nights, denied his wants in favor of hers—or what he'd perceived hers to be. How many husbands would do nothing to detract from their wives' pleasure even if it meant lessening theirs?

He'd released her wrists so his hands were once again gliding over her body, stroking her sensually. She'd come to love the roughness of his palms. No calluses, but still not smooth. They were large and she thought when he squeezed her breast or her hip or her thigh that she should have felt pain, but instead she felt only an exquisite loveliness. From the first night he'd made love to her, she'd been overwhelmed by the sensations, his administrations, his attention to the details. But now that he was kissing her fervently, as though he'd never have enough of tasting her, their lovemaking was rising to an entirely different level. It as though by finally gaining his kiss, she'd become acutely aware of what she'd been missing.

The heat was hotter, the pleasure more pleasur-

able, her skin more sensitive, the sensations swirling through her more intense, as though before
their lovemaking had been on the surface only
and now it was all consuming. No longer impersonal, but very, very personal.

He'd been right. Taste added a dimension that
made every aspect richer. And brought him nearer
to her in a manner that went beyond the physical. It ratcheted up her emotions as well. It was
so intimate, so personal, more personal than anything else he'd done with her—and he'd engaged
in some incredibly personal things.

And when his mouth left hers to sojourn over
her body, still she tasted the chocolate of his kiss,
still she was drunk on the flavor of wine that had
satisfied his pallet.

When he rose above her, she cradled his face between her hands and daringly brought his mouth
back to hers, their lips meeting as their bodies
joined, his mouth absorbing her sigh of pleasure
while she took in the low moan of satisfaction that
always escaped when she encased his body with
hers. It thrilled her beyond measure to know that
she had such power over him, to recognize that he
held the same over her.

How was it possible to find such joy in mating
without love?

She constantly asked him to please her and in
this one arena, she doubted he had an equal. He
was generous with his attentions, slow, deliberate,
and so very, very skilled.

The pleasure increased with each thrust of his

hips. Her body tightened and coiled. When her release came, he swallowed her cry. His low moan reverberated through her as he held close, lost in his own ecstasy. She tightened her arms and legs around him, relishing the feel of his spent body pressing down on hers.

And when he made no move to leave her, she smiled and sighed with utter contentment.

Michael awoke to find his wife still in his arms, her nose pressed flat against his chest. He wondered that she could breathe. He'd never slept through the night with anyone. He'd always found it too confining. But with Kate, he thought he could sleep with her wound around him every night and be glad of it.

There was a joy to be found in waking up next to her. Perhaps they'd never replace her furniture in the bedchamber at the estate. Perhaps she'd simply sleep in his bed, always.

He felt her eyelashes fluttering against his skin, tickling him as she awoke. She stretched along the length of his body, her foot rubbing his calf. She fairly purred, and he couldn't prevent his own moan in response.

Then she laughed, a joyous sound.

"You take pleasure in tormenting me," he grumbled.

"Mmm-huh." She pressed a kiss to his chest. "I like waking up to find you in my bed."

He didn't understand why it was that she had

the power to wretch confessions from him so easily, but he found himself telling her things he'd never told anyone.

"I don't usually . . . I've never before"—she peered up at him, her chin nestled in the hollow of his breastbone— "remained in bed with someone through the night. I always found it too confining. My mistress . . . I insisted she leave." In bafflement, he threaded his fingers through her hair. "Why is everything so different with you? Why do I care about your favorite color? Why does pleasing you bring me such pleasure?"

Her mouth curved into an impish smile. "Because you've grown fond of me?"

He suspected that she'd meant to announce her words as a statement of surety and instead they'd come out as a question. She'd had another man love her, marry her, want her. How could she doubt her own appeal? How could she not know that he adored her?

He should tell her. He should simply speak the words aloud, but voicing them would make him vulnerable, revealing them to her would open him up to being hurt. The test for knowing when he'd earned her affection had been that she'd allow him in her bed—but he'd not waited. He'd taken her in anger the first night, and every night since, he'd simply taken her because she no longer had a reason to object, because he'd informed her he wouldn't be denied. But she never sought him out, never came to his bedchamber.

And most telling of all, when he came to her bed, she closed her eyes.

So he held the words tightly inside, safe from ridicule, safe from harm, and merely smiled at her before demonstrating with his body what he dared not reveal of his heart.

Chapter 21

❦❦

"My goodness but you look happy," the Duchess of Hawkhurst said.

Smiling, Kate greeted her guest with a kiss to her cheek. "Why wouldn't I be?"

"Quite honestly, I was under the impression that things between you and Falconridge were quite strained. It's not every night that a young lady arrives on my doorstep cursing her husband and her father."

Kate led Louisa to the terrace, where biscuits and tea awaited them. "I can't thank you enough for providing me with a haven."

They sat at the round table and Kate began pouring the tea.

"You're always welcome in our home," Louisa said. "I grew quite fond of you and Jenny the short time that I was with you."

Kate handed her the cup and saucer. "Do you ever hear from your brother?"

Louisa shook her head and tilted her cup to sip her tea.

"I think Jenny might be seeing him."

Louisa's hand stilled momentarily before she returned the cup to the saucer. "Why would you think that?"

"I haven't seen him, it's nothing she's said. It's just a feeling I have."

"That could result in a disaster." Louisa shook her head. "I'm certain you're wrong. I've been accompanying her on outings with Pemburton. He's becoming quite serious with his suit. I expect him to ask for her hand any day now."

"That's good. It'll please Mother to have a duchess in the family."

"It'll please her not to have my brother in the family."

Reaching out, Kate squeezed her hand. "Sometimes we don't act rationally when we're in love."

"Have you fallen in love with Falconridge?"

"I've come to care for him, but love seems rather drastic."

"I've made you uncomfortable," Louisa said. "My purpose in coming here today was not only to make sure that you were well, but also to invite you to attend the opera with Hawk and me this evening. I know it's short notice but he has a box and it's hardly ever used. It would please us both immensely if you'd join us."

"I'm not even sure that Michael likes the opera."

"If he's like Hawk, he abhors it, but that's hardly the point in going."

She could already envision her conversation with Michael.

"The Duke and Duchess of Hawkhurst have

invited us to attend the opera with them this evening. Shall we go?"

"If it pleases you."

Hours later, sitting in front of her vanity, while Chloe settled an elegant diamond tiara on her upswept hair, Kate couldn't help but smile at her reflection. The conversation with Michael had gone precisely as she'd predicted.

Once she dismissed Chloe, she opened a drawer and removed the sheaf of paper that Wesley had given her yesterday afternoon. She wanted to be stronger than she was. She wanted to stop dwelling on what might have been. And yet, she seemed powerless to do anything other than unfold the paper and read his words.

> *You are the stars in my heaven.*
> *You are the green in my fields.*
> *You are the birds' sweet song*
> *in the boughs of my trees.*
> *You are the beauty, the everlasting*
> *beauty of my rose.*
> *You are—and will always*
> *remain—the love of my heart.*
>
> *—W*

He'd always referred to her as his rose. His perfect rose.

She heard the door between her and Michael's bedchamber open. She crumpled the poem and dropped it at her feet beneath the vanity, before rising and taking one last look in the mirror. The bodice of her gown was low enough to reveal her cleavage but high enough to hide the love bruise her husband had left on the inside of her right breast the night before. At the base of her throat was the tiniest of bruises that she hoped no one would notice or if they did perhaps they'd attribute it to the lighting. It never was very bright at a theater.

Turning to greet her husband, she found herself in his arms, his mouth locked on hers with an eagerness that promised wondrous things when they returned. His lips were pliant and hot, the kiss deep, as though he'd consume her if he could.

Having unleashed his kisses, she was now the joyful recipient of a good many of them. He never failed to cross paths with her without delivering at least one.

He pressed his mouth to the tip of her nose. "Must we go to this dreaded affair?"

Playfully, she pushed him back slightly. "I've already sent word that we'll be there. It would be rude not to show."

Reaching out with a bare finger, he touched the line of her collarbone, stopping his journey beside his love bite. "That might raise a few eyebrows."

"I have no evening attire with a higher neckline." And the string of pearls circling her neck certainly didn't serve as adequate covering.

"Maybe this will help."

He withdrew from his pocket an exquisite silver necklace, strands of silver woven into a fine netting that looked as though it had captured an array of emeralds. She looked at him, wondering if the awe showed in her eyes. "I recognize it. The first marchioness was wearing it in the portrait she had made following her wedding."

"A gift from the first marquess."

"Oh, Michael, it's too valuable, I can't."

"You're now the Marchioness of Falconridge. It belongs about your throat. Please honor my family by wearing it."

Hardly knowing what to say, she did little more than nod and remove her own string of pearls. He came behind her and draped the necklace around her. The top of it was like a collar that circled her throat as he secured it at the back. The front flowed down toward her bosom.

She thought of his ring that Jenny had secured from the jeweler. It was nestled safely in Kate's jewelry box. She wondered if this was the moment to return it to him, if their relationship was strong enough to sustain his learning that she knew of his sacrifice. Or was it still too delicate? In the end, she decided not to risk anything ruining the magic of this moment of his giving such a precious gift to her.

Turning, she lifted on her toes and kissed him, welcoming the feel of his arm snaking around her as he drew her closer. It was as though asking for his kiss last night had unleashed much of what he'd been holding back. As though, at long last, they were both embracing the promise of something special building between them.

"I know what you're thinking," she said, feeling the press of his hips against her. "But it must wait."

He laughed, a low sound that vibrated between them and filled her with excitement and anticipation over what would be waiting for her—for them—when they returned.

He began nuzzling her neck, just above the top of the necklace. "This is all I want you to wear to bed tonight," he rasped. "This necklace."

Her knees weakened with the onslaught of images bombarding her after lying upon the bed. Somehow the thought of wearing a single piece of jewelry seemed more sensuous than being completely nude. And judging by the reaction and tightening of his body, he was feeling the same. She stepped beyond his reach. "We really must go."

Michael studied the blush that traveled from his wife's cheeks, disappeared beneath the necklace, and reappeared across the exposed swells of her breasts. He could hardly wait to uncover the rest of her, to watch the blushes slip into hiding. Who would have thought that her wearing anything at all to bed would fill him with such anticipation?

"Very well," he murmured, removing his white gloves from his pocket and tugging them on as he followed his wife out of the bedchamber. "Promise me if the opera is boring, we'll leave before it ends."

"I'll promise no such thing," she said tartly.

"I've already deduced that no matter how enjoyable the performance, you'll be bored."

He couldn't help himself. He laughed, the sound traveling in his wife's wake as they reached the foyer. Suddenly she spun around. He thought she was going to comment on his laughter. Instead she said, "Oh, I forgot my wrap."

"I'll get it. Wait here."

"It's lying across the foot of my bed."

He couldn't stop himself from grinning as he bounded back up the stairs. They'd make use of the foot of the bed later. He could have sent up a servant, but his long legs made quick work of returning to her room. He was almost leery to put a name to what he was feeling. Intense satisfaction with his life, in spite of the hardships that might still await them. Something had shifted last night with that kiss . . . it was as though her request and the intensity of all that had followed had somehow managed to permanently knock down the last of the bricks that had encompassed the wall surrounding his heart. He felt a stirring, a hope for the future that he wasn't certain he'd ever known. It was quite possible that together they could find unlimited happiness. It was a notion that he was having a difficult time wrapping his mind around, but he wanted to embrace it. He wanted to give to her everything within him that he was capable of giving.

He strode into her bedchamber, snatched the silken wrapper from the bed, and turned for the door. His gaze fell on a crumpled piece of paper beneath the vanity. He wasn't certain what drew him to it. It was obviously of no importance and yet—

Bending down, he picked it up and straightened it out. An obviously unschooled attempt at poetry. Was it something old, something Kate was dismissing from her past? More likely, it was something recently received during an encounter in a night-shadowed garden. Or perhaps during a secretive rendezvous. He wondered what it was about Wiggins that appealed to Kate. Perhaps it was the man's ability to put into words thoughts Michael held only in an abstract sort of way. They were too powerful, too overwhelming, too large to attempt to narrow down into a few mere words.

He dropped it on the vanity, so it would be there for them to discuss later, but truly what was the point? He'd given her permission to love the bastard, to fantasize about him. Why should he find fault with her reading his poetry?

Because while her heart might never be his, her person belonged to Michael. He'd deal with it later. The money was in his hands now. He was the one who needed to be pleased. Taking a deep breath to regain control of his temper, he made his way down the stairs. Kate was standing by the door, talking with the butler.

"Bexhall," Michael said, summoning his butler over. There must have been something in his voice that indicated to Kate that he wished to speak privately with his servant.

"Yes, my lord?" Bexhall said once he was near enough to speak with the proper decorum.

"Did the marchioness have a visitor today?"

"Yes, my lord. The Duchess of Hawkhurst came to call."

"Anyone else?"

Bexhall swallowed.

"Anyone else?" Michael repeated through clenched teeth.

"Not today."

"Yesterday?"

Bexhall nodded. "A Mr. Wiggins."

"Was she home for him?"

"They took a stroll in the garden."

Michael nodded, reverting to his former skill of not revealing his emotions. He strolled over to Kate and draped the wrap around her shoulders.

"Is everything all right?" she asked.

"Everything is fine. I simply noticed an area upstairs in need of dusting. Bexhall will see that it's taken care of."

"It seemed like a rather serious conversation for a bit of dust."

"Now that I have the means, I'm very particular about the management of my homes. Shall we be off?"

She smiled brightly. "I'm looking forward to the evening."

Unfortunately, he no longer was.

Chapter 22

Kate was well aware that at the theater performances were not limited to those on the stage. Theatrics were at play as soon as one alighted from one's coach. Everyone pretended gaiety, everyone put on a show.

Still she wasn't quite prepared for the performance required of her when she and Michael crossed paths with Wesley and Melanie in the lobby of the theater.

"I love the opera. Don't you just love the opera? I love the opera," Melanie said, her horse-size teeth displayed in a macabre kind of smile that seemed terribly forced.

"I'm fond of the opera," Kate said, because responding to her seemed the kind thing to do.

"Wesley doesn't. Do you, Lord Falconridge? Do you like the opera?"

"Not particularly. I'm here because it pleases my wife that I be."

Taken aback by his words, Kate turned her head to look at him. He'd been unusually quiet in the coach, which she'd attributed to the busy day he'd had hiring the builder and seeing to things that needed to be taken care of before they returned to the country. Still it had been some time since he'd given the impression that he was doing something simply because it pleased her.

"How fortunate for her. And for me. I mean, Wesley's here because I want him to be. Isn't it wonderful to have such attentive husbands, Lady Falconridge? Although I'll confess to finding it strange addressing you so formally, but Wesley assures me I must. He's more familiar with what is proper than I. I don't like living here. Do you?"

Kate laughed lightly. "Well, except for all the rain. I thought I felt a few drops when we were walking inside. Oh, look, there's the Duke and Duchess of Hawkhurst. We're sharing their box tonight. We should probably catch up to them."

Wesley rubbed his right ear. It was a signal he'd perfected when he was secretly courting her. It meant he'd be waiting for her in the lobby after the performance began. She wondered how he intended to escape his wife, how he expected her to escape her husband.

"It was good to see you both. Come along, my darling, we should find our own seats," he said.

As he and Melanie strolled away, Kate couldn't help but think that even he had been performing.

"Did you know he'd be here?" Michael asked quietly.

"Of course not." She put her hand on Michael's arm. "You're very fortunate her father isn't as wealthy as mine. She's actually the least talkative of her sisters."

She'd expected him to laugh, at least to smile. Before she could question him about his somberness, Hawkhurst and Louisa had joined them and were escorting them to the box. The ladies sat in the front chairs, the gentlemen behind them.

"I'm so glad you could join us this evening," Louisa said, patting Kate's hand.

"It was kind of you to ask."

"Is everything all right?"

Kate nodded, not at all comfortable telling her that something was bothering Michael. Although she couldn't imagine what it might be. He'd been attentive before they'd left the house. Perhaps it was simply traveling in the confines of the coach. Maybe he needed time to shake off the effects of confinement. Or perhaps the crowds here made him feel as though everything were closing in on him. Or perhaps, as she feared, it was Wesley's presence.

She was beginning to wish they'd simply stayed home. Together. Reading in the library. Lying in bed. Kissing. Touching. Talking. They had so much to learn about each other.

The lights dimmed, the curtains parted. Fifteen minutes from now, Wesley would expect her to slip out and meet him outside the theater. He'd rubbed his right ear three times, one time for each five minute increment. It had seemed so adventuresome when she was sixteen attempting to escape from beneath her mother's watchful gaze. It had been fun, thrilling.

But to seek to escape her husband? To escape Michael? It seemed the worst sort of betrayal. It was the worst sort of betrayal.

Immediately she felt guilty. She'd not been firm enough the day before in explaining to Wesley that they couldn't engage in any sort of tryst. She knew the power of his allure, how difficult she found it to resist him.

No one in her family knew that she'd gifted him with her virginity three weeks before she'd married him. His taking of her gift had been quick, painful, and unsatisfying to say the least. She didn't regret it. How could she? She'd loved him.

But he'd been as a child tearing into a gift on Christmas morning.

A woman's initiation into lovemaking should be handled with patience, the sort Michael had shown her, even though he'd known she was experienced. He'd seemed to savor the discovery of what lay beneath her gown. But then he always seemed to savor it, as though each time would be the last. And now that she at long last knew the flavor of his kiss . . .

Honestly, how could Michael not comprehend the power he had over her? To think that she could concentrate on imagining another man in her bed. He vastly underestimated his prowess.

She realized quite suddenly that she was sitting

in the darkened theater, smiling so broadly that her jaw was beginning to ache. The opera had begun with her barely noticing.

Honestly, what was she going to do about Wesley? If she met him, she would only encourage him to pursue this path. If she didn't meet him, she had no way of knowing if he would realize that she was rebuffing him.

They couldn't have a relationship. She wouldn't be unfaithful to Michael. And even as she thought that, she couldn't help but wonder if a woman could be unfaithful with her heart and not her body. Michael thought she dreamed of being in another's arms. If that belief caused him any sort of pain, he certainly didn't show it. He never showed anything about what he felt. Even when his mother had attacked him, he'd been stoic.

Only later had the anguish become too much to bear. Did she cause him anguish as well?

In the past few days something significant had changed between them. He had the money now. He had no reason to be kind to her other than because he wanted to be. He no longer *had* to earn her favor. She touched the priceless necklace he'd given her. But it seemed he *wanted* to earn her favor.

Was trying to earn what he'd already gained.

She'd come into this marriage as damaged as he, knowing how love could hurt. Not realizing how it could also heal. When they left the theater tonight, she wanted nothing else to be between them. Which meant saying a final good-bye to Wesley.

She leaned over toward Louisa. "I'm going to the ladies' refreshing room."

"I'll go with you."

"No," she whispered. "Enjoy the opera. I won't be long."

Rising, she turned to find herself facing her husband, who'd come to his feet. She touched his arm and repeated the lie she'd told Louisa.

"I'll escort you."

"No need."

He studied her, then nodded. She could feel his gaze on her as she exited through the curtains.

With doubts flickering through his mind, Michael watched his wife leave.

"Is everything all right?" Hawkhurst asked. He'd come to his feet along with Michael.

"I'm sure it is. I'll return in a moment."

He slipped through the curtains and walked to the balcony that looked down on the majestic stairs and the grand foyer. His hands gripped the railing as he watched his wife hurry across the plush carpeted flooring, without once looking back, before leaving through the door that the footman opened for her. He knew beyond a doubt who she was going to meet. He had the money now. He had no need of her.

Let her go. Let her find her happiness in the arms of another man.

Turning back toward the box, he nearly doubled over with the pain brought on by the thought. He needed an heir. By God, she would remain faithful until he had his heir. Then she could take any lover she wanted.

He was halfway down the stairs before he realized where he was headed. The easy thing would be to let her go.

Damned shame for her that she'd taught him he gained more by not following the easy path.

Kate quietly slipped between the two buildings, the streetlamps casting very little light back here, just enough that she could see the gladness in Wesley's face as he stepped from the shadows.

"I was afraid you weren't going to come."

"Wesley—"

"Kate, there must be some way we can be together. Each time I see you, I realize what a mistake I made in marrying Melanie."

"Wesley—"

He pulled her farther into the shadows. "I love you, Kate. I always have. I always will. I know your father paid Falconridge five million dollars. If you could just find a way to get your hands on a portion of it, we could run off to America—"

"We're married."

"No one in America would know that. Melanie and Falconridge would be granted divorces on the grounds of abandonment. They would be free to marry others." He squeezed her hands. "But what matters most is that we'd be together."

Working her hands free of his, she reached up and touched his once beloved face. He'd always given so little thought to planning . . . to responsibility. He was a man who lived only in the present, who looked no farther than the distance cast by his own shadow, who put his needs and wants above all others. "Wesley, what I feel for you—"

"It's time to return to the theater, Kate."

Kate spun around at the familiar voice, and while there was a good deal of gloom in the alleyway, she didn't need a good deal of light to know that Michael was furious. The seething anger shimmied off him, in undulating waves, like lightning striking across the sky.

"Michael—"

"You're not leaving with him." He crossed over and took her arm. "You're coming back with me."

"I just have to explain—"

"The explainin' can wait 'til later, m'lady," a large man said, stepping out of the shadows, brandishing . . .

Good Lord. He was holding a gun and so was the fellow with him. Scruffy hats shadowed their faces, coats disguised their shapes.

Michael moved Kate back slightly, placing his body between hers and the unsavory men. His eyes wide, Wesley stood to Michael's side, but back a bit as though hoping he were lost in the shadows. Not that she blamed him.

"We mean you no 'arm," the first man said, obviously the leader. "We only want yur valuables. 'And 'em over, gents, lady."

Too stunned to believe this was happening, Kate watched as Michael removed his watch and chain from his vest as well as his money clip and dropped them into the outstretched hand of the second man.

The leader waved his gun. "The lady's necklace."

Kate's hand flew to her throat. "No, it's priceless—"

"Ev'rything's got a price, m'lady. Give it up now. Don't want no 'arm comin' to yur man, 'ere, whichever one it be."

How long had they been there, how long had they been listening? How long had Michael?

"No," she said.

"Kate," Michael said with a low rumble that would brook no arguments, turning slightly, holding out his gloved hand, but still managing to block most of her view of the men. "Give it to me."

Taking the glove off her right hand so her fingers would have more dexterity, she reached back and unclasped the necklace. "I'm so sorry," she whispered, setting it in Michael's hand.

"It's not important. They'll want the tiara as well."

It hadn't been in her family for four generations. It she gave up easily.

Michael turned back to the men and handed the things over.

"All righty, you there, gent. We'll 'ave your things now."

"The marquess is the only one with anything of value," Wesley said.

"We'll decide that. Give us what ya got."

"I have nothing."

"Wiggins—"

Kate heard the warning in Michael's voice.

"I'm not giving them—"

"Then it's yur life," the first man said.

Everything happened so fast that Kate did little more than stand in stunned silence. She was aware of Michael moving toward Wesley, shoving on him—

A noise like thunder echoing between the buildings.

Michael crumpling to the ground.

"Blimey! Ya killed a lord!"

The thieves running off.

"Oh my God. Oh my God." Kate's heart was hammering in her chest as she knelt beside Michael. He tried to raise up on an elbow, but collapsed to the ground, groaning. Kate opened his jacket, trying to determine—

Her fingers touched warm, sticky wetness . . . so much wetness. "Wesley, go for help." Removing her wrap, she pressed it against Michael's side. He groaned.

Wesley knelt down. "Let me see how bad it is, Kate."

She abandoned the pressure she'd been applying, moved slightly, and cradled Michael's face between her hands. "Why did you do that?" she asked. "Michael, why did you—"

"You . . . love . . . him." He went limp in her arms.

In a panic she pressed her ear to his chest, could still hear the pounding of his heart.

"He's alive," she whispered, before shifting

slightly to take over applying pressure—only to discover Wesley hadn't been. He grabbed her hands.

"Kate, it's quite bad."

"Yes, I can see that. Go get help." She hadn't realized how far back they'd moved.

"Kate, darling, listen to me carefully. Only Melanie would remain between us."

She stared at him in disbelief. Was he saying what she thought he was? To do nothing?

"The money is not entailed," he continued. "It would become yours. We would go to America. Together. You and me."

She shook her head. "Please go get help. Find a constable, Hawkhurst, someone!"

"Kate, this is our chance—"

"I love him, Wesley. I came out here to tell you that your pursuit of me must stop. I won't be unfaithful to him, and I will never abandon him. Now, please, I beg of you, I can't leave him while he's bleeding. Go get help."

"You can't possibly think I'll give you up so easily—"

"He saved your life, Wesley! Go get some damned help!"

His eyes widened, whether at her profanity or her fury, she didn't know, but he nodded succinctly. "Right."

He scrambled to his feet and ran back toward the street.

Leaning down, she pressed her cheek to Michael's. "Please don't die."

Chapter 23

❦❧

"**F**ootpads don't usually carry pistols," Louisa said.

She was sitting on a padded bench in the hallway outside Michael's room, while Kate, with her pacing, was in danger of wearing a hole in the carpet running its length.

"I don't care what they usually do. These two did."

Wesley had elected to seek out Hawkhurst rather than a constable, and Hawkhurst had taken over as though born to leadership. Kate supposed he had been. All the first born of the aristocracy were. He'd called for his coach and Michael's, sending a footman in Michael's to fetch a physician, and hoisting Michael inside his own because it offered a less bumpy ride. Kate had cradled Michael's head in her lap the entire journey. Now Hawkhurst and the physician, a Dr. Lensing, were seeing to Michael's wound.

Hawkhurst had wanted to take Michael directly to a hospital, but Kate had thought he'd hate that, being in an institutionalized building where others had control. No, much better to have him at home where he was master.

"What were you doing in a darkened alley anyway?" Louisa asked.

"Meeting with Wesley Wiggins," she said with resignation. Everyone would be asking. She'd considered creating some elaborate story, but in the end she'd decided to be truthful. It was time everyone was truthful, that everything was revealed. If Michael had known she'd been married before, he might have never taken her as his wife to begin with. And he no doubt thought if Kate or her father knew the truth about his mother's condition, that Kate's hand would no longer be offered in marriage.

"You and Jenny seem to think that dashing off to meet with young men in secretive corners is appropriate behavior for young ladies."

Kate heard the censure in Louisa's voice, but she couldn't bring herself to remind her that she was the one to be caught in a compromising position that had resulted in her own marriage. She brought her pacing to an abrupt halt, looking to Louisa for hope because she had none remaining. "What if he dies?"

Louisa rose to her feet, crossed the short space separating them, and took Kate in her arms. "I'm sure he's much too proud to allow a couple of ruffians to kill him. He'll insist on facing death on his own terms."

Welcoming the embrace, Kate let the tears fall.

"He is proud, so proud. I asked so much of him, Louisa. The impossible."

"To deduce your favorite color?"

Kate leaned back, swiping at her tears. "He said he'd gone to you for advice?"

Louisa nodded. "I greatly underestimated him as a husband. I think he'd do anything for you."

Together they returned to the bench. "Wesley paid me a visit two days ago. He brought me a poem. I'd planned to ignore it, but where he's concerned, I've always been so weak. I read it this evening before we left. I crumpled it up and dropped it to the floor, beneath my vanity. Michael returned to the room to get my wrapper as we were leaving. When we returned home . . . when I went to my bedchamber to change out of my . . . the clothes soaked with his blood"—she pressed her fingers against her throat where her pulse jumped erratically— "it was lying on my vanity. He must have seen it."

"Perhaps your maid—"

"She says she didn't." She held back a sob. "That man was going to shoot Wesley. Michael stepped in front of him, pushed him out of the way. Louisa, I think he did it because he believes I love Wesley, because he believes if given the choice, I would choose Wesley's life over his."

Louisa wrapped her arms around Kate, holding her close, rocking her while she finally let the tears fall.

"Oh, sweetheart, you can't think any of this is your fault."

"It's all my fault. I'll never forgive myself. And if he dies—"

The door to Michael's bedchamber opened and the doctor stepped out. Kate lunged to her feet. "How is he?"

"Fortunate, Lady Falconridge. Very fortunate. The bullet went through and he's lost a lot of blood. But no organs were damaged."

"So he'll live?"

"In all likelihood."

Kate dropped back to the bench, her knees too weak to support her. "Could you be a little more optimistic?"

"There is always the risk of infection."

"Then you'll stay and watch over him."

He gave her a quick grin that evaporated as soon as he realized she was serious. "I'm afraid I can't. I have other patients, but I'm leaving medication to help him sleep and I'll return in the morning to look at the wound and change the dressing."

"I think you should stay."

"He needs rest to heal. My watching him would serve no purpose."

Kate had never been in a sickroom. Still, she forced herself to her feet. "Tell me everything I need to do."

Kate had always known that she'd lived a pampered life, but she'd never really comprehended what that meant. She'd never truly tended to someone else's needs. Servants had always done everything for her. She supposed she could have hired a nurse, could have had one of the present servants oversee Michael's care, but she didn't trust anyone to tend to him with the patience and gentleness that she would.

Hawkhurst and Louisa had both offered to stay, but just as the doctor had said his presence would serve no purpose, so she'd convinced them that neither would theirs. Hawkhurst had promised to stop by her parents' residence and let her family know what had transpired during their evening.

"I'm sorry I ruined it for everyone."

Hawkhurst had merely given her a compassionate smile. "The blame lies with the blighters who robbed you."

"Do you think the police will ever catch them?"

"I doubt it."

"They took precious jewelry that had been in Michael's family—"

"Nothing is more precious than life."

"Michael might not feel that way."

"Did he do anything to prevent them from taking the jewelry?"

Kate shook her head.

"Did he do anything to try to stop them from taking a life?"

Kate felt the tears well in her eyes.

He nodded perfunctorily as though his point had been made. "Falconridge has been my friend for many years, Kate," he said, using her name, bringing an intimacy to his words. "He is not a man comfortable with expressing his feelings. I have always relied on his actions to speak for him. I am honored he considers me a friend."

His actions to speak for him.

Those words haunted her as she sat by his bedside, wiping a damp cloth over his bare chest. Earlier he'd begun breathing harshly, had seemed to be fighting the confines of the bed.

And she'd thought of his actions: riding his horse in the rain, leaping out of the coach. So she'd removed the covers and he'd settled down somewhat. She'd cut off the linen shirt someone had put on him as though they thought there was a need to protect his modesty. He'd calmed completely after that. He'd not even fought when she'd brought the sheet up to his hips when Jenny arrived to sit with her.

Jenny kept her company now in the dark, quiet room where only candles flickered. Kate dunked the cloth into the cool water, squeezed the excess water out, and once again began wiping Michael's chest. She'd never ventured into his bedchamber before. It was so masculine, so much like him. Thick, heavy wood. Simple carvings. Lines mostly. Nothing elaborate. She wondered how much of the room reflected his taste and how much that of the marquesses who had come before him.

She accused him of not knowing her, yet what did she know of him? What did he like to read? What was his favorite color?

She heard Jenny's quiet footsteps as she wandered around the room, the irritating sound grating on her nerves. She wondered if it would be rude to ask Jenny to leave, and yet, did she truly want to be alone?

If she were alone, nothing would distract her from her thoughts. Did Michael truly believe that if given the choice, she would rather watch him die than Wesley? That knowledge hurt most of all. What a terrible, selfish wife she'd been, to be so concerned with being loved herself that she didn't stop to think maybe she wasn't giving love in return.

She felt the tears burning her eyes, clogging her throat.

"Wake up, Michael," she whispered.

"Did you say something?" Jenny asked.

"No, not really."

A few more moments of silence passed before Jenny said, "Oh, Kate, look at this."

Kate glanced over her shoulder. Her sister was standing at a small desk. "I'm not certain he'd appreciate you rummaging through his things. As a matter of fact, I can guarantee you that he wouldn't."

"I'm not rummaging. This was right on top." Holding up a piece of paper, she approached. "It's from a dressmaker's. It's a listing of colors of fabric." She held it toward Kate. "Look. It must be where he got the names of colors you'd never heard of. Some are marked off."

With tears blurring her vision, Kate took the paper. "There must a hundred colors here." She felt a painful tightening in her chest as a sob escaped.

"Oh, darling, don't cry. He's going to be all right." Jenny knelt beside her, taking her in her arms as best she could from such an unfortunate advantage.

"Oh, Jenny, he never asked me to love him, and yet he tried so hard to do what he thought would please me. He doesn't know my favorite color, but somehow I fell in love with him anyway."

Jenny sat back on her heels. "Why?"

Kate sniffed and stared at her sister. "Why what?"

"Why did you fall in love with him? Tell me about him, Kate. Is it because he's a lot like Wesley?"

"Oh, my Lord, he's nothing like Wesley." She wiped her tears. "Did you know that he auctioned himself to the highest bidding American father?"

"No. I can't imagine Father participating in something that scandalous." She grew quiet for a moment. "Because of Mother."

"Yes."

Jenny got up, pulled the chair nearer, sat, and took Kate's hand. "So he didn't really ask for your hand in marriage."

"No, but I can't even begin to imagine what it cost him to place himself on the bidding block like that."

"It's not as though he was entering slavery."

"But still, Jenny, he's such a prideful man. But he was so desperate for funds—"

"Aren't they all? They have estates that need to be remodeled."

"He has a mother who's not well. He's making plans to build her a house."

"Is that why you fell in love with him? Because he cares for his mother?"

Kate shook his head. "He says he knows so little about love, but in truth, I think he knows everything. He's done nothing except try to see that I'm happy."

"Then surely a man such as that can*not* die."

Yes, Kate thought, surely a man such as that couldn't die.

She wouldn't let him.

"I've decided to accept Pemburton's offer of marriage," Jenny said, a few hours later.

Kate looked at her sister. She was sitting in a chair beside the foot of the bed, studying her hands as though she'd just discovered they resided at the end of her arms.

She'd been a source of comfort and strength while Kate had tended to Michael, who continued to sleep.

"Did Father talk to you?" Kate asked quietly.

Jenny nodded.

"Do you think that's a proper reason to marry?"

"I'm not sure there is a proper reason. Perhaps I'll be as lucky as you and discover after the wedding that he's the right one."

Was Michael the right one? Yes, she was beginning to realize he was.

"Can he give you the passion you long for?"

"I think so. He has a very attractive set of lips and his hands are large and I can feel strength in them when we dance. He's very proper. I hear those are the ones you have to watch out for. That behind closed doors they are quite improper."

"And will that be enough?"

Jenny peered up at her. "I suppose you think I should strive to find love."

"I think you can have both."

"I don't trust love. It's only served to muck up your life. With passion there's no doubt. You either have it or you don't. It's not judged by a frivolous heart."

"You think I've been frivolous?"

"Where Wesley's concerned. Don't you?"

Kate shook her head. "I was young. Naïve. What I felt for Wesley . . . it pales in comparison with what I feel for Michael."

"And yet you wanted to spend the rest of your life with Wesley. You thought it was love. How can you know if what you feel now is true love?"

Kate looked back at Michael. How did she know? Because she would do anything, pay anything to keep him alive.

Kate didn't understand why people felt a need to come when darkness settled in. Perhaps because it seemed that death could arrive without being seen.

Michael had yet to awaken. He was slightly fevered. The physician had cleaned his wound, changed the dressing, given him medications of one sort of another, some designed to help him heal, others to ensure he slept with as little discomfort as possible.

Jenny had left that morning and Kate had kept her vigil alone, until her mother arrived, late in the evening. As formidable as ever, as though she were preparing her own battle against death.

She sat in a chair on the opposite side of the bed from Kate, but her gaze would rest on Kate for a bit, before shifting to Michael, and then she'd sweep her gaze around the corners and shadows.

"I don't know how I'll survive losing two people I love," Kate said quietly into the night.

Her mother sat up a little straighter. "Your father told you about me I suppose."

"Yes."

"Well, I'm not dead yet and neither is your marquess. I suspect, like me, he has no desire to be mourned before he's toes up and six feet under."

Kate released a light laugh before settling into somberness. "Are you afraid, Mama?"

"Of death? No, but I shall miss your father terribly."

"I never realized how much you love each other."

"People love in different ways, Kate. They show it in different ways." She snorted, in a very unladylike manner. "Sometimes they don't show it at all, but it's still there."

"Why did you believe Wesley was a fortune hunter, but not believe the same of Michael?"

"Michael?"

"Falconridge?"

"Oh, he's a fortune hunter, no question there, but he's an honest one. And an honest heart is capable of great love."

"What is love? Wesley wrote me poems, he brought me gifts, he told me he loved me every time he saw me. Michael has never said he loves me. He's never even said he has affection for me. I didn't *know* until he stepped in front of Wesley. Why didn't he tell me? How can a person know if the words are never given?"

"Love isn't found in words, Kate. It's found in quiet moments, a look, a sigh, a smile, a gladness." She sighed. "And very often, it's shown with sacrifice."

Chapter 24

❦❧

"Lady Falconridge, I'm here to take you home."

Kate was surprised her voice sounded so calm, so authoritative as she spoke to Michael's mother. Kate's stomach was knotted so tightly it was a wonder she could stand upright. She'd brought one of her tall footmen with her and he now stood just outside the open door in case Kate should need him to pull the dowager marchioness off her.

But the silver-haired woman seemed as docile as a newborn kitten.

"Home," she murmured as though the word had no meaning to her.

Kate dared to step closer. "Yes, my lady. Your son is hurt—"

"Did he fall from the tree again?" Her gaze was wandering over the wall. "I should have it"—she made a chopping motion with her hand. "I told her . . . restrain his activities . . . can't risk . . . only heir."

Kate could only assume that the *she* was his governess, who'd locked him in dark closets rather than risk any harm coming to the only heir. Only she had harmed him, in ways perhaps worse than any physical harm that might have come to him.

"You should come with me now," Kate said. "I'm taking you home."

Holding her breath, she approached the woman as she might a skittish horse. Placing her hand beneath the woman's elbow she urged her to her feet. "That's it. Very carefully now."

She wore a soiled nightgown. Once Kate got her home, she'd have Chloe clean her up proper before taking her to see Michael.

The marchioness shuffled with tiny steps as though she hadn't the strength to lift her feet. Her gaze wandered as did her attention. She looked so lost that it tore at Kate's heart. She wondered if bringing Michael's mother home now was the right thing to do, but she wanted his mother to see him, wanted him to know his mother was there.

She needed to give him the will to fight—if not for her, then for the first woman he'd ever loved, the first woman who'd hurt him. Little wonder he guarded his heart so. The women who meant so much to him took such little care of his feelings. She included herself in that assessment.

The footman, John, stepped forward quietly, carefully, with as much tenderness as Kate had ever seen a man exhibit. Also with more patience. Kate dearly wanted to hurry the woman along, but she'd witnessed how little it took to set her off and the last thing she wanted was any sort of altercation.

The staff of Glennwood stood around, staring, as though they'd never seen someone being escorted from the facility.

"Don't you all have something better to do than gawk?" Kate snapped.

A few hurried off and Dr. Kent approached. "Are you certain this is a wise course?"

"No," Kate said with conviction. "But it is necessary."

It seemed to take an eternity to get Michael's mother settled in the coach. Kate gave her the honor of sitting forward while she sat across from her, not wanting to crowd her. As the coach lunged forward, his mother did little more than gaze out the window at the passing scenery.

As the miles passed, Kate began to relax. It would be all right. She would handle Michael's mother. With Jenny's help, she'd managed to hire nurses and additional servants. A staff whose only purpose was to see to the needs of the dowager marchioness. And once Michael recovered—he would recover; Kate refused to accept any other outcome—they would return to the country estate and build the house he wanted for his mother. She'd be happy there. They'd all be happy there.

"I yelled at him," Michael's mother said loudly, and Kate nearly leapt out of skin.

"I know," Kate said softly. "But he understands, he forgives you."

Michael's mother still stared out the window, and Kate wondered if she truly saw the buildings that were coming into view or if, instead, she saw another part of her life, a part now lost to her. "I was dressed for the opera. He ran into my bed-chamber . . . so excited to share some new discovery. So small. His arms closed around my knees. Hugged so tight. I yelled at him. He wrinkled my clothes." A small smile flitted across her wrinkled face and disappeared. "Such a good boy, eager to please. Never hugged me again." She shifted her attention to Kate, and Kate fought not to be frightened or nervous.

Michael's mother looked as though she was on the verge of weeping. "A mother should always have wrinkled skirts."

"You love Michael very much don't you?" Kate asked.

The woman sitting across from her creased her brow. "Who is Michael?" Her eyes took on a more vacant look and Kate realized she'd returned to the hell of her life.

"The man I love," Kate answered, tears burning her eyes. The man she didn't know how she would live without.

Michael was tired, so tired. He felt as though someone had set kindling in his side and set it afire and the flames were licking unmercifully, spreading throughout his body, consuming him. He felt the cool touch against his brow, heard the whispered, "Come back to me."

It was such an urgent plea that even if he'd wanted to, he couldn't have ignored it. He forced his eyes open. The room was dimly lit. The cool fingers continued to stroke his fevered brow. A soft cheek lay against his bristly one. While he couldn't see her, he recognized the fragrance of raspberries.

"Please don't leave me," she whispered.

Imagines flashed through his mind. Kate leaving the opera to meet with another man, the sight of them standing so near in the darkness. The thieves. A flash. The fiery agony. But the physical pain had paled in comparison to what he'd felt in his heart at the sight of what he'd witnessed. Another man offering to take her away . . .

And yet here she was. Was it guilt that kept her tethered to his side?

"I'm not the one . . ." The words came out as little more than a croak.

Kate jerked up as though she were a puppet whose strings had been yanked. "You're awake. Here, have some water."

Only instead of giving him a glass, she flung droplets at his lips. Not enough, not nearly enough as he gathered them up on his parched tongue. As though growing as frustrated as he, she mumbled something about the doctor and moved away, before returning to slip an arm beneath his head and lift him slightly, bringing a glass of water nearer. It was heaven. Or as close to heaven as he'd ever get.

After he'd taken a few sips, she took the glass away and returned with a damp cloth, wiping what he assumed was sweat from his neck and chest. It was so unbearably hot in here.

"Wiggins?" he rasped.

"He's fine. I can't believe you did what you did." Her hand stilled just above his pounding heart. "I wasn't going to leave with him, Michael. I wasn't. You must believe that."

"You love him."

He didn't know if he'd meant his words to be a statement or a question.

"Once, but no longer."

His head hurt, his eyes burned. There were so many things he wanted to ask her, questions he wanted answered, confusions he needed explained but they were shooting through his mind like a thousand falling stars. He couldn't seem to manage to latch on to one and hold it long enough to string the words together so they made any sense.

"Don't want to die—"

"You're not going to die."

"—without knowing your favorite color."

She gave him a tearful smile. "Green."

His fever, the ache in his side were affecting his hearing. He couldn't have heard her correctly.

"So common."

Tenderly she moved his hair back from his brow. "Not when I look into your eyes."

"Imagine that." The answer had been staring at him all along whenever he gazed in the mirror.

He heard her voice coming at him from a great distance, but he was too tired to respond. Too tired. He hadn't the strength to fight when the darkness swallowed him.

* * *

The past three nights had been the most difficult of Kate's life. If only his fever would break . . .

She'd snatched bits of sleep here and there, but her body ached to such a degree that she'd begun to fear that she might have a fever as well. Her father had sat with her for a while earlier tonight. It was as though each family member had agreed to take a turn. And while he'd wanted her to rest when he was there, she'd been unable to. Her greatest fear was that Michael would awaken, not see her there, and think she'd abandoned him for Wesley.

Near dawn, she heard a rap on the door just before it opened and Jeremy slipped his head inside. "Mind if I come in?"

"Is it your turn?" she asked wearily.

With a cocky grin, he walked in looking as awful as she felt, his clothing rumpled and askew.

"You smell like a brewery and tobacco," she said when he was near enough to lean down and kiss her cheek.

"I've been out all night."

"Madam Tussaud's Chamber of Horrors?"

He grinned. "Chamber of pleasures, more like." Turning somber, he sat in the nearby chair and nodded toward the bed. "How is he?"

"He woke up a few hours ago. There's so much I want to tell him, but I want him strong enough to remember it all."

He yawned. "He'll get strong enough, Kate. Not to worry there."

"You like him," she stated.

He nodded.

"Why?"

"Can't say really. Just do."

She and Jeremy had always had a special bond, different from the one she shared with Jenny. Growing up, she sometimes felt like the brother Jeremy had never had. They both understood numbers. When her parents had threatened to cut her off after she married Wesley, he was the one who'd convinced her that if it was true love it would still be there in five years. Wesley had barely waited three.

"Wesley was going to let him die," she rasped, mortified, ashamed of her past husband's actions. Jeremy didn't seem at all surprised by her words. "How is it that I'm the only one who couldn't see him as he was?"

"Because you were looking at him with your heart."

"How could my heart be so wrong?"

"Because it was such a young heart."

She laughed bitterly. "And you are so old and full of wisdom."

"Let's just say I've not been as sheltered as you and Jenny and leave it at that."

Michael was more tired than he thought it possible to be and still be alive.

Giving up would have been so much easier, but since Kate had come into his life, nothing had been easy, but neither had anything ever been so worthwhile. He'd spent his life traveling the path of least resistance, taking the easiest of routes, searching for the quickest of solutions, and with Kate, he'd discovered more satisfaction was found in fighting for something, in striving to meet her expectations. She brought out the best in him.

He opened his eyes to the shadow-filled room. Kate stood over him, bent slightly, using a damp cloth to wipe away the sweat of his fever. It had been a circus here, with people coming to keep her company. At the fever's highest pitch, he'd even hallucinated that one of the guests was his mother, holding his hand. It had felt so real, her hand frail and wrinkled, but warm, so warm. And gentle. Her eyes ever so gentle. For a moment they had been those of a woman who remembered him.

But such is the way of fevered dreams: to fill the mind with images that can never be.

"Oh, you're finally awake," Kate said, and abruptly turned away.

If he'd known she'd leave him so easily, he'd have kept his eyes closed and simply absorbed her tender ministrations into his soul. Then she was back, holding a glass of water, slipping one arm beneath his shoulders, lifting him—

"Here, you must be thirsty. Drink this," she ordered, pressing the glass to his lips, tilting it too high, nearly drowning him, spilling water over his chest.

"Oh, I'm sorry," she said, letting go of him, causing him to drop back with a groan. "I'm no good at this." She was dabbing at his chest, tears filling her eyes and rolling along her cheeks.

It took a great deal of effort, but he managed to capture her wrist and she stilled. "It's all right, Kate. Feels good."

"I'm so sorry, Michael. I've never taken care of anyone before, and I've been so worried that I'd botch it, that you'd die—"

He rolled his head from side to side. "No plans to die."

She swiped away at the tears that he wished he had the strength to reach. She sniffed. "Do you feel up to eating some soup? It'll help you gain your strength."

He nodded once, and the sweetest smile appeared on her face.

"I have so much to tell you." She squeezed his hand. "When you're stronger."

She was back in no time with a bowl of soup. She helped him sit up slightly, then very carefully spooned out a little bit at a time and brought it to his lips, tilting it slightly, watching it disappear as though she were witnessing a miracle.

He'd never seen her so disheveled. Her hair piled on her head but falling around her face in obvious disarray. He thought she might be as pale as he felt he might be. Her eyes were sunken with dark half-moons beneath them.

When the bowl was empty, she set it aside and began to tenderly wipe a damp cloth over his body. "Everyone's been so worried. They'll be glad to hear that your fever's broken and that you're going to be all right. You will be all right. I won't settle for anything less."

"If it . . . pleases you," he croaked.

She tilted her head slightly, like a lark that had spied something of interest just beyond reach. "I'm beginning to wonder if when you say that you mean something else entirely."

He gave it his best effort, but he wasn't certain his mouth shifted into the cocky grin he was aiming for because tears began welling in her eyes again. "Don't cry."

She swiped at her eyes and sniffed. "Sorry, I can't help it."

"When did you sleep?"

She shook her head.

"Will you lie with me?" he asked, wondering how long he'd sound like a frog.

"But you're hurt."

"I still have one good side. Let me hold you. You need to rest."

Leaning down, she pressed a kiss to his forehead, then smiled softly. "If it pleases you."

Standing, she unbuttoned her sacklike dress and removed it, revealing her cotton chemise and bloomers. She slipped beneath the sheet, nestling up against his good side. He didn't know if anything he'd ever experienced had ever felt so good.

Until he felt her warm tears running along his chest.

"Kate, please don't do that."

"I can't help it. I'm so happy, so relieved—"

"And to think I worked so hard to make you happy. Had I known tears were to be my reward, I'd have not tried at all."

She lifted her head and met his gaze. "You'd have tried. I've figured you out, Lord Falconridge. You concern yourself with everyone's happiness except your own. Your misfortune was in marrying a woman who cared for only her own happiness. And never gave any thought to yours. I shall spend the rest of my life making it up to you."

It took all the strength he could muster to cradle her cheek. "Lie still and quiet. You need your rest. We'll talk later."

Nodding, she lowered her head to his shoulder. He began stroking her arm, the motion bringing as much comfort to him as he hoped it did to her.

"Your mother's here," she said quietly.

He stilled his hand and glanced around the room. "Where?"

"Presently in her room. I've hired servants. She's never left alone. She's come in to see you several times. She loves you."

"She doesn't even remember me, Kate."

"Still, she does love you."

He was too weary to argue. Instead he commanded, "Go to sleep."

He felt somewhat better that she actually obeyed without question. Almost immediately he heard her gentle snoring. He thought he'd probably never been so clean in his entire life. The woman must have bathed him a thousand times in the past . . . how many days had it been? And she'd been by his side nearly the entire time. Only once had he awoken to not find her there. It must have been when she was fetching his mother. That was a situation he'd have to put back to rights. Only how could he even contemplate returning his mother to that awful life? He'd pay the builder extra to get the house finished as quickly as possible.

Other matters needed to be tended to as well. Most importantly the matter of their marriage.

Chapter 25

It was several nights later before Michael finally found the strength to leave his bedchamber, not that he was fully recovered but he was damned tired of being bedridden, and the walls of his room were beginning to close in on him. And time spent with his wife was coming close to driving him mad.

He had a feeling—as loath as he was to admit it—that he was receiving from her the sort of treatment she'd received from him when they first married. There was a cautiousness to everything she said, everything she did. A distrust. A fear of opening her heart. No doubt a good deal of guilt.

He understood guilt, remorse, and the things it would cause a man to be willing to do to ease the burden of carrying both. It would make a man sell his pride to provide her with a haven. It would make a man try to guess a lady's favorite color simply to please her.

He'd placed his mother in an asylum because he couldn't be bothered to care for her.

He'd auctioned himself because he couldn't be

bothered to court a woman—and yet he'd found himself courting her anyway. He wasn't certain when the appearance of courting had transformed into an earnest desire to win her over. Perhaps the first time he'd heard her laugh as she sat in mud. Or perhaps when her eyes had blazed as she informed him she wouldn't continue to pay for his mistress, or the sympathy she'd expressed at learning he no longer had one. There were a thousand moments that shifted through his mind like an elaborate kaleidoscope and he was unable to pinpoint the exact one that had turned the tide on his affections toward her.

That she had cared for him during his recovery gave him hope. That he'd discovered her with another man made it impossible for him to hold on to it for any substantial length of time.

He had his valet prepare a bath for him, the water shallow, rising no higher than his hips, because his physician had warned him it was too soon to get his wound wet. It was healing nicely but would leave a nasty scar. Michael had yet to determine if he should look upon it as a badge of courage or stupidity.

Unencumbered by clothes, he lay with his back against one side of the copper tub, enjoying the warmth of the water, tempted to call for more. He'd instructed his valet to give him a few moments alone so he could simply enjoy the quiet of solitude. Kate had spent little time with him today, this evening, for which he was grateful. He needed to think and when she was with him, he couldn't. Her presence overwhelmed his senses. As weak as he was, he found himself reacting to her nearness as though there was something he could do about it, as though he could find the strength to bring her pleasure, to bring it to both of them.

He heard the door click open. A little more time alone would have been nice, but he suspected Nesbitt was anxious to get his duties over with so he could retire for the night. Michael rubbed his hand over his rough beard. "I believe we'll start with a shave."

"Why now when you told me no earlier?"

At Kate's voice, Michael quickly twisted around slightly, gasping when his body protested the awkward positioning. She had offered to shave him earlier, and while he longed for her attentions, he knew he was better off not receiving them. He needed to be strong, to lay down ultimatums, to—

"I wasn't aware you had the skills to shave a man," Michael groused.

"How difficult can it be?"

She gathered up his shaving cup, his straight-edged razor, and knelt beside the tub. "I might trim your hair afterward. It's beginning to look a bit unwieldy."

"It's always unwieldy. Besides, we pay a man good money to take care of my needs. Fetch him."

"I've already dismissed him for the night." She was wearing a thin nightgown that revealed a hint of shadows. His body, miraculously, reacted.

Perhaps he was more recovered than he realized.

"Kate—"

"I want to do this."

"You've tended me enough."

"But none of that was fun. I think this could be fun." She was busy using his shaving brush to whip up his shaving lather as though he weren't protesting, as though she'd made up her mind to do exactly as she pleased. But then that was her way—as she was accustomed to doing exactly as she pleased.

Only as she rose up on her knees and began to spread the lather over his jaw, he had to readily admit that her doing precisely as she wanted wasn't exactly true. She'd not necessarily wanted to marry him. Her parents had insisted. She'd wanted to remain married to Wiggins. Her parents had denied that request. They'd somehow managed to arrange an annulment. Michael knew absolutely nothing about the process. Had Wiggins's consent been needed? If they removed all of Michael's funds, would he easily give Kate up?

Her brow was furrowed in concentration.

"Laughter usually accompanies fun . . . or perhaps even a smile," he murmured.

She snapped her eyes up to his and offered him a slight grin. "I just want to make sure I do it right." She set the brush in the cup and put it aside. She picked up the razor.

"Have you a clue what you're doing?" he asked.

"When I was little, I'd watch my father."

"You and he are close."

She nodded. "I always wished I'd been born a son."

"I'm rather glad you weren't."

He had the pleasure of watching her blush, and he was left to wonder how differently his marriage might have been had he married Jenny. She'd have never denied him the opportunity to offer her passion, but would she have allowed him to give her love?

"Why the stricken look?" Kate asked. "I assure you I'll be very careful."

"A pain in my side, nothing more." A lie, easily spoken because the truth was almost beyond bearing. The cold jealousy, the icy fury he felt when he'd seen her with another man had nothing at all to do with the possibility of losing coins from his pockets. It had everything to do with losing her from his life.

He angled his chin, felt the steadiness in her hands as she scraped the blade along his throat, heard the rasp of bristly beard. Appearing civilized would do much to improve his well-being.

After a few scrapes, she went to dip the blade in water, to rinse it off—between his legs!

He'd barely opened his eyes in time to jerk back and grab her wrist. "Let's not swish it around down there, shall we?"

She giggled, actually giggled. "I had no intentions of getting it anywhere near your"—she cleared her throat— "well, near your . . ."

"Still, use the water beside my hip."

"Don't you trust me?"

Did he?

Her smile withered as she returned to shaving him. "When you're strong enough, you should visit with your mother."

"Perhaps tomorrow. Before this moment, I looked like such a ruffian, I would have no doubt terrified her."

"I was beginning to like the beard. Perhaps I should leave the mustache."

"Perhaps you should not."

"Have you given up on trying to please me?"

"If I wanted conversation I'd have gone to the parlor. I wanted a bath. That is usually managed in silence."

"Getting shot puts you in a foul mood."

"Kate—"

She pressed a finger to his lips. "I'll be quiet . . . if it pleases you."

If she was of a mind to be so agreeable, he considered insisting she leave. Instead he angled his head back and closed his eyes. He desperately wanted to be rid of the itching beard, and he wasn't certain his hands were steady enough. He had moments when he felt completely recovered and others when he thought he'd be on the losing end if he entered into a fight with a kitten.

Her touch was gentle, not quite as sure as that of his manservant, but neither did Nesbitt smell as sweet. Kate had obviously had her own bath, was herself ready to retire for the night. He wondered if she'd come to say good night and found him in the tub as alluring as he'd once found her.

When she was finished, she wiped away the remaining lather with a warm, damp cloth, her breast pressing against his shoulder as though she needed the nearness to accomplish her task.

"Bend your head back farther and I'll wash your hair."

He did as she ordered, keeping his eyes closed, concentrating on the gentle kneading of her fingers against his scalp. He thought he could grow accustomed to the spoiling. Her hands weren't as strong as Nesbitt's, but they were still capable and much more pleasant. Why did valets have to be men anyway? Why could a man not have a female servant? Other than the impropriety, it was certainly a more pleasing experience. Surely a man could be expected to behave when being ministered to by a woman.

Although based on the tightening of his body, he might be giving a man credit for more control than he deserved.

When she'd finished using a towel to dry his hair, she began to wash his back, careful to avoid his wound, her fingers stroking and rubbing the slick soap over his shoulders, down his right side, around his buttocks. Over and over until he was surprised she'd not worn away the skin. She added a little more hot water before shifting over to begin work on other areas.

As her hands glided over his chest, he opened his eyes. She'd somehow managed to dampen her gown in strategic areas, her taut nipples pressing up against the wet fabric, leaving nothing at all to his imagination. His body hardened in response.

Her hand, wet and slick with soap, moved lower. He groaned and accepted her touch when he should have pushed her away.

"If you're not careful, I'll give you another mess to clean."

"I have no intentions of being careful."

He glared at her. "What game are you playing?"

"No game. I want to . . . pleasure you. The bath is only the prelude."

"I don't want to be pleasured."

"I don't think you have the strength to fight me on this."

"I'm more recovered than you realize."

"I wasn't talking about physical strength."

"What are you trying to prove?"

"I'm not trying to prove anything."

She was obviously surprised by the harsh laughter echoing through the chamber, because her ministrations ceased, affording him the opportunity—with much less grace than he'd have liked—to get to his feet. He reached for the towel, only to have her snatch the towel from his hands.

"Step out of the tub and I'll dry you."

He shook his head. "I can't do this, Kate. I'm not nearly as strong as I thought. I thought I understood the price I was paying when I decided to be auctioned but I hadn't a clue.

"If I'm honest, I'm not as comfortable with our marriage as I thought I'd be. The reality is far different than I expected. I've tried to make the best of what I brought upon us. I've spent a good deal of my life in debt, but never have I felt I owed anyone as much as I owe you. It is overwhelming to owe one person so much. I find it more difficult than I imagined. I thought there was nothing you could ask of me that I would not grant. From the moment we exchanged vows, I became your servant. Someday, I'd hoped to rise to the level of your husband. But I know now that it's an impossibility.

"Your heart will always remain with him"—he couldn't bear to say the name—"and I thought I could accept that. But I can't. I honestly believed your demand for love was frivolous and trite. I thought a marriage could be made to work without it. But I want a wife who looks at me the way you do him. I don't want you thinking about *him* when I'm touching you. I don't want you meeting him in darkened alleys. My curse is that I can't deny you what brings you happiness. But neither can I live with it any longer. Take most of the money your father gave me and go to America with him. Leave me enough to see to my mother's welfare. That's all I ask. That and that you be happy."

Tears had begun to stream down Kate's cheeks. Much to his surprise, tears of happiness very much resembled tears of sorrow. She still clutched the towel between her breasts, which only served to jut them enticingly toward him. He was a man in short supply of restraint.

"Will you please hand me the towel so I may dry myself and prepare for bed. We can finish discussing the particulars in the morning."

"Do you know what will happen if I leave?" she asked softly.

"I shall seek a divorce on grounds of abandonment."

"I'll never forget you."

He couldn't stop himself from laughing again, not as harshly but just as bitterly. "You'll forget. I'm not easily remembered."

"Your mother—"

"My mother aside, do you know my mistress had another protector within a day of leaving me?"

"Did you love her?"

"Of course not."

"You tried to earn her affection."

"Don't be ridiculous."

"It had to have hurt . . . you had so little money at your disposal and you put it toward trying to please her."

"It is the nature of the relationship that one has with his mistress—"

"And yet she left."

"I satisfied her not at all. Is that what it would please you to hear? For me to acknowledge—"

"You chose the wrong mistress."

She'd been beautiful, talented in bed, and distant. She'd seen to his physical needs but a man needed so much more than that. But yearning for more than the physical was terrifying, because when the heart reached out, and found no purchase, it fell and shattered, resulting in unbearable pain.

"And the wrong wife," he said quietly.

"You didn't choose me, Michael. If you'd been given the choice, you'd have chosen Jenny."

He had nothing to say to that. "May I have the towel?"

She stepped forward, draped it around his shoulders, and held the ends together in front of him. "I'm not going to America with Wesley. I never think of him when you're in my bed. As a matter of fact, I never think of him at all except when he's standing in front of me. Yes, he came to see me here. Yes, he gave me a poem. Yes, I read it. Yes, at the opera, he signaled that I was to meet him. And I did. To tell him to leave me be. To alert him that never again would there be anything between us. To inform him that somehow, against all odds, I fell completely and madly in love with a man who couldn't even deduce my favorite color. Yet somehow he stole my heart." Tears welled in her eyes. "If you send me away, I won't forget you. When I gasp my last breath, I'll carry memories of you into heaven with me."

"Kate . . ." He swallowed hard. "I won't survive if you die."

"Exactly how I felt when you stepped in front of the gunman, you dolt. Never, ever do anything so unselfish again. I won't stand for it. I'll cut you off without a penny—"

"You no longer have that power over me." He skimmed his fingers along her cheek. "I wish I didn't need any of it, Kate. I wish I had asked for your hand. I wish I could say . . ."

Reaching up, she pressed a kiss to his throat. "I

know, Michael. All that matters is that I do know."

"I wish I had the strength to carry you to my bed." He grimaced. "Although after my spending far too much time in it of late, I fear it's not suitable for a lady."

"A good thing I changed the bedding before coming in here."

He narrowed his eyes at her, and she gave him an impish smile. "My sole purpose in coming into this room was to seduce you."

"Then all my blabbering—"

"Wasn't necessary, but was very much appreciated."

He cradled her face between his hands. "I adore you." He couldn't say why those words were easier to speak, didn't seem to carry the weight of others. "I have for a good long time now."

"And I love you." She slid her hand in his. "Come to bed with me and I'll show you exactly how much."

He barely remembered the journey to his bed because his attention had been caught by the sight of Kate's bare backside coming into view as her gown slid to the floor and she stepped out of it without missing a beat. She scrambled onto his bed and he knew an intense moment of satisfaction. "Don't close your eyes tonight," he ordered.

"I'll try not to but I can't promise. When I close my eyes it's only because you've delivered such exquisite torment. I swear to you, Michael, he's never been in bed with us."

"Never?"

She slowly shook her head. "I tried to hold on to him that first night, but you effectively sent him away."

He sat on the edge of the bed. "So all your cries were always for me?"

"Always. Lie down. Tonight I wish to torment you."

"I'd rather we torment each other."

Stretching out on his side, his bad side, he groaned, before falling to his back. Before he could apologize, she'd straddled his hips. His body reacted with a ferocity of purpose that had him smiling as he reached up and threaded his fingers through her hair. "I wasn't certain I'd be up to the task. I'm glad to see I misjudged my strength."

She furrowed her brow. "Once clothes are removed you don't usually talk . . ." Awe filled her eyes, then tears. "Oh, my Lord, you kept silent because you didn't want to interfere with my fantasy."

He stroked his knuckles along her cheek, capturing her warm tears. "Don't cry, Kate. I'm not worth tears."

"You're worth everything, Michael. I shall spend the remainder of my life proving it to you."

Michael became acutely aware that when someone *wanted* to touch a person the sensation of it was very different than it was when someone was required to touch a person. Kate's touch was tender and gentle, brazen and fiery. She did what she'd never done before. She touched every inch of him. Every inch. With her soft hands, her hot mouth, her velvety tongue. He writhed in torment, writhed in ecstasy.

Kate was determined to bring Michael as much pleasure in one night as possible, the total of all he'd brought her during so many other nights. But he was impatient, her husband was. When she returned her mouth to his, he used the opportunity to cradle her hips, to lift her up, to guide her down.

He murmured sweet words, praising her beauty, praising her skill, praising her. She felt for the first time, that tonight finally, she had all of him. And she wanted to leave him with no doubts that he had all of her.

As she rocked against him, with the pleasure building, she held his gaze, never once closing her eyes. Not even when the rapture threatened to cause her to pass out.

It was the strangest thing to hear his joyful laughter filling the room afterward, to feel the rumble of his chest beneath hers.

"You're truly mine, Kate Rose Tremayne. You're truly mine."

"I truly am," she whispered, as she snuggled in contentment against him and fell asleep.

Kate loved him. Michael woke up in awe, with her still nestled against his side. They'd made love that morning, not once, but twice. He'd have kept her in bed all day except she'd insisted she had matters that needed her attention. The Season was coming to an end. They'd be closing up the house soon, and she was ready to return to the country where they could begin working on all the plans they had there.

He was making his first foray beyond his bed-chambers. His valet had helped him dress, but he still didn't feel quite civilized. Nor was he particularly hungry, even though he was certain breakfast had been set out. What he wanted was a walk about the garden, a chance to smell flowers, to touch silky petals that reminded him of the silkiness of his wife's skin. He wanted to feel the sun on his face, the breeze in his hair. If he didn't think it would reopen his wound, he'd take a hard ride on Obsidian.

He stepped out on the terrace, surprised to discover his mother sitting there. It had been so long since he'd seen her tidy. She wore a pale pink dress, her hair upswept in a simple style. The young woman sitting at the table beside his mother rose and smiled at him. "My lord."

She tilted her head slightly as though issuing an invitation for Michael to take her place. He'd not seen his mother since she'd attacked him. She hardly seemed aware of his presence now. But she did appear calm. He took the chair while the young lady poured him tea before moving away to give them a moment of privacy.

It was some time before his mother finally looked over at him. "Dreadful stuff."

"Pardon?"

"Tea. I've never understood—"

"The English fascination with it?" he finished for her.

She smiled and nodded, before giving her attention back to the garden. Michael watched as tears welled in her eyes.

"Lionel?"

Michael's heart lurched. That had been his father's name. Was she having one of her delusions, imaging that she was sitting beside her husband?

"I know it's our way to have"—her brow creased as though she searched for the word—"nannies . . . but how will our son know how much we love him?"

Michael felt a painful tightening in his chest. Her mind may have taken away her memory, but it seemed in far corners some bit of him remained real to her. Reaching across the table he laid his large hand over her frail one. "He'll know, madam. I swear to you, he'll know."

"You absolutely will not believe this," Jenny said.

Kate had arranged for her family to join her and Michael for dinner, and her family had only just arrived. She wanted a last evening with them before she left for the country estate. She'd escorted them into the parlor where Michael was pouring a bit of brandy for the men. His color had returned and he was moving around less gingerly. And whenever he looked at her, his eyes promised pleasure when they retired for the evening.

"Wesley has left for America."

Kate felt Michael's gaze come to bear on her, and she hoped her face revealed exactly what she was feeling at the news: absolutely nothing. Not the tiniest bit of loss. "Melanie will be happier there," Kate said.

"Here's the thing, though, he didn't take Melanie with him. He's abandoned her."

Kate stared at her sister. "You can't be serious."

"Deadly. Her sister told me she's been in tears ever since he left. She'll no doubt seek a divorce."

"How will he survive in America?"

"Apparently he came into a small fortune."

Kate narrowed her eyes as suspicion began to dawn. She turned her attention to the three men who were studying their snifters of brandy as though they'd never seen the shade before. "All right. I want the truth and I want it now. Which one of you paid him off?"

"I did," her mother said.

Kate spun around and stared at her.

Her mother angled her chin. "Money well spent."

"How much?"

"Don't be vulgar, Kate. A lady does not discuss monetary details."

"What were the terms?"

"That he put as much distance between himself and you as possible. I suggested the width of an ocean."

"You didn't have to do that, Mama. I was quite determined to steer clear of him myself."

"Would you deny me an opportunity to meddle?"

Kate rolled her eyes. "I'm so glad to be leaving for the country tomorrow."

"You will return for your sister's wedding in October."

"No one will be in London in October."

"I hadn't considered that."

Kate looked at Jenny. "Why don't you get married at Raybourne?"

Jenny smiled. "I'd like that."

Much to Kate's surprise, dinner was a pleasant affair until Jenny remarked on how much she detested the constant rain that had descended on London of late.

Michael had lifted his wineglass and swirled the ruby-red contents. "I'm rather fond of rain, especially the sound it makes as it dances across leaves."

And Kate had known he was thinking of their time beneath the tree at the pond. She'd grown warm with the thoughts, finding it difficult now to comprehend why she'd resisted his touch so fervently for so long.

She didn't get a moment alone with Jenny until after dinner. Her father, mother, and Jeremy had gone on out to coach when Kate had stopped Jenny at the door.

"Are you really going to marry Pemburton?"

"Yes, and you'll have to address me as Your Grace."

"Mother can arrange a fabulous wedding in two weeks. Why are you waiting two months?"

"Because I have something I want to do before I get married."

Kate squeezed her sister's hand. "Is it something foolish?"

A sheen of tears appeared in Jenny's eyes before she blinked them back. "Probably. I want to say good-bye to Ravensley . . . properly."

"Do be careful lest you find yourself married to an earl instead of a duke."

"There's no chance of that happening."

"I'd once thought I'd never have a marriage filled with love. But I do, Jenny. I've never known such happiness. Never."

"You have love. Do you have passion?"

"I'm not certain you can have one without the other."

Jenny smiled. "Still I shall try."

Michael decided that he didn't like this tradition of husbands and wives having separate bedchambers, especially since he could no longer envision a night when he wouldn't want to sleep with Kate.

He walked into her bedchamber, surprised to find she wasn't in her bed. Nor was she sitting on the sofa. She had to be in her bathing room, but as he headed toward it with visions of washing her, he spied her sitting on the floor before the fireplace, removing items from a box and tossing them onto the writhing flames, watching them burn one by one.

Sitting beside her, he grabbed her hand before she could toss the next envelope into the fire. "Kate, what are you doing?"

"Ridding myself of Wesley's poems."

"You don't have to do that for me."

She gave him a wistful smile. "I'm doing it for me."

"You loved him once. You shouldn't discount that."

She tossed the envelope into the fire, watched the flames licking at the edges of the paper. "I'm not so sure I did." She looked at him and he could see the struggle in her eyes. "I think I gave him up too easily."

Michael felt as though she'd taken the poker and struck him with it. "You mean you wish you'd gone to America with him?"

Leaning over, she brushed her lips over his. "No. When Wesley and I were married, it took very little for Father and Jeremy to convince me that we should have the marriage annulled. No one would be able to convince me not to remain married to you."

Michael released a huge sigh. "I'm very relieved to hear that."

She shook her head. "I don't think you quite understand. They could take away the money and I'd stand firmly by you. They could tell me they'd disown me, and I wouldn't leave you. There is nothing with which they could threaten me that would cause me to abandon you. And with Wesley, in truth, it took very little."

"You were young, Kate."

"That's what Jeremy said."

"I think you should keep the poems. God knows I'll never write you one."

She tossed the entire box onto the fire, watched it flare, before turning back to him. "I don't need poetry, Michael. All I need is you."

Then she was in his arms, holding him close, kissing him tenderly.

Epilogue

Several years later

"**C**ome give Mama a hug before she goes."

Standing in the doorway of the nursery, Michael watched as his wife bent down and gathered their two sons and one daughter against her, somehow managing to effectively hug all three at once. He didn't know if he'd ever seen a mother of the aristocracy who doted on her children more than his Kate did.

Their children harbored no doubts that they were loved and loved deeply. Kate played games with them, took them on outings, read to them, and hugged them fiercely every chance she got. Michael still found it difficult to be as free with his affection, but Kate more than made up for it. He loved these moments of watching her with them, loved when he had time to join them on their outings to the zoological gardens or on picnics. But between managing his estates and working to improve the conditions at asylums, he found his days never seemed to have enough hours in them. With

Kate's acumen for business, they'd made some wise investments and Michael had never taken another shilling from her father after that initial payment. As a matter of fact, as their own wealth began to accumulate, he'd wanted to return the five million dollars to her father, but the old man wouldn't hear of it. "You'll just get it back when I die and I certainly don't need it. Put it to good works."

And so they had.

On the first anniversary of their wedding day, Kate had returned to him his father's ring. He'd been deeply touched. His gift to her had been a very badly written poem.

Kate gave the children one more hug. "Now be good. Go to sleep when Nanny says, and Mummy and Papa will slip in and give you each a kiss when we get home."

Michael bade his children good night as Kate joined him in the hallway.

"Your skirt is all wrinkled," he said.

"A mother should have wrinkled skirts," she said, wrapping her arm around his. "Your mother taught me that."

His mother had slipped away in her sleep one night. The house near the pond remained unfinished. Kate and Michael had turned their efforts elsewhere, building a much larger residence on a distant corner of their property: Tremayne Convalescent Hospital. Michael thought it a much gentler name than insane asylum. All the residents there suffered from some sort of mental affliction, but their stay was not dependent upon their likelihood of being cured. Nor were the families of those who lived within its walls likely to pay. It catered to those who didn't have the financial means to pay for such services—and yet the care was the best money could buy.

Kate was not one for collecting trinkets. She'd rather their money be spent helping others. Michael didn't know if it was possible to love her anymore than he did.

He decided it wasn't, hours later, when he lay in bed beside her, sated and lethargic. He wouldn't leave her tonight since they were in his bed—and had been sleeping together ever since he'd recovered from his wound some years back.

As always, she bent down and kissed the scar on his side as though to remind herself not to take him for granted. His wife had developed a lovely habit of not taking him for granted.

She peered up at him and smiled. "Why the frown?"

He threaded his fingers through her hair. "What if my mother's affliction . . . what if a time comes when I can no longer remember you? I can think of nothing more cruel than not remembering you."

Easing up, she straddled his hips and kissed him sweetly. "You won't forget me." She kissed his forehead, his nose, his lips. "Will you make love to me again?"

"If it pleases you."

And in his words, as always, Kate heard the echo of I love you.

Author's Note

Today, we would know that Michael's mother suffered from Alzheimer's, a devastating and heartbreaking illness. But it was not until 1906, when Dr. Alois Alzheimer, a German neurologist, performed an autopsy on the brain of a woman named Hannah who had died after years of experiencing severe memory problems and confusion that the disease began to get attention. His discovery of abnormalities in the brain led to further research, although it was Hannah's own descendents who provided much of our understanding of Alzheimer's.

Because I long for happy endings, dear readers, rest assured that Michael did not inherit the genetic disposition toward Alzheimer's from his mother, and he will forever remember his Kate.

NEED SOMETHING NEW TO READ?

Download it Now!

Visit www.harpercollinsebooks.com
to choose from thousands of titles
you can easily download to your
computer or PDA.

Save 20% off the printed book price.
Ordering is easy and secure.

HarperCollins e-books

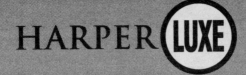

AVON

DANGEROUS ADMISSIONS

JANE O'CONNOR

978-0-06-124086-7
$13.95 ($17.50 Can.)

Secret Confessions OF THE *Applewood* PTA

ELLEN MEISTER

978-0-06-082481-5
$13.95 ($17.50 Can.)

TRUE CONFESSIONS

RACHEL GIBSON

978-0-06-082481-5
$13.95 ($16.50 Can.)

bed rest

SARAH BILSTON

978-0-06-088955-1
$13.95 ($17.50 Can.)

MEG CABOT

QUEEN OF BABBLE

978-0-06-085199-6
$13.95 ($17.50 Can.)

JACK'S WIDOW

Eve Pollard

978-0-06-081705-3
$13.95 ($17.50 Can.)

Visit www.AuthorTracker.com for exclusive
information on your favorite HarperCollins authors.

Available wherever books are sold, or call 1-800-331-3761 to order.

ATP 0907